COWBOY

SEAL TEAM ALPHA

ZOE DAWSON

BLUE
MOON
CREATIVE
LLC

ACKNOWLEDGMENTS

I'd like to thank my beta readers and editor for helping with this book. As always, you guys are the best.

To Bruce, the inspiration for Triton with his sweet mix of German Shepherd/Pitbull mix. You are a sweet, sweet boy. And, to Pip, the inspiration for BFA, a Tortie with tortitude.

If you don't fit in, then you're probably doing the right thing.

Unknown

1

The rope felt rough against his fingers as he coiled it up, the big gelding beneath him broadcasting his readiness—and this big fella, a palomino named Sunshine, was one of the best. Hanging the rope over the horn, he pulled out his gloves and slipped them on. The sun blazed in the bright blue cloudless sky and beat down on the rolling rangeland, the relentless heat shimmering up in waves. The rises and gullies lay like laugh lines in the earth's surface, the folds held in place by sharply defined mountains rising up in the west.

A vast cloud of dust hung in the air, forming a golden aura that cloaked the landscape and distorted the horizon. Overhead, two red-tailed hawks circled, watching for unwary gophers.

The bawling of calves and the shouts of cowhands carried on the warm air, echoing against a bright sky Hundreds of cows and their spring calves plodded onward through the rolling terrain, marshalled into a long meandering column by watchful riders. The cloud of yellow dust hung suspended above the undulating herd, the fine grit coating the newly unfurled leaves of the oaks and sweet-gum, finally settling on the new shoots of grass struggling through last year's thatch.

Cowboy pulled up his mount at the crest of a small hill, giving the reins a light jerk as the big palomino gelding danced and tossed his head, impatient, already seeing what needed to be done. The slant of the late afternoon sun angled beneath the brim of his Stetson. With his gaze fixed on the rim of a far-off ravine, he squinted into the distance.

A series of shrill whistles pierced the din, and Cowboy's attention shifted to his dad as he gave signals to their two hardworking border collies to move up and turn the lead cows into a narrow draw. Yet when his eyes moved to his dad, he was indistinct, blurred, not as if by distance—they were close—but in definition. With an unsettling feeling in his gut, Cowboy kicked his heels into Sunny and the gelding jumped into a gallop from the get go. All cow ponies knew what they were about, and Sunny was one of the best.

Two other riders assisted him as he hazed the outside stragglers back into the ranks and crowded the herd into the gully, forcing them through the natural funnel. A sense of foreboding settled between his shoulder blades when he tried to make out his father again. The lead cows complied, calves crowded against their sides, lumbering through the wide gate while other riders flanked the herd, trying to prevent any of the range-wary animals from bolting.

He wheeled the big animal around. Sunny tossed his head, prancing, and Cowboy handled the spirited horse as easily as breathing. He gave him his head as Sunny instantly responded, lunging down the hill, stirring up more dust as he headed toward two stragglers grazing down by a ring of cypress. Cowboy grinned. Right on the money. He'd had cowhands who weren't as smart as this horse.

Then there was another shrill whistle and he turned his head, confused. His dad was now gone, his horse's saddle empty, the air heavy and humid. Something was wrong. The landscape was different—rain, darkness, water. The hair on the back of his neck stood straight up. *Something was wrong.*

Cowboy jerked out of sleep. The sound of the explosions was deafening. He was jarred out of his idyllic dream of what his life should have been and rolled right into hell. Mud flew everywhere in the tropical, water-saturated air.

He snatched his body armor and weapon out of habit, his uniform damp, ready in a heartbeat. They had been stuck here waiting out the intel before they could move forward, which seemed like a good time to rest. Clearing his head from being startled out of a deep combat nap, he put on his comm headset and listened in.

"Fuck! RPGs, ladies. I think we found the enemy!" Ruckus shouted. The enemy in this case was the *Abu Hurriyah,* or ABH for short, which in English stood for "Father of Freedom." A Jihadist militant group based in and around the Jolo and Basilan islands in the southwest Philippines, where the Moro, or Muslim, groups had formed into an insurgency for independence in the province. The group was designated a terrorist group by many countries including the US.

Another volley of rounds hit the wall outside, and off in the distance, he could hear other battles raging. "Kid, get up on the roof and get those guys to stop shooting at us, pronto!"

"Roger," Ashe "Kid Chaos" Wilder said, sprinting under fire to one of the buildings below Cowboy and disappearing inside. He didn't want to take his eyes off that roof with Kid on it, but he had a job to do. They had gotten a tip about a man who would have the intel they needed to rescue two

American hostages and a Filipino doctoral student who had all been taken by the ABH at a small eatery in Manila outside the university. The Americans were Harvard recruiters and the Filipino a much sought-after candidate who had designed a new state-of-the-art microscope.

To gain intel on the hostages, they were working with the Philippine Special Action Force with the SEALs on point. They were currently on the island of Basilan in Isabela City where there were still pockets of ABH fighting, but their objective was Farouk Bakil, a zealot who had in recent months been responsible for numerous kidnappings of foreign nationals in the country. With Americans targeted, the SEALs would run him to ground and get the information they needed.

With Kid laying down cover fire, Cowboy's team—Lieutenant Bowie "Ruckus" Cooper, or LT as he was known, Scarecrow, the comm operator, Blue, their corpsman, Hollywood, Wicked, Tank and Echo—started their assault along with the SAF guys. The rain was coming down in a steady sheet. Dirt, leaves, and debris eddying in the wind around them, Cowboy prepared to advance. Rubble from demolished buildings lay in heaps as they passed, keeping low.

"RPGs neutralized," Kid said over the mic. "Everything is quiet now, LT. Looks like they were reacting to the police in the area. I don't think they know we're here."

"Solid copy," LT said. "Let's keep it quiet, ladies." Cowboy, paired up with Tank and Echo, surveyed the windswept area. "Kid, get down here and get on point."

"Copy, LT." After a few moments, his voice came over the comm. "On point, plenty of tangos."

"Keep it stealthy. Let's hope we find this guy and get enough information to get those hostages out," LT said.

"If they're still alive," Tank muttered.

"Comms scrambled," Scarecrow said.

As Kid fed them information, they went through an abandoned and demolished house, and Cowboy saw the sentry at the same time Tank did. "Clear," Tank whispered. "All yours, man."

Cowboy moved up on the guard and with his knife made short and silent work of him. In front of them was a pile of debris and a burn barrel to keep the next sentry warm. Tank squeezed off a suppressed head shot and the guy went down.

After crawling through the mud and rain puddles, they made their way into the main part of the city and Kid said, "Tangos on the buildings surrounding your position, LT. Half a dozen. Maybe more inside." Cowboy, Tank and Echo had moved around the building to the back door.

"Copy that. They're going to know we're coming. We need to get inside a-sap. Cowboy?"

"Roger, LT."

"Are you in position in the back?"

"Affirmative, ready for assault."

"Go on my mark." There was silence for a moment, then, Ruckus said, "Kid, take them out. Cowboy breach. Get me Bakil. Alive."

As soon as Kid started firing, they back kicked the door, Tank tossed in a smoke bomb, and as the explosion went off, Cowboy smoked everyone left standing in the room. They made for the stairs as soon as the room was clear, took out two armed guys at the top of the stairs, and continued down the hall. Outside, Kid's sniping had grown silent.

"Moving," LT said. "Cowboy?"

"Standby," Cowboy said as they breached another door and took out the two guards, recognizing Bakil. He wasn't about to be taken. When he raised his arm to fire, Tank gave the apprehend signal and Echo was on him so fast, he never had a chance to discharge his weapon. Faced with the dog hanging on his arm in a vicious bite, his jaw locked, Bakil screamed, "I surrender! Get him off me!"

Tank covered him while Cowboy kicked the weapon away. "Target secured," he said over the mic.

Challenged with the growling threat of Echo, Bakil soon spilled the beans that the hostages were being kept at an *Abu Hurriyah* safe house deep in Isabela City close to the coast. The op ran like clockwork after Bakil's intel and hours later even through a chaotic op, they took down the ABH fighters, securing the hostages.

"LT," Kid's tight voice came over the comm. "You need to see this." They were currently at the safe house, a single-family home near the beach.

Cowboy and LT walked downstairs to the basement. Bodies were strewn across the floor, a testament to how well guarded this area was. Kid stood in front of a crate. He turned when they walked up. Kid moved out of the way, and Cowboy's gut clenched.

"Warheads."

"Yeah, I recognize them. These are from the undercover operation in Bolivia, ones in a cache that the Kirikhan rebels got away with," Kid said, his eyes bleak. "But there's only one here."

"Where are the other five?" Ruckus growled.

"That's a good question," Kid said.

A question Cowboy was pondering as he kept his eyes peeled while they headed toward transpo at the back of the island—rigid hull inflatables, sleek high-speed boats.

"Angel One, this is Ruckus, proceeding to the boats, Rally Point Delta."

"Roger that, Ruckus."

Cowboy spotted them a second after Echo, who jumped into a sprint and took the guy with the RPG down. The chopper was coming in fast through the gray sheets of rain, but still distant. They had to get to the boats. Automatic gunfire sounded all around him, but he stayed with the group. Echo jumped into a sprint and lunged at a rebel with an RPG even before Cowboy realized he was there. While Echo hit several other targets, the dog caused disorientation to the hostiles. He was the best damn dog. Cowboy hustled the rescued hostages toward the boat when one of the recruiters went down, blood coating his neck and shirt. Cowboy covered the wound with his hand, stemming the flow of blood. The guy's eyes were wide, his mouth gaping with the shock and pain of the wound.

"Blue!" Cowboy called out, but he was already responding, already next to Cowboy, taking over.

Blue's mouth pulled into a grim line, his hands working fast over the injured man's wound. Cowboy was always in awe of their corpsman's calm under pressure.

"Took a round in the throat. Not good! We need to move." Blue shouldered him into a carry and headed for the boat.

Tank whistled shrilly, and soon Echo was back with them. He had blood on his muzzle, but it looked like none of it was his. The dog flanked him as he rushed toward the RIBs. Helping the other two terrified hostages inside, he registered Tank's warning. "Cowboy!"

He spun to find several ABH bearing down on them. They wanted either the hostages back or the warhead they had confiscated; Cowboy was determined it would be none of the above.

Cowboy took out one, and Tank double-tapped the

second. Soon they were in the boat and speeding out of the canal.

"This guy is going into shock, Angel One."

"Roger that. Trauma is standing by. We're almost to Rally Point Delta. Coming in hot."

"Hit it, Cowboy," Blue shouted, and the RIB surged forward as Hollywood manned the gun and took care of the tangos along the banks that were shooting at them. Spray from cutting through the waves and the rain drenched them, visibility obscured. When they were almost out to open sea, a gray landscape with occasional whitecaps, an explosion hit a dock nearby and rocked the boat, but Cowboy muscled them through the debris stinging his face and into the open ocean. The helos buzzed over them, and they hooked up the two boats to the chopper's underbelly. As they were lifted into the air, Cowboy could only think it was a job well done.

They were heading home after this, the brass obviously concerned about the warheads. If they were still in the hands of the Kirikhan rebels, it was bad news.

Very bad news, but Cowboy would be off on leave to attend his reunion and spend some time with his family. The team was in store for some much-needed downtime.

His battle-focused mind relaxed, he remembered his combat "dream," and it hit him hard. That life *was* now a dream when it had felt so real. There was no ranch anymore, no legacy, no birthright. Now Cowboy was just the son of that no-good coward, Travis McGraw. He had never even tried to change anyone's mind—not that he could. But he would like to go back to Reddick and be able to hold up his head without this shame dogging him, reconnect to his family. They had become the casualties in his battle to deal with his betrayal. Cowboy had lost his connection with

Reddick a decade ago and felt nothing but humiliation when he thought about the area now. Going home meant nothing to him. He'd lost that a long time ago.

The day his dad had put a bullet through his brain.

Then a thought occurred to him. If he could get the ranch back, show the people of Reddick that he wasn't like his dad, maybe that would be enough. He had the money tucked away. He'd saved every last cent of all his bonuses. His renewal for his tour of duty was coming up. Maybe it was time to reclaim what he had lost.

THERE WAS someone in Kia Silverbrook's house.

Kia turned off the water of the shower, the sudden chill producing pin prickles of fear that blossomed like goose-bumps all over her wet, tired body.

She listened intently, her body frozen, her muscles locked. But heard nothing.

Maybe her imagination? But lately, she had the feeling that she was being watched. She'd felt it in The Back Forty, her bar/diner/rooms for rent where she worked behind the bar and fed the people of the small town of Reddick, twenty minutes from Galveston and thirty from Houston. She felt it at the grocery store while she was squeezing cantaloupe and smelling them for freshness. The persistent ache between her shoulder blades was now a constant companion.

There was never anyone there, but the feeling had persisted, making Kia edgy and paranoid.

She waited as cool air slid across her just wet skin, the warmth from the water a fleeting memory. A shiver cascaded over her, a combination of physical and mental energy co-mingling.

She listened intently, her eyes fixed on the door, her ears attuned. Water trickled down the drain like an indrawn breath, adrenaline shocking into her system, twisting her stomach into knots.

Just when she thought she was hearing things and had reached for the tap to turn the water back on and finish her shower, she heard it.

A scuff of a shoe.

Her heartbeat quickened, and the hair on the back of her neck stood to attention.

Slowly so as not to make a sound, Kia stepped out. She didn't know much about self-defense, but she knew trying to defend herself in a wet, slippery shower didn't put her at any advantage.

She approached the bathroom door, and with a deft flick of her wrist, she set the lock. She pressed her ear against the gap between the frame and the door. Maybe she was mistaken. Maybe it was her overactive imagination.

She could hear him breathing.

Her heart dropped straight into the pit of her stomach. Gasping, she backed away, her gut tightening in ever-increasing spirals of fear until it was a huge roll of panic.

She looked frantically around her, but there was simply no place to hide, no place to run.

Just as she reached for her discarded clothes on the floor, she heard the bathroom doorknob jiggle. Kia gasped and froze.

Her stomach flopped, turned upside down. "Oh, God," she said softly.

HE KICKED THE DOOR OPEN, ready for a fight, ready for

anything, but the bathroom was empty. He knew she'd been in here. Suddenly he felt the air on his face, and his head jerked toward the left. He strode over to the open window and stuck his head out. The little resourceful bitch. A ladder to the ground swung against the house.

He swore softly. He looked back at the empty bathroom and the clothes lying in a heap on the floor. The woman was running around buck-assed naked?

He would like to see that. What an exotic beauty, with her alluring mix of big dark eyes and elfin features, her rich black hair and her very curvy body. But he wasn't here to admire her. He was here for a very specific purpose.

Her accidental death.

KIA BREATHED SHALLOWLY. It was all the space she had for her lungs to expand. It was the only time in her life that she cursed her five-foot, nine-inch frame. She suddenly wished she was smaller.

And had someone she could turn to, someone tall and strong. Someone so handsome he made her lungs seize. Someone that she hadn't seen in ten years. She sighed. Dammit. Now was not the time to daydream about Wes McGraw.

She could only be thankful that she hadn't washed and dried the majority of the towels that would have occupied the space she'd wedged her body into. A space that barely accommodated her. Bone-deep fear tightened her stomach and froze her limbs as she heard him swear. She realized that he was at the window she'd opened. Thank God she'd gotten that fire escape ladder. He went for the ploy.

But it seemed that her sense of relief was premature. She

heard his footsteps stop as he stood right outside the closet. She bit her lip. Her hands tightened into fists that she pressed against her mouth to keep the whimper of panic from slipping out.

Her heart was beating so hard, she was worried that he could hear it. If it occurred to him that she had hidden herself instead of running, she was dead.

Finally, he moved away. She heard his retreating footsteps and then the closing of her front door. Breathing a sigh of relief, the panic and adrenaline receding, Kia let out a shaky sob. Tears of relief squeezed from her tightly closed eyes.

When she was sure she was alone, she extricated herself from her fetal position, groaning softly as her stiff muscles protested.

She clutched the edge of the doorframe as blood rushed to constricted extremities, the pain spikes almost welcome.

They reminded her in vivid detail that she was alive.

As soon as she got dressed, she found her cell phone on her coffee table and called the police. She sat on her sofa just breathing deeply to waylay the panic that kept climbing up her spine.

It hadn't been her imagination. Someone had been watching her. Was her secret out? Did it have to do with her very long, very clandestine investigation that had brought her to nothing but dead ends?

She opened the door when the police knocked. After settling down on her couch, she answered all the questions they asked.

"We're sorry about what happened to you, ma'am, but it was most likely a vagrant looking for what he could sell."

She looked from the local fresh-faced deputy to his more experienced partner and realized that they hadn't taken what she'd said seriously. That shouldn't really surprise her. As a woman always looking in, she felt like the establishment, i.e. the Sheriff's Department, had written her off as a kook a long time ago. But she wasn't going to allow that to bother her. She was pretty much an elastic band, and she always snapped back. She was determined to act normal.

"I don't think so. I think this was the man I believe has been following me."

"Yes, you did mention that, but you don't have a description or any information for us to go on. You never saw this guy, right?"

"That doesn't mean he doesn't exist."

"Yes, ma'am. We'll let you know if we come up with any leads."

Which basically meant she was screwed. They were right. She didn't see his face; she had no description, no proof that he was following her, watching her.

As she closed and locked the door, she felt that same panic crawl up her spine. She backed away from the door, her senses heightened.

She went back into the bathroom and closed the door. Stripping down, she turned on the water, but she tucked her vanity chair under the doorknob. No one was going to intimidate her, not here in this place she had built for herself.

She showered, hyperalert to any noise. Maybe she should get herself a dog. A big one with a deep bark and a menacing growl. At least she would have another warm, dependable body in the house. She decided that was an excellent idea. She was going to get herself a guard dog.

She dried her hair, leaving it loose and dressing in a sheer black blouse with bats all over it, a black bra underneath, paired with a pair of ripped fishnets and a black

denim skirt, and her kickass black studded cowgirl boots
with the metal heel that made her feel invincible. She
smudged her dark eyes with black eyeliner, forgoing
mascara as she was blessed with thick, dark lashes. She
swiped on a shade of red lipstick that contrasted with her
pale skin. She worried the lip ring at the corner of her
mouth as she grabbed her black cowboy hat, bag, and keys
on the way out of the house, locking the door behind her.
Her shoulder blades tingled as she walked to her car. Her
three horses all nickered at her: Quicksand, a big tan buckskin gelding who was a challenge, Twilight Star, a black and
white paint gelding with beautiful brushed patterns who
loved apples, and Saragon, a brown appaloosa with a
blanket of white with rust dots on his hindquarters, a solid
trail horse. She'd already fed them early this morning, so
they were set for the day.

"See you guys later. I might have a friend for you to play
with soon." She got into her Jeep, all silver and black,
looking like a mini-hummer. As the house disappeared in
the distance, the feeling of being in danger passed.

She'd lived here for eight years. She had her money-
making business—hacking. She had her bar. She had her
horses and the four-stall barn on her meager ten acres. She
was on the outskirts of town, a bit isolated. She was solid
and stable. She had never wanted for money, the hacking
had made her a teenaged millionaire when she was still in
high school.

When she reached her bar, she parked behind the structure and entered through the alley. Reddick was a mid-sized
town, mostly comprised of ranchers and people who
supported the cattle trade. But it was more than that, and
with a population just under six thousand, it had grown
since she'd been in high school. Between history, food,

shopping, the beautiful scenery, and being close to the ocean, Reddick was a tourist magnet. People loved soaking up the charm of the Texas Gulf Coast.

Her cell rang as she slipped the key in the lock. "Hello," she said, entering the building and walking toward the bar.

"Howdy, Kia. This is Evie Marshall. We're all getting together next week for the decorating party at The Barn." A meeting and multi-purpose venue at the edge of town would serve as their site for the reunion. "Just checking to make sure we're ready to go."

"Yes, I've assembled everything." Kia had gotten roped into this reunion committee, and she'd been thrilled at first until she realized the group wanted her to do all the work. She rubbed the back of her neck, her stomach twisting. This was silly to immediately think about how many times in high school Evie had called her a freak. That was so long ago. She saw these people every day, but her isolation, her fairy bubble, kept her protected. Did these people still think she was a freak? Probably. She still was too different and weird for anyone to understand her. Why wasn't being herself enough?

"Well, girl, with your businesses, I'm sure you're always straight out. This won't tax you none, will it?"

"Nope, I'll be there."

"Good. We'll have plenty to do. I'll see you then."

"Wait, Evie, do you know someone I might be able to get a dog from?"

There was silence, and Kia realized that she was probably wondering what the hell Kia was asking her for. Yeah, keep building that freak cred. Then Evie said, "I can't think of anyone right now, but check the local paper. There might be some ads in there."

"Good idea. I'll see you soon."

"Bye."

Kia went to the front door and unlocked it. She could already hear movement in the kitchen. The breakfast crowd would be in soon. She walked to the curb, slipped in a coin and grabbed the paper out of the bin. Walking back inside, she opened it to the want ads, setting the newspaper on the bar. She looked under "Dogs for Adoption" and found several prospects that might work, one with a fine description for a German shepherd/pit bull mix. That sounded like an excellent combination, a herder with a pit bull mentality. The companionship was also going to be nice as people drifted in and out of her life just like when she'd been in foster care. Dogs, like horses, gave their owner unconditional love. Unlike people, once the bond of trust had been forged, there was no going back. Animals were uncomplicated and lived in the moment.

She could provide a good home for him.

But as an orphan, a foster kid, home was an intangible concept. And that summed it up. She went from home to home because most people thought she was weird or strange.

She was sure she was a changeling, one of the fairy folk who had replaced a human baby, a dark fairy, one who could never find her way home. That elusive dark den where she belonged. A place that defined her with all the other dark fairies. Strangely, her magic was technology based. The computer world was where she felt most at home, a language of zeros and ones that, when she saw it, gave her a vast, open universe of not only discovery, but creation. A life she'd never known. It was her dark Oz.

She'd had the ruby slippers for a long, long time, but the question was: How could she click them to get back home when she'd never had one in the first place?

2

After Thorn "Tank" Hunt settled Echo at the base kennel, he headed home to a modest-sized house in the San Diego foothills. He wished he could keep Echo with him, but that's not the way MWDs operated. They weren't pets, but highly trained and valuable navy assets. Tank knew that but still wanted the Malinois with him. There was no doubt that Echo was an alpha dog. He proved that every time in the field, like the interrogation of Balik. Echo had just sat there, looking fierce as hell, and Balik couldn't stop giving him fearful glances. Every so often, Echo would growl low in his throat. Balik wasn't as intimidated by eight US Navy SEALs brimming with automatic weapons, but he was daunted as all get out to have Echo's intelligent, feral eyes on him. Ruckus used it to his advantage. Their LT was so damn good at his job both in leadership and in getting information he wanted. That guy was top dog, and Echo knew it; the pack of them ran like wolves.

Tank knew about being a wolf, being an alpha and making sure that all the other wolves were aware that he was the one who was large and in charge. It didn't really stem from being half-Hispanic or anything as simple as being macho. It was all about survival on the streets of East LA. That urban battlefield prepared him not only for BUD/S, the navy SEAL Basic Underwater Demolition/SEAL training, but for battle.

When he pulled into his driveway, he groaned softly at the powder pink Porsche parked at the curb. It even had a frothy name—Cabriolet—and cost a hundred grand and a quarter—*for a car*. Yeesh. He hit his head a couple of times against his steering wheel. He needed a shower and some downtime, not the pink cotton candy juggernaut that was so self-absorbed she wouldn't know empathy if it hit her in the head.

Princess Rebecca Dassault, or Becca for short, always had a sixth sense for when he'd be home. She didn't hesitate to show up unannounced because...well...the world revolved around her. Truth be told, she would take his mind off battle, conflict, the fact that Echo was getting on in years. Anyone who looked at that dog wouldn't see it, but Tank noticed him slowing down, which meant he'd be retired and Tank would have to contend with another dog.

He didn't want another damn dog.

"Yoo-hoo, Thorny!" she called out, totally ignoring the person she was currently talking to on her phone. She flitted through the grass in a pair of high heels that had pom-poms on the instep. Fluffy pink balls of spiky fur that jiggled when she walked. She wore a lot of pink, and when he'd remarked about it, she said: *I love pink and pink loves me back. It's that simple.* As he emerged from the car, she threw her arms around him. She was such a tiny little thing—most people were compared to his two-hundred-and-forty-pound, six-feet-four-inch frame. "Ooh, you feel delicious. Hop, skip into the house and shower and change. We've got a night of clubbing ahead."

She didn't even bother to wait for his answer, but just kissed him on the mouth and returned to her phone call as if he wasn't there. He shook his head, used to her antics. They had a loose relationship. When he was in town, they fucked. When he wasn't here, she fucked who she wanted.

"Ah, no, sweetie, not tonight. Winding down. If you want to stay home with me and give me a BJ, that works for me. I haven't had a woman in months."

She stopped talking and turned to look at him. Her mouth curled up at the corners. "BJ, huh?" She said into the phone, "I'll call you back, Lacy. I'm busy right now…serving my country."

He chuckled, grabbed his duffel, and headed for the house. He heard her lock her car and follow him.

He was of the Gaston mindset. You give women books and before you know it, they're reading, getting ideas, and thinking. Actually, he enjoyed intelligent women, but Becca was nothing but froth and foam with a slamming body he enjoyed as much as she enjoyed him. Uncomplicated was what he liked at this point in his life—really malleable women who did things his way.

He dropped his gear at the front door and headed up the stairs. When he turned around, she was already shedding her clothes. The pretty little heels looked so out of place near his dirty, muddy, olive drab kit. In fact, she looked like an exotic bird in her colorful print sundress that was now a heap on the middle of his stairs. Dressed in hot pink satin and lace, the sight of her made his dick rock hard.

She removed her bra and he had to admire her generous, pink-tipped breasts. His back hit the wall, and she walked right up to him. "I love it when you come off deployment looking so rough and tough." She ran her open palm against his dark beard, her direct eye contact stimulating. She might look like a demure princess, but there was some good ole bad girl in there, too.

She molded her hand to the hard length confined beneath the fly of his NWUs, and she nipped playfully on his lower lip, sending a shock of arousal straight to his already aching groin. "I'd rather blow you than go clubbing." She tugged his head down and followed that comment with a gust of warm, damp air into his ear that made him shudder.

"I'll make it up to you, honey," he rasped, aching for her mouth. "They don't call it a job for nothing." She laughed softly, and he dragged her into the bathroom. "Take my clothes off."

"I do love a man in uniform, but I love one even better out of it." She reached for his waistband while he twisted and turned on the water, getting it to the right temperature.

Divesting her of her panties, he dragged her inside the shower. "Wash me."

She complied, using her soaped-up hands to touch every inch of him. "That's no hardship. I love your muscles. There isn't an ounce of fat on you. Every inch of you is so lickable." She proved it by sending her tongue over him, and he leaned back, closing his eyes. She bit and stroked her tongue over the ridges of his abs, then settled on her knees. The soft wet warmth of her mouth closed over his dick, enveloping him in the moist heat of her mouth. She took him all the way to the base of his shaft as a deep, tortured groan rumbled up from his throat.

His mind was now totally on his pleasure. Mission accomplished, princess pink.

KIA GOT no response when she knocked on the modest ranch house door. The guy had just texted her to come around and take a look at the shepherd. She walked around the house to the barn and called out, "Hello?"

A tall, lanky man poked his head out of the barn door and said, "Howdy, ma'am. Come on over."

She walked toward the man even as he gave her a once over, and immediately she could see that he'd pegged her as different. He took in the ripped fishnet and the unique cowboy boots. "You're an interesting one," he drawled. "You here about the dog?"

"Yes. I'm Kia Silverbrook. Nice to meet you." She reached out her hand and they shook.

"Marty Carpenter. Likewise." He set down the brush he was using to groom a beautiful bay gelding. Kia rubbed his forelock when he sniffed toward her curiously.

"He's beautiful."

"Samson is that, but spoiled." Marty smiled. "I'm happy to show you the dog, but I want reassurances that you have the right disposition to handle him, and he'll have adequate exercise and nutrition."

"I love animals and have three horses, one of them a challenge. I can handle him." She followed him. "Why are you giving him away?"

"I have too many puppers as it is with a hound giving birth just a few days ago. My wife is giving me the evil eye. This is a stray I found on the side of the road. He's a good dog."

Already she was hooked. A stray, like her. "I need a guard dog, one who will protect me and my home."

"Then you've come to the right place. He's very vigilant. He's been herding my small flock of sheep since he got here." The affection in the rancher's voice was evident, and Kia already liked him.

He brought her to a pen and emitted a shrill whistle. The sheep parted, and she got her first glimpse of the dog. Her eyes connected with his warm amber eyes and...*powie*. It was like she was struck by lightning, as if it was kismet.

"Come here," Marty said. Wow, he was muscularly built, very solid, but that wasn't a surprise. He was almost completely fawn-colored except for totally black ears and muzzle and a streak of black on his back. But his snout was shorter and his face showed the influence of the pit bull: wide head, powerful jaws.

"Someone trained him very well, and I've tried to find the owner, but no luck. Maybe he died or some other issue keeps him from claiming him. Either way, he needs a home. I'd keep him in a heartbeat if it wasn't for—" His cell phone rang and he said, "Excuse me," and walked off.

The dog trotted over and sniffed her, and she reached down and petted his wide head. He closed his eyes and butted up against her leg. What a sweetheart. Already her heart was getting taken over, but she had to wonder what he would do with strangers. Would he just cuddle up to them?

Marty turned then, and his jaw dropped. He stared at her and the dog, then went back to his conversation. Just then a woman came out of the house with a cat carrier. There were plenty of low growls, threatening meows and general disgruntles. She stopped a few feet away and set down the cage. Kia crouched down to find a chocolate and cream cat—what was called a tortoiseshell or Tortie. She had copper eyes and a direct stare.

"She looks like a handful."

"It's a he. Rare for a Tortie, I know." She reached out her hand and smiled. "I'm Emma, Marty's wife."

Tucking the phone into his back pocket, Marty walked back over to her. "So what's the verdict?" The cat made a hissing noise and caught her on the ankle. Kia stepped back, her skin smarting.

"I'll take him."

"Him?" He looked at his wife and then back at her.

"I didn't get a chance to tell her."

"Oh." He shuffled his feet. "Um...the cat goes with the dog."

Kia absorbed that information and looked back down at the cat carrier. "What?"

"I found them together, and I'm afraid they're bonded. If you take the dog, you've got to take the cat."

She looked at the placid animal now sitting at her feet looking up at her with adoring eyes and the cat who was hissing up a storm and protesting as all get out.

"He just puts up a fuss. He's really not that bad," Emma said, and Kia had to wonder if she just wanted him gone.

"He's a very good mouser and can live outside," Marty offered.

"I do have a barn and horses," Kia said. The fear of the morning break-in fresh in her mind, she figured it couldn't hurt to have a guard dog and an attack cat. "All right," she said, biting her lip and worrying the ring. "I'll take them both."

A few days later, after three shredded pillows, plenty of caterwauling, spilled food dishes and general tortitude, a

word Kia came up with to describe BFA's disposition, she
was determined to win this animal over. He was a gorgeous
one at that, all cream and chocolate. She was a good person
and she loved animals. He would come around. His name
came out of a hacking term for an alternative phishing
method called Brute Force Attack. BFA sounded so benign,
like BFF, but this cat wasn't exactly interested in being best
friends with her. More like mortal enemies. No matter what
she did, he just wouldn't warm up. Finally, she set him out
in the barn where he proceeded to kill mice and leave them
on her porch. But he'd bonded with her horses, especially
headstrong Quicksand. When she came out in the morning
to go to work, he was perched on the big buckskin's
hindquarters, mocking her, pretty much a cat middle finger.

And when she looked down, another mangled mouse.
She got a tissue and raised it in the air. "Thanks! This is such
a great present," she said, then under her breath, "you little
monster." She buried it with the others.

Unlike BFA, Triton, her new guard dog, was fantastic.
Several times, he'd barked enthusiastically and after a few
tense moments with him on alert, he would settle. She
worried less and less about break-ins now. He had some
amazing training, and he was easy to manage, energetic, but
she loved running with him, walking with him. He was even
good with the horses when she rode. A genuine little hero.

She wasn't going to examine too closely why she had
named the dog that, for the same reason, she didn't exactly
examine the reason she was enamored with forty, Wes's old
football number. She closed her eyes when she got into the
car and gripped the wheel. Even a ten-year-old memory
could make her giddy just thinking about Wes McGraw. The
fleeting glimpses of him here and there had been few and
far between over the years.

But her stomach lurched and tied itself into terrible knots. She had kept a terrible secret from him. One that had lingered for ten long years, her biggest failure, her deepest regret.

Once she got to work, she had no idea why Wes was so heavy on her mind. He'd only been back to Reddick a dozen or so times since he'd left just before his father's funeral. She'd heard that not only hadn't he finished college, but he'd gone into the navy.

She'd overheard Annette McGraw say that her son had become a SEAL, part of the elite, tough fighting force. Wes in the military was hard for her, at the time, to get her head around. He was a cowboy through and through and had been born and bred for the range. She often wondered how he'd fared on the battlefield.

He and his father had been so close. She knew every one of Cowboy's dad's hopes and dreams because Travis McGraw had told her. He was such a good, kind man, a former rodeo cowboy who was a legend in Texas before he'd quit to take over the running of Sweetwater.

She'd met him at the business end of a shotgun, but he wasn't threatening her, just the boys who thought she would be an easy mark for some sexual fun.

As morning flowed into afternoon, the crowd was heavy during the breakfast rush, plenty of tourist dollars flowing into neat, tidy Reddick and into her coffers. She thought she might like to spruce up the place a bit with a new sign and some paint both inside and out. She'd have to think about that. Probably do it before next summer's bookings.

As soon as the lull started, Kia began inventory of the liquor. A tedious task, but it had to be done. Running out of booze, especially on a Friday or Saturday night, wouldn't do.

The bell over the door sounded as a customer came into The Back Forty.

The tapping of boot heels sounded, a familiar cadence in Texas. Kia looked up and everything in her froze. He was tall, so very tall and lean, standing by the door, a black Stetson on his head, the brim shading his eyes, but she'd know the man anywhere, anytime.

Wes McGraw had come home.

Big, wide-shouldered, he stood framed in the light, his thumb hooked in the front pocket of his jeans. His hands were long and well-shaped, and there was something almost deceptively casual about his stance, about the way his fingers splayed out against his thigh. Something lethal and a little too careless, as though he had small regard for danger.

Experiencing a strange flutter at the unexpected thought, Kia clenched and unclenched her hands, recognizing the flutter as an extreme case of nervousness. Wes McGraw did that to her, another constant where he was concerned.

He took in the room, a quick once over as if gauging the lay of the land and assessing everything there in one quick sweeping, tactical glance.

He took a few steps forward, then they faltered when he was close to the bar.

Taking a fortifying breath, she watched him come toward her, trying to quell her stupid girl crush on him. She wasn't going to make a fool of herself. She was *not*.

Wes was and had been a stranger to her. They had only exchanged a few words to each other. He'd been the jock and she the freak, from two different worlds. And even though she thought she had perceived something there, it was all in her imagination. High school was all about fitting in. Everyone wanted it, and it was so hard when a square peg could only seem to find that round hole.

Feeling as if her heart was going to actually thump against her chest wall like in the movies, so visual she could almost see it, she stared at him, her heartbeat stopping completely when he took off his hat and she could see the lean angles his face. Ten years had taken a handsome boy into a rugged, gorgeous man. Some things hadn't changed, like the thick, coal-black silk of his hair, or those intriguing, thickly-lashed whiskey eyes. He might have more lines around them now, but he was still simply an arresting man with his big body, knee-melting face, and his strong, beard-shadowed jaw.

Ten years wasn't enough to mitigate her guilt, or her doubts or the way she felt about him. Her pulse was racing with an awful mixture of surprise and anticipation, and a truly horrible excitement at just seeing him again.

Even a square peg could dream.

"Kia?" he asked, his voice going through her and reverberating in her bones, the kind of deep timbre that melted her and probably every woman within earshot. His voice was deeper than deep, sending vibrations through the air, commanding attention and sending skin-prickling, hair-raising chills through her body. His voice was the kind that people listened to and trusted. It hit her deep in her gut and drew her in.

His Texas roots were both in his voice and in his dress—a dark blue plaid western-style shirt that fit him like a second skin, faded blue jeans molded to lean hips and powerful thighs, a wide, hand-tooled belt that sported an engraved silver buckle threaded through the loops of his jeans, and on his feet, a pair of scuffed cowboy boots. He leaned forward, the edge of the bar pressing against his lean torso as he extended his hand to her.

Kia felt vaguely untethered as she met his steady gaze. Placing her hand in his, she was bombarded by the warmth, texture, and strength of his skin, his grip. "Yes, it's me. Wes McGraw back in town. What brings you home?"

He met her gaze with an unreadable expression, his tanned skin and honed body a testament to his active, outdoor lifestyle. "My sister's nagging and the high school reunion."

Her stomach lurched again for different reasons. He was going to be part of the festivities? Part of next week's Thursday night mixer, then the car wash Friday to raise money for the high school football and band uniforms, followed by Friday's tailgate and local football kickoff game, with the dinner and dance Saturday night, closing with a brunch on Sunday here in The Back Forty.

She'd see him all weekend. She glanced down at his left hand and breathed a sigh of relief when she saw no ring. Not that it was any of her business and didn't mean that he wasn't with someone.

His eyes were the color of aged whiskey and, like the spirit, teemed with multiple layers and a complex presence, an irresistible and seamless blend of character and personality.

She was so lost in those eyes she didn't realize that she was still clasping his hand. Unwilling to break physical contact with this man, she self-consciously let go. "There's a lot planned," she said lamely. "So, what can I do for you?"

"My mom said you have rooms for rent that are reasonable. It's much too crowded at my sister's house with my mom, sister, brother-in-law and niece and nephew."

"Let me guess, short couch, long legs?" God, she'd

forgotten how potent he could be in person, an attractiveness that was unfeigned and indestructible.

He chuckled and a brief grin lit his face. Wes could look so stoic, but when he smiled... Watch out.

"And old springs."

"Gotcha. I think we can help you out." She checked him in, ran his credit card, then she called out, "Sally Jean, I need you out here." A blonde woman came out of the back, her hair in pigtails, a bright grin on her face when she got a load of Wes. Kia said under her breath, "Not for him."

"You are no fun," she whispered.

"I'm taking him up to the apartments. Watch the front for me."

"You bet." She smiled at Wes and said, "Hey, cowboy."

He'd just settled the Stetson back on his head. He nodded, brushed the brim, and smiled softly, walking along the bar to where Kia was watching the exchange. When her ribs connected painfully with the hinged bar top, she realized that she had been too caught up in staring instead of paying attention.

Stupid girl crush, one—Kia, a big fat zero.

Wes didn't say anything, just reached out and lifted the partition for her. She slipped through, and while she stood in the shadow of his body, he gently set it down. She tingled everywhere. "This way," she said, her voice even more breathless than before. Geez, Kia get a damn grip. She was almost out the back door before she realized that she didn't have the key. She stopped, turned, and Wes plowed right into her.

"Whoa," he said, "You need to give a cowboy a warning before stopping on a dime, darlin'." He caught her against him with lightning quick reflexes and *oh, boy* was that one *hard* body. Startled at the contact, she grabbed for his arm and snagged one of those biceps—and it was a good thing he was holding her so tightly, because swooning was a definite possibility. The bulge was thick, hard, and rounded, but she held on.

She looked up into those warm eyes and said, "Um, I forgot..." Then got lost.

He was staring right back, and it was a moment before he cleared his throat and said, "What did you forget?"

"The key," she said sheepishly, and the sound of his laughter rumbled against her breasts and stomach. Stupid girl crush, two—Kia, no surprise, a big, fat zero.

"Oh, well, that's important."

He released her, probably expecting that she had already regained her balance.

Not likely with this man.

She went around him and there was Sally Jean, eyes sparkling as she held out the key. Kia gave her a scrunched-up warning look not to laugh, but Sally Jean was irrepressible. "You got any more of them stashed somewhere?" she asked under her breath, sneaking another peek at Wes. "That's one rodeo I want to ride."

"Shush, you hussy," Kia said, taking the key and a deep, much-needed breath.

She turned back around and headed out of the bar and around to the back. "You can use this entrance and park your vehicle in this lot. Be careful coming up the alley, though, because people are always coming and going, emptying trash, stuff like that."

"Got it."

She opened a wooden gate and went through, walking toward the stairs, trying to keep her voice even. "There are ice machines, one down here, one up on the porch at the end in case you want some. Although, the fridges in the apartments have ice trays if you prefer to make your own."

She went up the stairs, Wes right behind her, and walked along the porch until she got to their best apartment. Inserting the key, she pushed it open and went inside.

"This is nice," he said as he followed her. "Very western." He walked up to some paintings hanging on the wall depicting cowboys on the range. "These are great. I also like the cowhide chair. Tasteful without being too kitschy."

His praise made her smile. "I've never been accused of ever being kitschy. Maybe weird, strange, and odd, but not that."

He turned to look at her. "I would never describe you that way...different maybe, but that's what makes things interesting."

There was something about the way he turned his head, the way he looked at her, that made her insides knot up. As if he'd contemplated long and hard about what made her unique. Did it just get hot in here? "I got them at flea markets, redid the frames, recovered the chair and there you go. Cowboy stuff."

He cast her another look, only this time she caught a trace of amusement around his mouth. "Cowboy stuff."

She shrugged. "It's big business. I do it my way, but people seem to like it."

The corner of his mouth quirked again. "I bet they do." All of a sudden it felt like they weren't talking about her decorating prowess. It felt like the temperature rose a few more degrees.

He pressed his forearm against the wall, his hand hanging inches from her face, and leaned in toward her. The light from outside slanted through the windows and exposed his eyes beneath the brim of his hat. There was something oddly disconcerting about the way he scrutinized her, as if he was peeling away layer upon layer, looking for the person within. Kia didn't move a muscle, her heart suddenly pounding, her breath stuck in her chest. Awareness churned through her, making her heart beat even harder, and she was struck by a nearly paralyzing fascination with his hand, making her wonder what it would be like to be touched by him. A disabling weakness pumped through her, and it was all she could do to keep her eyes from drifting to his mouth, wide and full and looking very kissable. The amount of time she'd thought about kissing him filled many hours. A need so strong filtered through her. More than her next breath, she wanted to reach out and smooth her hand across that strong jaw, to experience his strength and his warmth. More than anything, she wanted to experience his warmth.

His expression suddenly shuttered, and he jerked his gaze from hers, his jaw bunched.

The moment was past; maybe it had never been there. Sometimes it was easy for a square peg to mistake a round hole for a square one—the desperation quotient. She stepped back. "You can expect fresh linens every day and housekeeping comes around about ten or so." She backed up some more and he straightened. "We serve breakfast downstairs until eleven-thirty, and of course we have lunch and dinner. Tonight, it's cornbread and authentic Texas chili. Yum."

She had reached the door, and she turned to go.

"Kia?"

"Yes?" She whipped back around.

"The key."

"Key?"

"To the door." That amusement was back.

Her words weren't quite so steady when she responded. "Oh, right, ha. I'm so lame." Yeesh, she was such a head-in-the-clouds dope. Feeling suddenly very foolish and very small, she eased a breath past the funny sensation behind her breastbone. Stupid girl crush, three—Kia, still a big, fat zero. She set it down on the end of the table. With her cheeks flushing, she closed the door behind her.

She was with Sally Jean. She so wanted to ride that rodeo.

3

Damn. He was in trouble, and he'd been in enough to realize it from the get go. Kia Silverbrook. He had to wonder if his mom knew she was running this place, but it wouldn't have mattered. No one...well...except his whole freaking team knew about her. It had been private until he'd been talking to Kid, but those nosy knuckleheads had overheard. And, of course, they couldn't give him enough advice.

Well, he could keep his own counsel just fine. Sure, he'd fantasized about her, but seeing her in person made him realize how gorgeous she was—really, truly beautiful. The otherness of her intrigued the hell out of him, with her pierced lip, the dark, expressive eyes, her pretty, pale skin, the purple streak in her dark, silky hair, and her strong features made him want to get closer. There was a look about her that told him she was a fighter, a scrapper, a tough warrior.

But he was just here to attend the reunion and visit with his family. His real life was in San Diego, overseas, wherever Uncle Sam wanted to send him. Reddick, its folks, and his time here were nothing but memories, most of them filled with anger, resentment, shame, so much guilt. Bitterness tightened his mouth at the renewed pain of that day his dream had come to an end. He shook it off, his throat tight from nostalgia, feeling gritty from the trip. So far no one had treated him any differently. He'd get his truck and unload his luggage, take a shower and try out some of that delicious sounding cornbread and chili. He had to wonder if Kia would still be tending bar or if her shift would be over.

Thirty minutes later he was down in the bar, and he knew he'd been kidding himself. He hadn't just come here for the reunion or to investigate buying back Sweetwater. He had come here for her. To fulfill his curiosity, to find out if the fantasies he'd had could even come close to something... ah hell. He didn't know why he was compelled now of all times to be here. He just was, and the reunion was just an excuse.

When he showed up, the perky blonde came right over to him. "Hey there again, cowboy. A table?"

He glanced toward the bar and saw that Kia wasn't there. Ah, damn. "Yeah, a table is fine."

The waitress smiled. "She'll be back any minute. She just went home to take care of her animals."

Damn, he was that transparent. He'd have to work on his poker face. "Thank you kindly, ma'am."

She brought him over to a table near the window, and he sat down. She handed him a menu, and he gave it back to her. "I'll take two bowls of the cornbread and chili and a beer for now."

"I gotcha. One of them bowls is for Kia. Well, that's good. She rarely takes the time to eat because she works so hard." She nodded. "Two bowls o' Red coming up. Excellent choice."

She served him the beer, and he took a gulp looking out

the window at the busy street. The main street was packed with people looking for a place to eat, and plenty of them were coming into The Back Forty.

Several people shot him glances when they came in, and he could see the recognition in their eyes. Yeah, there it was...the look that said they remembered him *and* his dad. His mom had tried to get him to go out to his dad's headstone, and he'd given her some noncommittal answer. He took another sip of the beer, the bitterness flowing back after so many years. He'd thought he'd put this life firmly in the past but being back here reminded him of everything he'd lost.

He'd saved every penny he'd made over the ten years he'd been in the service and now had a sizable sum. He'd been gung-ho to buy back his family's ranch, but as the time passed, it got less and less urgent as he immersed himself in training hard, staying elite. All his energy had been to become something more.

He wasn't sure he'd done that and wasn't sure that had stemmed from his need to prove to these people, to himself, that he wasn't that coward's son. He stuck it out, even when the going got rough.

Unlike his old man.

Even now, his dad could provoke him into that rage, a rage he'd channeled into the gumption he'd needed to kill other human beings. It was a fact of war, people died, he just made sure it was the enemy.

He didn't question what he did now. There were things he liked—the brotherhood of his fellow men in arms was priceless and something sacred. If someone messed with one of them, they messed with all of them. But he would never love killing. To him it was a necessity.

But as long as his dad could goad him into that kind of

reaction, Cowboy didn't have control, and he knew it. And he rebelled against giving a disgraced, dead man that kind of weapon.

He happened to glance over to Millie's Feed and Grain, and a distinct memory of sitting on the tailgate of his dad's truck as he loaded feed into the back came out of nowhere. It had been a bright, sunny day, and Cowboy was all of seven or eight. He had a shiner from a fight with Red Sweeny at school over some unflattering words that had been spoken.

Pride's a tricky thing, boy, his dad had said. *On one hand, we have pride and on the other vanity.*

Aren't they the same? he'd asked.

Nope, they ain't. He threw one of the huge feedbags into the truck, then wiped his brow. Cowboy couldn't have wanted to be more like his dad that day, strong, tall and smart.

To be proud, boy, is to know that you are worthy of great things. But, if you go for the petty stuff, that makes you not only petty, but vain. It's all about hard work and being the best man you can be. Think you're worthy of these things?

I think so. I want to be good.

There you go. You can be proud of that. His father had grasped his shoulder and crouched down so he could look him in the eyes. *Fighting for name calling and such is not a worthy situation. Makes you undeserving of great things, makes you vain and cowardly. Vanity and cowardliness are vices, Wes, but pride and temperance are virtues. Walk away unless you're threatened, then defend yourself. But don't let words and small people affect the way you handle your own honor. Am I making myself clear here?*

Yessir.

Good. He'd squeezed his shoulder again. *Because I think you have great potential, boy.* He'd lifted him off the tailgate and set him down. *Now let's go get you a cone and we won't mention this to your mom when we get home being it's close to dinner.*

Cowboy's throat tightened up. *But is that honorable, Dad?* he'd asked.

His father had given him a sly wink and a grin. *Your mom's a fine woman, but sometimes rules can be broken every so often. She doesn't have to know about it. So, yes, ice cream is always worth a little honor where your mom is concerned.* He'd ruffled Cowboy's hair, they had gotten ice cream, and to this day, it had been their secret.

Cowboy had to work to get his head around what his father had said that day, and despite what had happened, he'd taken it to heart, even though, now, it was a bitter pill to swallow.

He'd always believed his dad was an honorable man.

"So, this is a backhanded way of asking me to dinner?"

He jerked out of his musings to find Kia standing at his table with two bowls in her hands. He immediately stood up in deference to her, and she inclined her head, a soft smile turning up the corners of her mouth at his chivalry. She had delicate bones, a single silver band around her middle finger with skulls on it. Her skin had been soft when he'd clasped her hand, her palm showing that she was a working girl. She set his down in front of him, and the aroma made his stomach grumble. The savory chili with chunks of beef, a helping of sour cream to the side, along with a wedge of lime and the two triangles of moist cornbread, crunchy at the corners just the way he liked it, made him want to dig right in, but his manners won out.

"I heard that you don't eat much when you're working hard and that won't do. Hard work deserves reward. Now set that bowl down and get yourself something to drink. I'm sure your boss won't mind."

She did just that and handed him a spoon. "No, my boss is a pussycat," she said with a grin. She turned and went to the bar, which gave him too much of an opportunity to watch her.

Compact, not an ounce of wasted movement, the girl was put together with fishnet on top and on the bottom. Underneath a sexy cropped motorcycle jacket, covering the oh-so-feminine parts of her tantalizing anatomy and beneath the mesh, was a black bra with rollicking horses in shades of brown, and on her smooth, rolling hips, a barely-there strip of brown suede that would probably be identified loosely as a skirt. But there was nothing loose about her shapely backside, nicely curved and tight. A silver and black concho belt decorated with iron crosses nipped her waist. On her feet she wore a pair of edgy black cowgirl boots with metal at the toe and heel. But the kicker was a piece of leather around her neck with spikes. It conjured up the image of bondage and being submissive, but there was nothing at all submissive about Kia. He suspected, to her, it was a simple choker. It, nevertheless, turned him on.

She sauntered back over after taking the bottle the bartender handed her. He stood and held her chair while she settled into the seat. "I know you're itching to dig in. Have at it," she said. He didn't hesitate, but picked up the spoon and scooped up a heaping helping and popped it in his mouth.

"Mmhmm." He groaned. "Just the right amount of heat. What are you waiting for?"

"I just wanted to see your reaction to my cooking."

"Your cooking?"

"I'm a multi-faceted woman, and I wear many hats." She smiled and took her own bite, nodded. "A good batch."

"Yes, ma'am."

"I heard you joined the navy and became a SEAL. Is that true?"

"The God's honest."

He expected her to ask what everyone asked. But she took a totally different tack. "Maybe some time you could teach me to shoot or throw a punch."

He smiled because it was so unexpected. "Yeah? You got someone you want to beat up?"

"No questions about me wanting to shoot someone?"

"I'm leaving that one alone for now." She didn't smile, and he leaned forward. "Kia? Is there something wrong?"

"No. Well, I had a break-in and it scared me."

Cowboy stiffened, inhaling abruptly as every primal instinct in him surged to life, and he automatically went into military combat mode. His sudden, intense reaction caused her eyes to widen.

"That is a scary look I'd rather not have directed at me."

"Details?" he ground out.

She hesitated, and he deepened that menacing look that had seasoned SEALs backing down and subordinates running to do as he ordered. She gulped and her gaze hardened. "I'm going to tell you, but not because you're getting all hot and alpha bothered."

"Kia, what happened?"

"I was in the shower at the time and completely unprepared for the intended violence. I didn't like that either. It's not great to be exposed to someone who wants to do you harm, but even worse when you feel helpless."

"Do you know who this son of a bitch is? I can go have a talk with him."

She jutted her chin out. "I don't." She shook her head. "I also don't expect you to beat the shit out of him."

Terrorizing a woman was at the top of his "Beat the Shit Outta" list, and the fact that Kia had to endure that kind of fear made him a little crazy. "That's just a perk," he growled.

Her features softened, and she reached out and touched his hand in a neutral way, but he felt it all the way down to his groin. It also affected him that she was trying to soothe him when she'd been the one frightened. "The deputies say it was most likely a vagrant."

"Still scary." She nodded, the look in her eyes breaking his heart.

"I got myself a dog."

"You bought a dog? What kind?"

"I didn't exactly buy him, he was a stray, but I did get a guard dog, German shepherd pit bull mix."

"Interesting combination. What other animals are you feeding?"

"Three horses and one ornery, untrusting cat. He came with the dog."

"As in a pair?"

"Yeah, they're inseparable, and I didn't have the heart to be the one to come between them. Triton is wonderful, well-trained, and I already love him, but BFA—"

"BFA?"

"Ah, short for Brute Force Attack. It's a hacker term."

He chuckled. "Go on."

"He's impossible, and I don't get it because animals usually love me."

He bet she got a lot of attention, and not just from the animals. He'd like to give her his, but he was stymied by the distance and the fact that he just wasn't keen on getting involved with a woman in his hometown when he disliked even being here, the memories crowding around him like torturous ghosts. Everywhere he looked, he saw his dad, their life together, the promise that was long gone.

But she was so damn delectable. She leaned even closer over the table, her voice softly tender, her gaze darkening with concern—her breasts pushing toward the overfill maximum of that lively bra. She'd pulled all that silky hair into a ponytail, but as she spoke, an errant strand slipped free and fell in a silken purple curve to her chin.

Something inside Cowboy turned over, and it was all he could do not to lean across the table and take her mouth with his, to slide his fingers up into the violet and ebony silk of her hair and bend her into his kiss. He wondered if there was a name for this kind of reaction to a woman. Obsession might cover it. Horny certainly did. When she looked at him all starry-eyed and tenderhearted, like she wanted to take care of him instead, reassure him that she was okay when she wasn't, he wanted to make his fantasies his reality and take that second chance.

"I'm sure the cat will come around, darlin'. He is a male and you do have some charm."

Telling himself to slow down, way down, he stayed put on his side of the table and did no more than hold her gaze. He did have a point he was trying to make, and maybe he better make it.

"If you ever need me to 'talk' to anyone ever, all you have to do is ask me."

She gulped again, but this time it wasn't about his scary look at all, and he wasn't sure if he had made the smartest decision by coming here.

A man caught his attention in the dim light and the crowd. His hackles went up, his gut tightening. He couldn't quite make out the guy's face, but when Cowboy focused on the guy, he rose and threw some money on the table. Even though Cowboy tracked him toward the door, he got lost in the exiting crowd.

Kia looked over her shoulder, but there was nothing to see. When she looked back at him, he just shook his head.

"I should get back to work." He went to reach for his wallet, and Kia held up her hand. "No, it's on the house."

When he went to protest, her mouth firmed. "Wes, it's my treat, and it's wonderful seeing you after all these years." She rose and stepped back. "Stay and have whatever you like on me."

Whatever he liked on her? He'd like to be on her, all over her. She walked to the bar and lifted the hinged partition, slipping through. It was really getting crowded, and when the music sounded from the loud speakers, people got up to dance.

He watched them twirl around. His own two-stepping was pretty rusty. In fact, he couldn't remember the last time he'd danced.

Making a decision, he rose and threaded his way through the patrons now crowding the place. It seemed that the hours he'd sat there the restaurant had closed and the bar was now open. He leaned across, waiting for Kia's attention from the customers lined up for orders. When she spied him, she smiled and came over. "You need a refill?"

"No, a dance. Any chance your boss will give you a break?"

She gave him that secret smile again and nodded. She walked to the end of the bar and called into the kitchen. A young guy answered and took over. She came around, and he offered her his hand. "I'm a little rusty," he confessed.

She giggled and said, "It'll come back to you like riding a bike."

He walked her out to the dance floor and joined in. The quick-quick, slow-slow of the two-step was like slipping into a broken-in pair of shoes that he hadn't worn in a while. Second nature to a cowboy born and bred.

She followed his lead, and he took a chance, twirling her, getting rewarded with her soft laughter. "See, I told you."

After the song finished, the music went to something slow and sweet. Before Cowboy could even think about letting her go, he swept her up against him, the slow song giving him a reason to pull her close. Were second chances possible? Did he miss his window with this woman a long time ago? Was he fooling himself into thinking that he could seduce her into his bed and then disappear for another ten years?

The loneliness pressed in on him from so many deployments and not enough of a personal life. Had he been waiting for this? He had to take everything into consideration, especially Kia's feelings in the matter. He wasn't the kind of guy to keep mum about his intentions and ghost out of a woman's life. Serving his country made personal relationships complicated and his history with this town made it even doubly so, regardless of the distance.

The song ended, and he stepped back, suddenly wary of his own ability to keep this simple. With Kia, simple didn't fit.

She felt his withdrawal and blinked a couple of times. "Break time is over," she murmured and left the dance floor. He caught her arm and said, "What time do you close?"

"Usually about one-thirty, but I have to cash out and clean up, so realistically not until two." There was a hopeful look on her face, and he couldn't shake the feeling that he needed to stick close to her. It was just a nebulous feeling his gut kept broadcasting. He wasn't sure if his instincts were getting mixed up with his desire. He hated like hell to destroy her expectation.

"I'll walk you to your car."

She shook her head. "That's not necessary. It's just in the back lot. I'll be fine."

"I insist."

"That's terribly late and very noble of you, but I can make it from the bar to my car all by myself."

"Two it is," he said firmly.

She patted his arm. "Good night, Wes."

I'LL WALK you to your car about summed it up. Getting close to that man had made her go stupid girl crush again when he was just being polite. Maybe he was reacting to her story about being attacked. Whatever it was, she was fooling herself into thinking that a man like Wes McGraw would actually think getting involved with her was a good idea. After all, they lived hundreds of miles apart and he was a Navy SEAL, which meant he was gone a lot of the time. She lived here in Reddick and him in San Diego. Then there were these world-changing, axis-tipping secrets she'd kept from him. She had no idea how he would feel once they were out. Did she actually think he'd just take it in stride? Not really. It was best to just keep her distance, too. If only her silly heart could get the message. It was again no contest: stupid girl crush, four—Kia, still such a big, fat zero.

How could she be that naïve? She'd learned the hard way that people pretty much saw she was a freak and steered clear. But she answered to no one but herself and didn't really feel like opening herself to ridicule. That's why she was shocked that she had agreed to this damn reunion. But her years of isolation and the need to fit in even after ten years compelled her.

"Did you close the deal?" Sally Jean asked.

Kia let out a snort and reached for a bottle of Jack. Pouring it and the Coke into a glass, she served it with a lime wedge. "What deal would that be?"

"Okay, really? You have to be blind and dead not to want rodeo over there. Did you see that man?"

"I don't think he has any kind of deal with me, and my sex life isn't really up for discussion. He has different priorities." She uncapped a Corona and added the bottle to Sally Jean's tray.

"He has a dick, Kia," she said wryly, sticking a lime into the open lip. "Trust me, getting laid is a priority."

"I'm sure it is," Kia said, thinking about getting naked with Wes, reaching for a bottle of Jose Cuervo, pouring three shots. She grabbed the ingredients for a margarita. Not like she hadn't had that fantasy in...yeah...forever, but he was putting the brakes on, and she wasn't going to push. She had her own life to worry about. Except his offer to walk her to her car did melt her bones. She hit the blend button on her blender and gave it a few twirls with ice, then set the drink on the tray.

"Okay. Fine," Sally Jean conceded, and Kia was relieved. Opening two more bottles, she set them on the tray as well. She didn't want to get into an argument with her employee over her love life. Or, apparently, her lack of one. She hadn't missed the way Wes had given her the once over. She was sure he was thinking about the fishnet. All men thought about fishnet when a woman was encased in it from head to toe. This little number happened to be crotchless, too, but fat lot that would do if she couldn't get him interested.

Case in point, his offer to walk her to her car like a little old lady.

Sally Jean picked up her drink-laden tray and balanced it on one hand, unable to stop from giving Kia a sad look.

"Thanks for the girl talk," Kia said with a hint of sarcasm in her tone. Then she leveled a look at Sally Jean as she cleared dirty glasses off the bar. "Get those orders out before I fire you for being much too concerned about me."

"Sure, sure," Sally Jean said with a smirk, not at all fazed by Kia's words.

When she saw Wes leave the bar through the back, disappointment crowded her, and she spent the next few hours handling the bar, delivering drinks to the increasing deluge of customers flowing into The Back Forty.

Before long, the place was absolutely packed; the crush of people in the bar got thicker, the music amplified to a throbbing beat, and the crowd grew loud and boisterous from too much liquor and a whole lot of fun.

As the bar started to empty near closing time, Kia groaned. Exhaustion was settling in after working two shifts in one day, but with a man short she'd had no choice. Her employees had pitched in and had done such a bang-up job of cleaning up, for which she was eternally grateful. She just cashed out and called it a night. It was one-forty-five, and lost in her haze of fatigue, she simply headed for the back door.

She rolled her shoulders as she stepped through, then closed and locked the door.

When she turned, she was faced with a man in a black ski mask. She jumped back as he swiped at her, something glinting in the glow from the moon. A burning sensation erupted from her lower abdomen to her belly button, and she gasped at the cold, strange discomfort. He advanced, backhanding her across the face. Pain exploded out from her cheek and jaw. The man rushed her, and she was again completely vulnerable. She growled in anger and hit him a solid blow upside the head with her bag, knocking him back a couple of paces, thwarting him again, swinging her bag like a club. But he ducked, and she desperately used her bag to deflect his thrust toward her heart. She wasn't going to hold him off indefinitely. He was stronger than she was and so damn fast. But suddenly something huge hit her attacker, and the two figures grappled. It was Wes, and without much effort, he disarmed the guy, the knife clattering to the pavement. Punches were thrown and many blocks, kicks and general mayhem. Two powerful men locked in combat.

She tried to reach into her bag for her phone but felt weak all of a sudden. The burning sensation got worse. She reached down to cup her stomach and, when she felt something wet, lifted her hand to her eyes.

It was covered in blood.

4

"Wes," she said softly, even as the two men moved so quickly they were a blur to her. The man countering Wes's moves was a match for him. That was important, but she couldn't hold on to her thought, her fear for Wes acute. She clutched her side, the blood still flowing, her back against the wall for support. Finally, Wes got in a good blow and the guy sailed back and slammed against the wall. "Wes!" she called out again. He froze, turned toward her, and the guy who had attacked her rabbited away.

Wes rushed over.

"Christ," he whispered.

"I'm sorry, he got away."

"Fuck him. You're bleeding."

Without a word, he parted her jacket, getting all handsy with her.

"Aw, darlin', he caught you good." He reached for the opening of his shirt and with one pull had the snaps popped. Before she knew what was happening, he was pressing the cloth against her wound. "Hold that there, tight."

She closed her eyes, then opened them. Nope, still the amazing, gorgeous sight of Wes McGraw half-naked. She just stared at him, feeling woozy. "I'm feeling lightheaded, and I'm not sure if it's blood loss or you."

"Me? What did I do?"

"Really?" She reached out and bumped her index finger over the heavy muscles of his abdomen. Kia didn't have impulse control problems at all, but faced with that body, who could blame her? "Damn, Wes. Like wow. I don't think I've ever seen a body like that. Well, except in those male fitness magazines."

She took in the hard, chiseled cut of his jaw and beautiful mouth that she wanted to kiss. She'd like to see him smile more—not right now because that would be creepy. But like he did when she'd first met him, making all the girls in school swoon just waiting for him to work it in their direction, including her. She hadn't seen that sexy smile since his father had passed.

At this point, Wes was all about getting her help. It was in his body language. His focus was to stop the bleeding. He watched her, his seductive whiskey eyes intense and searching, as if he was trying to figure her out, who she was beyond the leather and fishnet, body piercings and purple streaked hair...*and what she was hiding from.*

In that moment, she felt a sudden shift between them. Her pulse leapt, and she realized she didn't like being on the receiving end of such an analyzing stare. For as much as she loved observing and scrutinizing people to get a clue how she should act, she'd also used her freakiness to shield her own emotions and soul-deep pain.

She'd always felt safe behind her computer, always peeking in on other people's lives and feelings but keeping her own hidden away. She'd never felt threatened that someone might realize her ploy, and that Wes might have that ability made her feel too vulnerable. Because her scars were on the inside, buried deep, and she had no desire to allow anyone close enough to unearth them. As a result, her relationships had always been short-lived, with her ending things before they got too serious. Before she gave her heart and opened herself up to the possible loss and rejection. She swore she'd never give up her personal power.

She realized that Wes had that power, and it was a realization that shook her to the very core of her being.

She'd had three boyfriends in ten years. One had been a biker, and she had really liked him. He thought she was cool, accepted her for who she was, but there was no spark there to keep the relationship from petering out. Then she'd met a cop in Corpus Christi, and he'd been serious and sweet, but it was clear he wanted her as an undercover girlfriend. She believed he was the one who wasn't comfortable with who he was more than he was embarrassed by her. Then she met a gamer online, and he'd been a blast. She'd flown back and forth to Georgia for a couple of years, but with him it was about the sex and the sheer joy of his just as quirky personality. He broke it off when he met a woman he wanted to pursue for real. She'd been single now for three years.

She closed her eyes. Man, did he smell good. So damn good. She wanted to bury her face in his neck and breathe deep. Once, when she was standing in line behind him in high school waiting to get into an assembly, the scent of him had stuck with her all day. The cut started to sting, and his shirt was soaking up a lot of blood. Her knees buckled a little.

He caught her against him, then bent those powerful legs and slipped his arm under her knees. Lifting her like she weighed nothing, he headed toward his truck. "Enough talk, darlin'."

He did smell good, the heat of his chest pressed against her arm, the smooth feel of his skin registering. She let her head fall against his shoulder, bringing the scent of him deep into her lungs. He leaned against the truck, supporting her while he dug in his pocket for his keys, unlocked the door and tucked her inside. When he came around the driver's side and slipped in, he urged her to lie down with her head in his lap. "Elevate your legs," he said.

She was feeling queasy. "Press it tight," he growled, his big hand covering hers, his forearm right between her breasts. My, God, every time the man talked, the smooth, deep sound of his velvet voice went right to the core of her and made her swoon.

"I'm so tired," she whispered. As her hand slackened, his pressed down.

"You're going to be all right. I'm going to get you to the emergency room. Hang in there."

Her head pounding, her stomach protesting, she so didn't want to throw up. That would be mortifying.

"Kia?" He shook her. "Stay with me darlin'."

She opened her eyes and tried to focus on him, but she was so tired. She felt cold and she couldn't seem to regulate her breathing, her heart pounding. The dizziness got worse.

She didn't want to die here and never tell him how she felt all these years. "I had a crush on you all this time," she whispered.

When she opened her eyes, he looked so calm as if he raced through the night with a bleeding, semi-conscious woman in his truck on a regular basis. He was such a rock, so solid. Wes was the epitome of conventional—hard working, capable. He was the description of a cowboy, from the deep whiskey of his eyes to the tips of his worn cowboy boots.

She was so different, isolated, not part of a team, different in her thoughts and dreams. The odd woman out. She wondered if he'd heard her at all.

When he pulled up at the hospital, he left his truck right there. By this time, Kia was really feeling awful. He came around and gathered her against him and moved briskly toward the sliding emergency doors. When he came inside, a nurse looked up and said. "Sir, you can't come in here without a shirt."

"My shirt is busy right now and this pretty thing needs medical attention. She's been cut." The nurse might have had the same malady Kia had when she was faced with a half-naked Wes. She just stared at him. "Now," he ordered, and she moved.

"Bring her this way."

"I think she's in shock," he said, but she heard it as if through a pipe, his voice indistinct and far away.

"Lay her here," another voice said, but she couldn't make out the face.

"What happened?"

"She was mugged and some guy cut her from just above her hip to just below her belly button. The guy got away. I brought her here."

"How long has it been?" a male voice asked, and Kia tried to turn her head. Her hand stung, then subsided.

"Twenty minutes. I timed it."

"Jo, call the sheriff, and sir, I'm afraid you'll have to leave."

Fear surged in Kia so hard she almost choked on it. "Wes," she called out, reaching for him, frightened with these strangers, even though they were medical professionals. If it hadn't been for him…if he hadn't been there, ignored her independent woman's nature, she'd be dead.

"I'm not going anywhere and you're wasting time here," Wes growled.

"Get this man some scrubs," someone ordered.

He clasped her hand. "I've got you, darlin'. Hang in there. You're safe."

She closed her eyes; the comfort of his hand meant so much. No one had ever held her hand. She drifted off, but he kept his fingers tight around hers.

For the first time in her life, someone had saved her. Really saved her, and of all the things she'd always wanted to feel, security was at the top of her list. That's what this feeling was that was radiating through her at his touch. Safety.

Wes would protect her.

COWBOY HAD BEEN PRESSURED to move further back now that Kia was sedated. He was still bare-chested as none of the scrubs could fit over his broad shoulders. His arms were folded across his chest as he watched every move they made, his gut tight. Christ. If he hadn't been impatient to see her again and had waited until two, she wouldn't be here. There was no doubt the guy was trying to kill her. If he had been closer… He closed his eyes. Rage flowed through him, and he wanted to kill the bastard who'd dared to attack a defenseless woman in a dark alley. He felt physically ill when he'd seen all that blood and realized that her smooth, creamy flesh had been cut. His rage boiled over into a white-hot violence, and it took everything in him not to slam his fist against the wall in fury and frustration.

Kia was in trouble. That guy wasn't a run-of-the-mill mugger. He had serious moves, and Cowboy knew an elite fighter when he came up against one.

Finally, the ER doctor pulled off his gloves and walked over to him. "Your friend is very lucky. The knife only sunk into the first layer of skin. I put in a couple of stitches so it'll scar less. I'll give you a box of waterproof bandages. The scrape part of the cut doesn't need a covering and should heal very quickly, but keep the stitched part covered. It's a superficial wound and she had some blood loss, but nothing significant. No organ or muscle damage. Once we get some fluids into her, she can go home."

"Thanks," Cowboy said.

A man in a tan uniform materialized at the door. He gave Cowboy a once over, then said, "Wes? My God, I haven't seen you in ten years."

"Uncle Jerry, how have you been?"

"Can't complain, but I don't like this business at all. How is she?" Jerry Jones had been Wes's dad's best friend and at the time of his father's death, a deputy. He along with the others who had responded to his mom's call had been tight-lipped and white-faced in the wake of his dad's suicide. Jerry was a good man, and he seemed not only devastated by his dad's death, but guilt-ridden as well. He kept saying he should have seen the signs.

"Kia is a trooper and the wound is superficial, but they sedated her. "

"All right. I'll get a statement from her when she's more aware. What can you tell me?"

Cowboy gave Jerry the breakdown of what he saw, but he couldn't identify the guy except that he was about six feet tall. He had on a ski mask and dark clothing. That was it. Not much to go on.

Jerry hooked his fingers into his belt. "Hmm, my deputies responded to a break-in call from her last week. I'll send a patrol around her house to start. But this is a small town and our manpower is always stretched thin this time of year. But we'll do what we can to keep her safe."

Cowboy wasn't impressed, but he got it. The local cops were going to do their best, but where Kia was concerned that wasn't going to be enough.

Not for him.

He waited some more once Kia came around, but he didn't go far. He stood within eyesight of her. She kept looking at him with bruised, faraway eyes, which only pissed him off some more. He wanted that warm, bright Kia back, the one he'd had dinner with, the one he'd danced with. Jerry was gentle and the consummate lawman asking her all the right questions. His competence made Cowboy feel much better, but once again memories of his dad surfaced. Fishing trips, hanging around the station, cattle drives, and just plain fun trail riding. He'd cut off any contact with Jerry as he had with everyone associated with his old life. His mom and sister only got cursory reports and short visits from him. They had often made the trip to San Diego to see him. It was the only reason he'd gotten the apartment in San Diego, or he would have stayed in the bachelor barracks on base.

He kept his eyes trained on her, the smudged eye makeup, her neat ponytail now in disarray, the ragged edges of the fishnet where the mugger had swiped at her, the bandage on her abdomen. But his eyes turned from assessing to caressing as he took in the belly button ring—another iron cross—the flatness of her midriff, the soft, touchable look to her skin. The jacket had hidden a lot, but with it off her, the fishnet covered her from her sweet, delicate shoulders all the way down to her toes. His mouth went dry, and he shifted. Damn his freaking libido. He shouldn't be ogling her after she'd been through so much tonight.

It was time to get her home, and they both needed sleep.

Jerry shook her hand, then squeezed her shoulder, leaning down to say what Cowboy was sure were encouraging words. Afterwards he came over to him. "Not much to go on, but we'll get on this. Are you going to stay with her tonight?"

"Yes," Cowboy said, the one word coming out strong and firm.

"All right, then. I'm afraid we're going to have to take your shirt as evidence, but I see you have nothing to be ashamed of there."

For the first time in a long time, Cowboy smiled.

"You have your dad's build," he said absently, his tone indicating not only how much he missed Cowboy's dad, but pure regret and some measure of guilt in his tone.

Uncomfortable with the mirror of his own emotions, Cowboy said, "Let me know if you find anything. I'd like to have a word with this son of a bitch."

"Now, don't go taking the law into your own hands, son."

He clenched his jaw. He couldn't promise Jerry a damn thing, so he kept his mouth closed. "I'll be in touch."

As soon as he left, Cowboy pushed off the wall and walked over to the gurney. Kia was sipping at some water a nurse had gotten her. The IV was gone. He reached for her leather jacket and helped her into it.

"You're my hero," he whispered, kissing her temple as he slipped the jacket up her arms.

She reached out and clutched his forearm, her fingers tight for a moment. He noticed she still had blood on her hands.

He lifted her off the stretcher and right into his arms. He held her close and gave the nurse outside the room a shake of his head when she indicated the wheelchair. He had told her he had her, and he did—safe in his arms.

The nurse looked disapproving, but she could go fuck herself. He wasn't giving Kia up to anyone.

He'd taken fifteen minutes to move his truck, and he walked steadily with her nestled against him. "You're very strong," she whispered.

"You're very brave," he said. He tucked her into the cab then settled himself behind the wheel. "Address?" he ordered, and she told him. He punched it into his GPS.

He headed out of the parking lot, keeping an eye on his rearview mirror to make sure they weren't being followed by anyone.

She didn't speak, and he looked over at her in the dim light from the dashboard. She had wrapped her arms loosely around her waist, staring out the window. He flipped on the heater when he saw that she was shivering. Luckily, the hospital had taken care of the shock concern, but now that the rush of adrenaline had worn off, she was beginning to come down.

"What's happening over there, darlin'?"

She slowly turned her head to glance at him, and even in the dimness of the cab, he could see the vacant, distracted look in her gaze. "I never thought of myself as a woman who needed to be saved by anyone. No one has ever saved me from anything, but I'm so very glad you were there tonight."

Cowboy's hands clutched the steering wheel in a punishing grip, his knuckles going white as he returned his attention back to the road. She'd almost died tonight, and if it had been an isolated incident, she could feel safe again after some time.

But with the information that she'd had a break-in last week and a *professional* had tried to kill her tonight and make it look like a mugging...there was something much more sinister going on here.

Tonight, he'd cut her some slack. After her attack, she wasn't exactly in the right place to hear about the danger or to even deal with it.

But come morning, when she was aware and had gotten some rest, they were going to have a little chat.

He had planned a simple week of R&R, but now he was involved up to his neck. His second chance girl had just become his number one priority. As a SEAL, he had vowed to protect the weak and innocent against all threats. Just because he wasn't on the battlefield didn't diminish his duty one bit. He might not be in uniform—shoot, he didn't even have a shirt on—but that duty was engraved on his soul.

He was going to protect her come hell or high water. There might be debate, and she might not like it, but he'd deal with that tomorrow.

There was one thing he learned in battle: being calm served everyone, and it was infectious. So he tamped down his anger and his frustration to make everything better, knowing that giving her his stillness would be the best thing he could offer right now. Going all combat black ops badass on her wasn't going to help her.

But later, when he found that fucker, combat black ops badass aside, Cowboy was going to kill him.

5

"You bought the old Hobson place?" he asked. Nothing more than a wreck of a barn, a ramshackle house with an outhouse, and about ten acres of land that butted up against Sweetwater.

Still huddled in her jacket, she said, "Mrs. Hobson died of pneumonia, and with his kids grown and no interest in the land, they left for greener pastures, leaving Mr. Hobson to either sell the land or let it fall to ruin. Unfortunately, he let it go."

He had no idea what to expect when he drove up her access road dotted with small slender trees and shrubs, wolfberry, hog-plum, and buttonbush. He came to an open gate with a cross bar with a stylish butterfly in silver, the letters spelling out Gray Havens.

As he drove, he was just hoping he wouldn't have to defend something falling down or, more importantly, have to use an outhouse.

The lane curved down into a sheltered hollow, and he felt a rush of warmth as the house and buildings came into view. The plantation-style home, painted a charcoal gray with white trim as was the decent-sized barn, sat in an L-shape with easy access. There was a garage, but he parked just by the front door. The corrals with wide white panels held three horses in the enclosure. Several acres of land adjacent to the road had been left untouched with a two-acre pond glinting in the moonlight. Thick stands of sweetgum and oak were scattered across the rolling terrain, and magnolia flanked the house on either side.

The driveway, which angled sharply across the yard, separated the raw, untouched land from the lawn surrounding her home. It butted up against Sweetwater. He'd made an inquiry with a local real estate agent, and he was waiting for her return call regarding his former ranch.

This place, though, was as surprising as she was—fresh, stylish, and well-maintained with plenty of landscaping touches, an unexpected and oddly disconcerting oasis in a night of violence and fear.

He stared at it a moment. Too many openings to defend. Too much landscaping, built in cover. A definite challenge if anything started going down.

Cutting the engine, he reached back for a small black case with a handle, then exited. Rounding the vehicle to the passenger side, he opened the door for Kia, but she didn't move—except for the tremors still running just below the surface of her skin. She seemed to have folded in on herself. He gently helped her out of the truck and onto the porch, her movement sluggish and unsteady. She stumbled a few times and looked around.

"Where are we?" she mumbled.

"Your place." With a firm hold around her waist, he led her to the front door, but when she made no move to extract her keys from her purse, he set down his case and grabbed her bag, rummaging through it under the lantern-style outdoor light until he hit pay dirt.

A sharp barking made her jump, then throw her arms around him and hold on. He dropped her purse and held her as her trembling went through him, breaking down his formidable defenses. Dammit. He was going to need a buffer here. A big buffer.

"It's all right," he whispered. "Your dog, Triton."

She looked up at him, her dazed expression clearing. "Right. He's a good boy but let me go first to make the introduction. After all you've done for me tonight, I don't want him to go for your throat. He's very protective."

She stepped away from him, and he unlocked the door. The sixty-five-pound, well-muscled dog poked his head out, but calmed a bit when he saw Kia. "Triton, sit. This is Wes McGraw. He's my friend." She patted his head and muzzle while he licked her.

Cowboy watched the dog, but, as she said, he was well-behaved and highly trained. To his total surprise, she was a natural as she put her body between them, exerting her alpha control. He snagged her purse and his case, then closed and locked the door.

The house was neat and tidy with a southwestern chic to it. Colorful striped rugs covered a glossy wood floor, and there was a fieldstone fireplace with plenty of wood to start a fire. It wasn't exactly freezing in the Gulf of Texas in September, the temperature at about sixty-eight, but a fire tended to boost the comfort level in the home. The brown suede couch, tan upholstered love seat, and armless leather chairs were set in a square grouping with a tan upholstered ottoman/coffee table in the center with two wooden trays, the TV on a wooden chest just behind the chairs. The pillows picked up the colors in the striped rugs and on the walls where several large horse paintings in violet and lavender hues hung along with silver spurs and a grouping of horseshoes and snaffle bits. The windows reached from the floor to the open beamed ceiling with brushed silver boxes of succulents at the base of each one. "Curtains?" he murmured.

She pointed to an iron table, and he grabbed a remote and clicked it. Shades made a soft whirring sound as they descended, closing out the night.

"Why don't you shower?" he said. "Get yourself cleaned up. You'll feel better. I'll start a fire."

She turned to look up at him. "You're not leaving?"

It was a plea, and he reacted to it, tenderness filling his chest.

"No, Kia. Not until this is resolved. Let's not get into this tonight. You're exhausted."

She just stood there as if he'd said a flying saucer had just landed on the lawn. He nudged her, and when she didn't move, he took her across the glossy wood floor to the stairs and helped her up them. He found the master bedroom and took her across the vibrant rugs, past the colorful bed with purple and red accents to the large tiled bathroom, noticing the splintered wood. His lips tightened.

Yeah, he was definitely going to kill that bastard.

He walked into the open shower and turned on the water. Immediately, nozzles in the wall and just above him started spraying water.

He helped her out of the leather jacket, his fingers catching in the fishnet as he went. Her skin was prickled with goosebumps, and he couldn't help noticing the stiff tips of her nipples outlined beneath the horse bodies on the bra.

"Get undressed and into the shower," he told her, meeting her gaze.

She gave a jerky nod, and he turned and left the bathroom to give her privacy to strip naked and step into the shower. Less than a minute later he heard a soft sound and turned to look back at her. Still fully clothed, she was looking down at her bloodied hands and plucking at the severed mess of fishnet.

"He ruined my body suit. I've had this...forever." She blinked, her eyes going glassy, filling with tears.

He reacted because she looked so upset and on the verge of a total meltdown. He went back inside the bathroom. Pushing her hands aside, he was lost for a second. The mesh was severed just in the area where she'd been slashed, partly intact on the right-hand side. No zipper, no buttons, no snaps, no nothing, and not enough stretch. What kind of witchcraft had she used to get into this thing?

"Damn, woman," he muttered. "I can break down a firearm and put it back together in minutes, but—" Then something gave way, a loose thread at the ragged edge just at her ribcage, and suddenly the whole top of it was unraveling right into his hands.

"Oh," she whispered, watching it come apart, tears dripping off her chin.

"Oh, shoot." This was incredible. With a handful of black thread and more falling off of her every second, trying to control the release only accelerated the process. It was like the endless scarf clowns pulled out of their sleeves, only this wasn't funny...at all.

In less than a minute, he was left holding a whole lot of ruined fishnet, and she was left with just the seam of what had once been mesh.

He definitely needed a buffer. At this point, her skirt was keeping up the rest below her waist, but he was able to remove the partially undone upper part off her. He stepped closer and slipped his hands around her to reach the zipper to her skirt, sliding it down her endlessly long legs, trying not to notice that the skimpy matching thong was all that covered her. Without preamble, he cupped his hand under her armpits and lifted her right out of the circle of suede.

She made a surprised gasp, and the sound of it tightened every muscle in his body. He set her down on the vanity chair and knelt down, removing her cool boots and setting them aside.

Then he reached up and grasped the ragged edges of the fishnet, and she lifted up her bottom as he rolled the mesh down her legs and off her feet.

Standing again, he pulled her back up, too, unclasped her bra, and let it fall to the floor. Fuck him. Fuck him hard, but she had pierced nipples, tiny bat wings hanging from a metal bar through each engorged tip. That little triangle of silk going next, and one glance at her completely naked had his dick swelling, her shadowed cleft cleanly shaven. Up to that point he'd managed to remain detached and focused on undressing her as fast as possible, and even though his brain tried to remain neutral like Switzerland, his body obviously had a mind of its own.

He tried to remove the collar, but she protested and turned her head. He left that alone at her agitation. He didn't want to upset her; he wanted to soothe her.

Ignoring the tightening ache in his groin, he guided Kia into the shower, a surge of hot need tightening his balls and making his thick dick flex. Her tight, sweet backside had a simple tat on one side—a heart with forty in the center— and a colorful fairy with purple hair sat on a crescent moon on the back of her shoulder. So it hadn't been a rumor. He positioned her beneath the multiple nozzles. She dropped her head as the water hit her and sluiced down her trembling body.

Knowing he couldn't leave her alone, he toed off his boots and removed his jeans. Keeping his boxer briefs on as a flimsy barrier to all that dark beauty, he walked into the shower with her. Wrapping his arms securely around her from behind, he pulled her as close as two bodies could get in one space.

She was rigid and unyielding at first, dealing with her trauma in her own way. He reached down and grabbed her hands and lifted them to the spray, gently washing off the blood with his fingers. She relaxed her back against his chest as the water cascaded over her shoulders and between their bodies.

Without warning, she turned against him, releasing a soft, shuddering sigh, trusting him to keep her safe and protected.

He vowed he would.

Her release of tension had been his plan, yet he hadn't figured in the intimacy of the situation once he'd gotten her to this point. Now she was burrowed close with her head on his shoulder and her lips mere inches away from his neck. Then there was the soft cushion of her breasts pressing against his bare chest, and the exquisite feel of her silky-smooth belly and supple thighs aligning so perfectly with his.

Despite his best efforts to remain unaffected, arousal thrummed heavily through his veins. His dick pulsed with need, and he was grateful that he'd worn his underwear, which was the only thing keeping his raging hard-on confined.

Needing some kind of distraction, he swept his hands up the provocative curve of her spine and beneath the fall of her hair. The heavy strands were wet, and the nape of her neck was like satin. Gathering her hair, he gently tipped her head back so that the spray soaked her hair. With a low, appreciative moan, she closed her eyes and lifted her chin even more, so that the water cascaded over her face, down her slender throat, and across the rise of her breasts.

She looked so incredibly sensual, like a water nymph with her sleek, wet skin and the ribbons of steam swirling all around her. His gaze took in her slightly parted lips, then slid along her jaw—and came to a stop on the deepening bruise from the base of her jaw to the top of her cheekbone.

He'd make the bastard suffer for that.

He couldn't stem the surge of anger that gripped him all over again—directed at the man who'd terrorized her, at himself for not staying detached when he was the rock, the calmest man in the platoon.

The thought that she could have been hurt a lot worse, nearly choked him on a fresh wave of anguish and relief. Without thinking, he lifted his hand and gently stroked his fingers along the bruise. Her skin was so soft, so delicate and fragile, and he couldn't help but kick himself for not getting there sooner and saving her from that horrible trauma.

"I'm sorry, Kia," he rasped, his voice sounding like rough sandpaper. "So, so sorry."

She brought her head back down, and the water-spiked lashes lifted, revealing beautiful silver eyes that were far more lucid than they'd been ten minutes ago. Her face was flushed with warmth, and she met his gaze with a small smile that was so incredibly sweet and guileless.

"I'm better. You were right about the shower," she said, misunderstanding his apology for remorse.

"I should have been there sooner; stopped it before it happened."

As they stood beneath the pelting spray, a slow, seductive awareness gradually took hold. He could feel the subtle change in Kia from relaxed to aroused in how she shifted against him and the way her flattened palms slid around his waist and up the slope of his spine. He watched as she licked droplets of water from her bottom lip and felt himself respond to the desire darkening her eyes. His erection throbbed and ached, the material of his briefs too tight and confining against his stiff dick.

"Wes…" she whispered, the one word filled with a wealth of emotion that struck a chord deep within him, too. "You saved me. You were magnificent." Eyes closing, she leaned forward and pressed her lips to his. Her mouth was soft and yielding, a heavenly temptation he couldn't resist, so he didn't even try. Her lips parted, and he accepted the invitation to deepen the connection, to slide his tongue inside and curl around hers, dragging her into a hunger so dark and hot he burned with the intensity of it.

He wrapped his fingers in the leather, the spikes poking his palm, and pulled her up to her toes, kissing her with a fierce urgency borne of knowing that she was truly okay and unharmed. He kissed her with an abundance of relief and gratitude and something else far more profound that echoed in the farthest recesses of his soul—an emotional, intimate bond that rocked the foundation of the solitary man he'd always been.

Driven by pure sensation, encouraged by the uninhibited way her fingers dug into the muscles bisecting his back and the arch of her hips against his, Wes backed her up against the shower stall, pressed the length of his body along her lush curves, careful of her cut, and ravished her mouth with overwhelming need and heat. His craving for her seared through him like an out-of-control blaze—something that he'd wanted for so damn long.

More. He needed more of Kia. Needed to touch her and taste her and savor every nuance that was uniquely her.

With only that thought in mind, he tore his mouth from hers and trailed his lips along her jaw, licked his way down to the base of her throat where her pulse beat strong and steady. He savored the life of her in the palpitations, knowing what a knife could do in the hands of a professional.

His hot blood ran cold. That was reason enough to not only bring in a buffer, but to keep his mind totally on point. Except she moaned softly and sifted her hands through his wet hair, twisted the strands around her fingers and guided his mouth lower, to the firm swells of her breasts. He followed, his resistance breaking under her dark magic, wanting to make one of his fantasies a reality.

He drew a taut, pierced nipple into his mouth, flicked the rigid tip and metal with his tongue, and sucked her deep and hard. With his hand, he squeezed and kneaded her other breast, traced lazy circles around her areola with his thumb before lightly pinching and rolling the firm, aroused nub between his fingers. She cried out, urging him down.

"Make me feel alive, Wes." Her voice was nothing but a sensual puff of sound.

With his large hands, he traced the dip of her waist, careful near her cut, the bandaged section and the angry red shallow slash uncovered and marring her delicate skin. He kissed it softly, and she pulled at his hair in response to his tenderness.

He cupped her hips, sliding his hands around to the base of her spine and down her perfect ass to the back of her thighs. The feel of her smooth, sleek skin against his palms was a luxury he'd denied himself too long, and he memorized every sensual curve of her body, along with the sweet, uninhibited sighs that accompanied every stroke and touch.

If he thought touching her was pure bliss, then allowing his mouth to follow in the same direction as his hands and tasting her warm, wet skin was like dropping down into heaven. He licked and gently bit his way down to her stomach and dipped and swirled his tongue in her navel around the iron cross belly button ring. Another erotic moan echoed in the shower, and the slender fingers still wrapped in his hair tugged him lower still.

He dropped to his knees in front of her, his heart racing a mile a minute as a heady surge of desire tore through him. Knowing what she wanted, what she needed, he took one of her hands and wrapped her fingers around the small metal bar built into the shower to help keep her steady and balanced, then draped one of her legs over his shoulder to give him better access to her.

The water poured down on both of them, and curls of steam immersed them in a sultry warmth as he leaned forward and laved the inside of her thighs slowly, leisurely, until he reached the very heart of her femininity. He used his tongue to increase her pleasure, her fingers knotting in his hair, her pleasure moaning and sighing out of her. His dick flexed, and he fondled himself, unable to handle the overwhelming need to be inside her.

That wasn't going to happen. He took her with heat and possessive intent, and she inhaled sharply, jolted against him in shock, then gave herself over to his erotic oral assault. Before long, he felt her come. He kept her from collapsing with a strong hand pressed to her uninjured stomach. After giving her every last bit of pleasure, he stood back up and braced his hands on the wall on either side of her head, not trusting himself to touch her when he was harder than granite and there was just enough of a thread of his self-control intact.

He lifted his head and looked into her face, expecting to see her sated, but it was clear that he wasn't the only one who'd had fantasies.

She reached down to his waistband, but he caught her wrist. "Let me," she whispered, pressing her mouth to his chest.

He shook his head and placed a kiss to the top of her head. "No, Kia. You've still got drugs in your system, you're reacting to me saving you, and this is going way too fast. Do you think you can finish up okay? I'm about at the end of my rope. Don't push me, darlin'."

She dropped her head and looked up at him. "You are so honorable. I'd never think about pressuring you."

Those words hurt. He cupped her face and kissed her long and hard. Then stepped out of the spray.

He opened the linen closet, realizing that this is where she'd hidden herself.

If that guy decided to come finish the job, his life was going to be over.

He pulled out a towel and reached down for his jeans. While she watched, he shucked his boxer briefs and dried off. Then he wrapped the towel around his waist. It was going to be some time before his erection went down enough for him to actually get them on.

Shutting the bathroom door on Kia when he wanted her beneath him was harder than anything he'd done in his life.

Hell, the only easy day was yesterday.

He settled in a purple cowhide chair in the corner of her

room, wanting to be close to her. Pulling out his phone, he punched in a number and waited.

"Give me a good reason why you're calling or I'm busting you down to seaman."

Cowboy couldn't help the smile that curved up one side of his mouth. Ruckus sounded like he'd been in some deep REMs. But when he explained the situation, Ruckus was concerned. When Cowboy mentioned Tank, his LT was all for it.

The next call got him the same kind of response. "This better be a fucking emergency," Tank growled.

"It's Cowboy, and I need you here in Reddick. I cleared it with LT."

His voice was immediately clear and intense. "When?"

"Yesterday."

"What's up?" Cowboy explained what happened. "I'll be on the road as soon as I talk to LT. You need anything from your apartment?"

"My shotgun," he said, his voice flat. Specifically, it was a pistol-gripped Mossberg 12-gauge Cruiser 500 shotgun.

"Got it. I'll be there by tomorrow."

"Thanks, man."

He severed the connection and sat back, trying to relax, working on getting the sensuous memories of Kia out of his head. Dang, he wanted her. Knowing he needed to take the edge off, he wrapped his hand around his dick and jacked himself off, hard and heavy into the towel. He was so primed, it didn't take very long, but the powerful orgasm was all about Kia, the intense pleasure making his back arch as he continued to pump up and down until he felt wrung out. Standing, he slipped into his jeans, the fly snug over his semi-erection. Still aching for her, he went downstairs. He grabbed his case and headed back to her bedroom.

He set the case on her bed and opened it. Nestled inside was his personal Glock. He removed it from the case along with the clip. He jammed it into the magazine and cocked the weapon just as she came out of the bathroom.

Her eyes went wide and dipped from his face to the gun in his hand. Chambering a round signified that he meant business, and she was well aware of that.

"I called a SEAL buddy of mine. He'll be here tomorrow. In the meantime, you need to get some sleep. How is the pain?"

"It hurts."

He tucked the Glock into the small of his back and walked past her into the bathroom. He dug in her jacket pocket and pulled out the pill bottle they'd given her. He filled a glass at the sink and popped the top, shaking out the prescribed dosage.

He set the pills into her palm and snugged her other hand around the glass.

"Get some sleep, darlin'. I'll be downstairs."

Then because he couldn't look at her without wanting her, he left the room. Triton stayed where he was on her bed, his tail wagging.

Thank God Tank was coming. He really needed a buffer.

He built a fire and got comfortable on the couch, the Glock now in his hand. A few minutes later she came into the room with an oversized T-shirt in her hand. On the front was lettered: *Feminine. Beautiful. Powerful.*

She reached out, offering the garment. He set down the handgun and pulled the shirt over his head in silence. She had on a pink top depicting a donut and coffee lettered with: *Donut Disturb*, the shorts a mosaic of donuts and coffee cups. She was freaking adorable.

She bit her lip and stood there, and he sighed. All he

wanted to do was take her upstairs, strip her out of that freaking cute getup and make love to her, lose himself, mind and body and soul, in her giving body, her sweet, drugging kisses, and forget about a killer out there stalking her. She was more than a one-night stand lady, more than a body to guard. It was emotionally complicated and freaking personal. And as a result, he couldn't take the chance that he would lose his edge and his ability to remain focused. Lose those instincts that kept his senses sharp and honed, enabling him to keep her out of danger.

But he also couldn't refuse her any comfort either. She was still a little out of it, scared and trying to deal with her own trauma. He made room for her on the spacious couch, and she came over and plastered herself against him. He reached for the purple fuzzy throw and covered her up.

"Did you take those pills?"

"Yessir," she said with a salute in her voice. He smiled slightly. "You are very pushy when you're in protection mode." Then she snuggled deeper into his embrace and promptly fell asleep.

He tightened his arms around her, listening to the coyotes howl in the distance. Tank would sleep while Cowboy guarded her, and he would sleep while Tank guarded them. He would keep her safe, use every ounce of training he possessed, go the extra mile. They would find and neutralize this threat.

Then he'd go back to San Diego. Back to duty.

6

Tank's phone rang as the sun was coming up.

"Hey, you need to make an appointment with my vet."

"Do I need my distemper shots?"

His little brother Jordan laughed softly. "Rabies more like it."

"Hey there."

"No, Doc's part of the Working Military Dogs network and doing great things. I thought you could meet, give Doc a real chance to see you guys in action. It's just a little bit of your time. Doc's all about this brochure to outline and promote the MWD program. Some people still think MWDs are euthanized as a matter of practice. Will you do it?"

"All right," Tank said, never able to say no to Jordan. I'm heading out of town to help a buddy, but when I get back, we'll hook up. Deal, little bro?"

"Yeah, really? Oh, man, Doc's going to be over the moon. Thanks, Thorn."

"You bet."

"While you're there, do get the rabies shot."

"I'm hanging up now."

He smiled as he disconnected the call, set the phone down and fondled Echo's head as he reclined in the front seat. He and his two brothers grew up tough, simply because nothing came easy. His family lived in East Los Angeles, where his parents were associated with gangs and divorced when Tank was young. Their mother, who was Puerto Rican, cared for them as best she could; his father came and went. One of Tank's earliest memories was of the car accident that spared everyone but his little sister. He was six, she five. The rent was often overdue, and sometimes his family simply abandoned the current residence and it was on to another house, another school—fifteen in all. He was always the new kid, the outsider. In high school, he lived in his garage, pumping heavy metal. He played drums in a band. He wore his hair in a mohawk and pierced his nose.

But even the extremes of Tank's rebellion were relatively tame: ditching class, drinking beer, smoking cigarettes, playing video games. Living in a violent world of real and wannabe gangsters, of random shootings, of drug dealing, a lifestyle they all wanted to escape. What he wanted most was the opposite of that world. He wanted to be a Navy SEAL.

At eighteen, he enlisted and found himself at BUD/S. Having grown up rootless and without boundaries, he immediately fell in love with the military's sense of tradition and ritual. He was nicknamed "Tank" for his big body, but he often felt isolated like a tank, a one-man killing machine. After several assignments, he was a standout not only in combat but in class. He was offered the chance to go to Lackland Air Force Base to begin training as a dog handler.

Tank had always loved dogs. During his erratic upbringing, they'd been a ballast. At various times, he'd owned a

Rottweiler, collie, and a black Lab named Bruiser. But Tank understood that a military dog was an instrument to master, just as a soldier had to understand his weapon or a diver work the water.

The military, with its sharp edges and unyielding discipline—the thing that was saving him from the streets and his parents' life—gave him purpose and when he worked with dogs, a sense of accomplishment because he was damn good at it. He instantly loved the work, inspired by its higher purpose. Even one IED, an improvised explosive device, sniffed out by a MWD's nose would equate to many saved lives.

He'd had many dogs through his career, but when he got Echo, he knew the Malinois was special. His assessment had gone fine, and he was cleared for his next deployment, but Tank knew that Echo was getting older and just a fraction of a second slower. He shook off his worries. That mutt had plenty of good years left in him.

His older brother Daniel had become a firefighter, and Jordan had gone for the animals and worked as an assistant in a vet's office. He had always been the most sensitive of the three of them. They had all gotten out of that life scot-free. To Tank, it was a miracle.

He had some clashes with his CO's over the years, but once he'd been assigned to his current team, with Ruckus at the wheel, it had been so much better. LT understood Tank and often gave him his head. In fact, Ruckus understood each one of them. Tank's biggest worry was the guy would get promoted. The brass had to know that their LT was admiral material.

He got along with most of the guys, but to be honest, Cowboy rubbed him the wrong way. That guy was always so damn calm, always in control. In the field, he was LT's right-hand guy, and maybe Tank was a little jealous of that, too. But he was part of the team, and when one of their members asked for help, he would drive twenty hours straight to lend a hand.

This Kia Silverbrook must be a babe, Tank thought. Cowboy had a hard on the size of California for her but had never sealed the deal. What was that about? Tank wanted a woman, he got her. Done deal, rocks off and everybody was happy.

He and Hollywood were of the same mind. Fuck them, but let them go, except Hollywood never slept with the same woman twice, ever.

Tank wasn't the kind of guy that stole a buddy's girl, but pulling Cowboy's chain did have its appeal. He'd just like to see that guy lose control. Just once. It would freaking make his day and show him that stoic, laid-back competent SEAL was just like the rest of them.

He'd heard still waters ran deep, and he wanted to stir the surface a bit to see if that big Texan bit. Would be real fun to reel him in.

He chuckled and stepped on the accelerator.

Get ready, Reddick, Texas. Tank was coming to town.

IT WAS WELL into morning when Cowboy woke, a heavy lethargy swimming through him, the weight in the middle section of his body anchoring him to the soft couch.

Then that pleasant feeling was suddenly dominated by a sensation of enormous responsibility. With the heaviness of accountability his whole life, he'd taken it in stride, wanting to do his father proud, wanting to live up to what his dad had said to him on that tailgate when he'd been young, not sure if he'd fulfilled it.

His doubts shamed him as much as his bitterness and resentment at what his dad had done— humiliated him, his family, tarnished their name. Nothing after that had ever been the same, and Cowboy struggled with the weight of his emotions, keeping them hidden, moving on stoically and calmly to put the pieces of his life back together.

He wasn't sure what that would look like if he could get past the fact that he'd been labelled by association in this town.

For the first time in his life, he didn't want to be logical or practical. For once, he just wanted to follow his heart as he recalled how hard it had been to turn away from Kia yesterday. He was screwing up his second chance, and he couldn't seem to help it. His actions were dictated by his strict code of conduct.

He opened his eyes and wished he'd kept them closed. But then he would have missed this. Her dark hair was everywhere. Silky swaths had tumbled out of her ponytail with a mussed-up, just-in-bed look. Then he was stupid enough to look at her face. She was so arresting with her features relaxed in sleep, her mouth just as soft and lush, exotically full, begging for his lips. She was beautiful in a quirky way, her looks compelling, but not standard, not run of the mill. Her chin was delicately angled, but he loved it when it was set with determination. Then, because he wasn't foolish enough, he let his gaze travel down her body. One shoulder was bare, her little shorts tight over her sweet backside. Her pelvis was nestled right against his erection which had already made its early morning appearance, and the sight of her only made him harder. After his unfulfilling encounter last night or early this morning, he was aching with a set of blue balls that would put hypothermia to shame.

He hadn't realized he could physically hurt for a woman. Self-control was supposed to be his middle name. But damn, she'd sorely tested him in the shower.

His gaze travelled back up, and she shifted. He released a soft groan as the movement sent waves of pleasure from the tip of his dick all the way to the base, clenching his stomach muscles and riding him hard. The cute top had ridden up as she'd slept, showing her creamy midriff and her bandage. That doused the heat in him, and with careful, controlled movements, he slipped out from under her, away from the torture and the danger. Triton lifted his head from his prone position on the rug and gave him a quizzical look. He crouched and patted his head.

Slanting a look at Kia, he wanted to devour her whole. Start at her cute hot pink toes with his mouth and just not stop. Instead, he stood, rearranged the throw over her, and collected his Glock from the coffee table, tucking it into the back of his jeans.

There were many things they needed to accomplish today, including telling her he was now going to guard her with his life, interrogate her about this situation, and get his luggage from her rented rooms. But first coffee, then breakfast.

His cell chimed, and when he looked at the display, he swore softly. He was supposed to be at breakfast twenty minutes ago.

He immediately called.

"What's wrong? You're never late. Are you all right?" His sister's frantic voice burst from the receiver.

"Sis, calm down. I'm fine. There's just been a complication."

"What kind of complication? Dammit, Wes! You've been here for one day and already you're ditching us? We planned this breakfast for you! There are people here waiting to see you."

"I'm not ditching you. Something's come up."

He heard in the background, "Let me have the phone."

"Wes! What is going on? We have been waiting for you for twenty minutes."

"I know. I forgot. I've been busy with—"

"I'm so sick of this behavior. You avoid everything that has meaning to you because you can't overcome what your father did." His gut clenched at the tone of his mom's voice, anguished and teary. Shit, he hadn't meant to make her cry. He winced, realizing just now that she had probably shed more than these tears over his inability to face coming back to Reddick. "You've been away for years. *Years, Wes!* Holding onto your bitterness is more important than your family. Well, fine. You take care of your complication!" The phone went dead. His mom had hung up on him. Fuck, she must be mad to cut him off like that. He'd have to make the time to smooth this over, but his family had to understand. Kia had to be the priority now.

He wasn't going to listen to that niggling voice that said he was more than relieved. He didn't want the damn breakfast in the first place. Most of those people knew his dad... He'd make it up to his mom and sister.

When he went into the kitchen to start a pot of coffee, Triton followed, but Cowboy stopped dead. A cat sat near some food dishes, and when Cowboy entered the room, the animal gave him an unblinking, silent stare. This had to be the attack cat. He braced himself. But BFA rose and walked over to him and curled around his legs, purring.

He frowned. He looked at the dog and Triton looked at

him, then back at the cat, then back at each other. It was like some comical canine skit. "Are you just lulling me into a false sense of security? Are you an ambush kitty?" Hadn't Kia named him after Brute Force Attack? He didn't seem so bad. "Sorry, buddy, but humans first, and I'm not sure what to feed you." The dog grunted his two cents about being fed, and the cat meowed at him, purring some more. "All right, you two spoiled brats, I'll see what I can do, but first I need a shot of caffeine or no one's going to be happy with this grumpy SEAL."

Triton and BFA touched noses, then the cat wound around the dog's legs, purring even louder. There was a ruckus outside, the kind of noise he recognized. Horses wanted their breakfast, too. "Settle down," he muttered. "What a zoo, but everyone gets fed." Cowboy looked for the coffeemaker, but there wasn't anything on her counter that he recognized until his gaze rested on a black and silver monstrosity. He approached it, typical of any man who was fascinated with gadgets. He crouched slightly, and when he looked down, both animals were watching him like he was their own personal entertainment.

"What you both looking at? I'm a SEAL. We can adapt."

A soft exhale of laughter sounded behind him, and he turned to find Kia watching them all. "Can you?" she asked, her voice all husky and drowsy. "That remains to be seen." She crossed the kitchen and reached for the contraption. Cowboy stepped back and watched her. She moved efficiently, punching controls, setting in little colorful tins, then revving the machine up. It spilled out a brew of foamy liquid into a horse-themed mug she'd pulled from the cupboard above the steaming appliance.

As soon as it was done spitting, she grabbed the handle and set the mug in his hand. He took a sip and exhaled the pleasure of that first taste. "Chocolate? This is a mocha. How did you know—"

"You had a chocolate bar every day for lunch in high school." She muscled him aside and smirked at him. He took another drink as she started her own cup, yawning. He stared at her, and she shrugged. "Hey, I'm observant."

"Mmhmm," he murmured noncommittally. That meant she was watching him in high school just like he'd watched her.

She looked down at the dog and placid cat, then frowned. "Are you BFFs with BFA?" she asked as if it was an accusation.

"Um, he was the one who made the first move," Cowboy said.

She frowned, then reached down to pet him. The cat hissed and jumped back as if he'd been scalded. He made the kind of deep, I'm-pissed-as-hell feline warning growl deep in his throat, then swiped at her.

She hastily drew her hand back and gave him an exasperated, quelling look. "Great. He'd rather make nice with a stranger than me." She took a deep breath. "But I will win you over, mister. Mark my words."

Damn she was adorable. She went to the fridge and opened the door. He saw her wince, reminding him how close she'd come to meeting her maker last night. He set down the cup and took her by the shoulders, steering her toward the bar and stool facing the kitchen. Her dining room, situated to the right of the open kitchen, had a rough-hewn table with six cool-looking copper chairs around it. He really liked her style, the soft/hard décor with the metal accents and the soft furnishings.

He pulled the pill bottle out of his jeans pocket and set it on the counter. She gave him a scrunched-up face. "I'm fine."

"Don't be a macho, tough guy, Kia. Take the pills. I'll take care of the food."

She was quiet for a moment. He'd always sensed she was a strong, capable woman. Most women would be frantic, panicked and emotionally distraught, yet Kia was sitting here having this crazy conversation with him.

She released a deep sigh. "Well, it's much more than you and me. There's Triton, un-hello kitty," she stuck her tongue out at the cat, "and three horses. I have a huge delivery of hay due soon, and it all has to go in the loft, stall mucking, and horse care. I have a bar to run, computer stuff to do, errands and girly stuff."

"You own the bar?"

Her smile was sheepish. "Yeah."

He narrowed his eyes. "I can handle most of that. I'm just not sure about the girly stuff."

"I have to wash my delicates by hand and paint my toenails," she said deadpan.

He grinned. Damn this beautiful, complex, funny woman. "You can give me some direction on the domestics, but I know how to take care of horses, no instructions needed there. And, at Sweetwater, I was the Hay King. Delegate the bar management, computer stuff is okay because that's not going to tax you none. We'll do the errands together. I can dang well hand wash delicates and paint toenails."

"Wow, a Renaissance Man. How did I get so lucky?" She grabbed the bottle and popped two pills, chasing them with a gulp of coffee. "There's more. I am part of the whole reunion—"

"Cancel."

"I can't miss it. These people are depending on me." She met his gaze head on like a freight train. "If you think I'm going to stick my head in the sand and disappear, you might start rethinking that pushy, alpha attitude right now." There was that determined chin. "I have commitments and a life to live. He's not going to take that away from me. Now that I'm aware, I will be more careful—"

"Damn straight. With me you will be."

"So, what gives here, Wes? Are you really sticking around?"

He turned to look at her. "Yes, I'm moving in, and I'm not letting you out of my sight until we get to the bottom of this shit storm you've fallen into, darlin'."

"Whoa, back that Pony Express up. You think that deep, sexy *darlin'* is going to soften me up there, cowboy?" she asked breathlessly. "I'm not saying it isn't working, but what exactly are you going to do, be my twenty-four/seven bodyguard?"

"That's my call name in the SEALs."

"What?"

"Cowboy, cuz of my Texas accent."

"Oh, I was just referring to the run of the mill, range-riding kind."

"Yeah, I know. I'm not that anymore. I'm a badass, highly-trained, spec ops wall of muscle that guy is going to have to go through to get to you."

"Are you going to answer my question?"

"Not exactly. Tank and I are going to be your bodyguards."

"What the hell is a Tank?" she squeaked.

After her direction, he found the frying pan. Peering at the stove, he tweaked the right knob. "Petty Officer Thorn

Hunt, Team Seven, big but stealthy and as dangerous as they come. But, you can call him Tank."

"Tank," she said incredulously. "He's on his way here?"

"Yes, I told you that last night." He cracked eggs, scrambled them, added ingredients.

"I was a little out of it last night, so excuse me."

"Yeah, I was a little, too." The heat, the taste of her all came rushing back at him. The metal and bud of her nipple against his tongue, how sensitive the tips were and the sound of her pleasure as he'd tasted her. He'd vowed to keep his hands off her, but his awareness of her couldn't be more on edge.

She blushed as she seemed to understand where his thoughts were right now. *The shower* hung between them like the overheated air between their lips, whispering against their skin with a raw longing, beckoning them to give in.

He swallowed and dished up the western omelets, garnished them with tomatoes and a dollop of sour cream and served her. Was it really him needing to stay on point that was holding him back from being with Kia? Or did it really boil down to the fact that she lived here in Reddick, a place he didn't want to be? That something couldn't work out between them because even with the purchase of the ranch, he wasn't so sure he could ever get over the deep, to-his-roots betrayal he'd experienced. How could he be proud of all his accomplishments when his core, his foundation, was rotten?

"I NEED A FORK," she groused. When he looked at her blankly, she blew out a breath and said, "Drawer right below you."

The rattle of the drawer was loud in the still air as he pulled out a fork and handed it to her.

She loaded up a bite and after tasting it, she said, "Wow, this is good."

"Kia—"

"I'm not ungrateful. I just hate being corralled and... dammit...afraid."

"There's no other way to deal with this. You need protection from that man. He was a professional."

She blanched. "What do you mean?"

"Trained. I'd say former special ops."

"Oh, God. Special ops."

"You were lucky with both the break-in and the attack."

"You think he broke in, too?"

"Yes, I do."

She bit her lip.

"Why does this guy want you dead?"

"I have no clue." She looked up at him and he could tell she wasn't done. "Wes, I'm still a hacker and in the past, I've done some illegal jobs. I was angry when I was a teenager, and I wanted to rebel against the world. Typical orphan who no one really understood or cared about."

"You were an orphan?"

"I might as well have been. All of my foster parents couldn't stand me and thought I was a freak. So, yeah, I lived pretty much alone, but that's beside the point. I took on any job that I thought would stick it to the man. You know...the establishment. I'm not proud of that, but there it is. Everyone has some secret they're ashamed of...that's one of mine." She toyed with the food. "Anyway, I covered my tracks extremely well. I'm pretty much a ghost online."

"Quicksilver."

She got even more white.

"I was in the office when you were accused of that grade database break-in incident. That's the hacker name Mr. Jackson used. Yours. It fits perfectly."

"Yes, I'm Quicksilver, but I denied any knowledge of that, and he couldn't prove a thing, the old goat. He might have been our counselor, but he wasn't very encouraging."

Cowboy laughed softly. "He thought I was nothing but a dumb jock."

"He was a jerk and fool," Kia said. "I ran rings around him in high school, even hacked his bank account and transferred all his money from his checking to his savings account. He always gave me the evil eye after that. I think he was a little afraid of me." She let out an evil giggle.

"So, you've dealt with some shady characters, then?"

She sobered. "Yes, I have, but I gave it up years ago. Now I'm a Black Hat."

So she was hacking to find breaches or bypasses in internet security. Also known as crackers or dark-side hackers who legitimately broke things for a living. "Working for the Department of Defense?"

"I can't talk about the DoD, Wes. It's proprietary information, confidential."

"I get that," he said with a wry shake of his head. "Hard to hear that come back at me, but we might have to investigate everything to figure this out."

"We'll cross that bridge when we come to it." She finished off the omelet. "So what we have is a dead end."

"For now."

THE HORSES STARTED in with more neighing from the corral. "The natives are getting restless," she said. "If we don't want a stampede, we better feed them. We should get at it."

"There's something else we need to talk about. Those animals can wait."

She slid down off the barstool. It didn't take a genius to figure out what he wanted to talk to her about. She got it by the reserved look on his face, coupled with the gruff, direct tone of his voice, that their conversation was going to be about that heated pleasure-burst in the shower in the early hours of the morning, and what she wanted from him now. Who was she kidding? She had always wanted something more with Wes.

"About the shower—"

"If you're going to apologize, you can stuff it." She faced him squarely, and it was hard not to get distracted. He was wearing that ridiculous shirt that she'd given him, and he filled it out nicely. The man had a chest that was made for a woman to press herself against, the kind of chest that was just as solid for her head as it was for her hands, filled with heavy-muscled contours that made her want to touch, to lick and suck. He was disheveled, unshaven, scruffy, and it was not fair that men looked so delectable in the morning. She was sure she looked like a complete mess. But not her cowboy. He looked like one of those Ralph Lauren ads for cologne. He didn't have to project the cowboy image; he was the cowboy image making unkempt so damn sexy. She should be fighting the lust he inspired, but she'd always wanted to know what it would be like to be with him, and that small taste wasn't nearly enough, but she feared that Wes's noble character was going to nix anything else between them. She didn't have to like it. "I'm not sorry one bit."

The cat yowled, and she huffed out a breath as she

headed for the cupboard. She had no idea what had stopped him from making a move in high school, but they were grown now, adults. There wouldn't be anything that she would regret with Wes. He might want to protect her, but what was developing between them was as real as it got. She opened the cupboard, the food container clearly marked. Wes moved in and took over.

"Genghis Cat gets half a cup. His food is in the second container marked *Beast*. Triton three-quarters." She handed him the measuring cup, then continued, "I had some pain killers, and I was a little out of it, but I knew what I was doing." He filled the bowls and set them down all in complete silence. "I wanted to be with you, plain and simple," she went on before he could say anything. "In my opinion, we didn't go far enough."

"Are you done?"

"No, but you can talk now."

"By all means."

She tilted her head and wished he would give her some indication how he was feeling. Calm, still waters was really irritating right now. "I'm not a demanding woman, and I don't cling...well, except when I've been knifed, and I'm freaking scared." *Oh, Kia, you're so full of horse hooey.* He raised a brow. That rodeo knew when he was dealing with some bullcrap. "Oh, all right. I can be demanding." But she had a right. Last night she had been so close to that heat, it had burned her badly, and she wanted more. He was everything she'd yearned for as a teenager and now as a woman, yet so much more. The desire between them had been mutual and real, soul-stirring, and deeply, irrevocably emotional.

And he obviously didn't have a clue. He was a typical, stupid, stubborn man when it came to admitting anything that had to do with his feelings or emotions. And she wasn't one to push or cling to false expectations. She'd learned with her last relationship that you couldn't force someone to love you back.

She leaned back against the counter for support.

"Apologizing didn't cross my mind, darlin'."

"Huh? It seemed as if you thought you were taking advantage of me."

"Your capacity to resist was low."

"Resist? That never crossed my mind."

He chuckled. "This is about focus. My attraction to you is too damned distracting, and I can't allow it to affect my ability to fully protect you," he admitted roughly and dragged his fingers through his hair. "I need to stay on point and ride the herd like wolves are snapping on our heels. Thinking about having sex with you is counterproductive to maintaining vigilance. I'm not about to make a mistake here, Kia. Not with your life hanging in the balance. Besides, I'm visiting, and being a SEAL isn't conducive to a long-term situation, especially when my home base is San Diego. That's something you can think about while we work on this problem of who wants to harm you."

She stepped forward and wrapped her arms around him, thankful for his presence, his honesty, and his lethal skills. For a moment, he didn't respond, then he pulled her close and held her tightly. He was so honorable trying to create a professional relationship between them, even while admitting to their attraction all to keep her safe. That he had to physically and mentally remove himself from the temptation of sleeping with her said a whole lot about Wes and his true feelings—that sex with her wouldn't be easy, casual, or forgettable. Because if he'd just wanted gratuitous sex, he would be taking advantage of her fear and need for safety and taken her invitation in the shower last night.

She suspected that not having sex was going to be more distracting for the both of them, but Wes would have to come to that conclusion on his own. Giving in wasn't going to make her any less susceptible to an attack.

She had to respect his professional boundaries, respect his wishes until he changed his mind. Her mind was already made up. She would have him before he pulled out of Reddick. One way or the other, he'd realize that there was more between them already than there had ever been with anyone else.

"Is she dead?"

"No, somebody intervened. I was trying to make it look like a mugging. Your instructions."

"What? You're a fuck up! This is the second time you've missed her. Who was this somebody?"

"I don't know, but he was big, lethal and trained. I'd say special ops."

"Special ops? Son of a bitch!" It was only going to be a matter of time before they traced the hacking to her, and when that happened, she would figure out who had been behind hiring her. Panic crawled up his spine. He would lose everything. "I want her dead! I can't afford for you to miss her again. Get it done, or I'll get someone else who will do it."

"The big guy is hanging around, but I'll get her. No one escapes from me."

"Call me when it's over, and we'll make arrangements for payment. Are you sure you have to have it in cash?"

"Yes. It keeps me completely off the radar. Cash."

"No more screw ups."

"Nope, consider the problem solved."

He slammed the phone down just as his assistant came through the door. "Is everything okay?" she asked when she saw his face.

He schooled his features into blank lines. "Yes, everything is fine." Or it would be when Kia Silverbrook, aka Quicksilver, was terminated. "What's up?"

"The White House wants you."

"On my way."

BEFORE HE'D LET her leave the house, he did a perimeter check, and she indulged his need to make sure it was safe for her to be outside. She had said she wasn't clingy, but, man, she wanted those arms around her as they stepped onto the porch. She felt marginally better that Triton was right beside her. He would alert her to any danger with his heightened senses.

But still, her skin prickled with fear, residual from her break-in and almost being gutted earlier. Every day of her life, when she left the safe nest she'd built for herself and ventured out into the world to expose herself to its ridicule, she found reinforcements that she didn't belong in normal, that her normal was beyond the here and now in the dark, shadowy ever after where people like her thrived.

She didn't *know* how to be anything other than what she was, and that person never seemed to quite fit in.

Wes turned toward her when she hesitated. She wanted to be brave, be the kind of woman that deserved a man like Wes, link into this existence. The kind of man that so belonged here. She pushed back at her fear and took a step. He extended his hand—that small gesture made her chest explode with newfound admiration for this big, tough guy. He had the presence of mind to understand how she was feeling and the sensitivity to offer this small gesture to show her that she wasn't alone.

She clasped it with a slight smile, and he gave her hand a quick, tight squeeze as they walked close together to the barn. She'd been okay with leaving the horses out for one night. It was still warm in Reddick and would be for a couple more months. But by this time, the hay would have been depleted, and her guys loved getting their daily ration of grain.

"The stalls are already cleaned. I did them yesterday. We'll just need to tidy up the corral, but we can do that when they are eating." Kia let Wes open the gate because she was the one who sensed he needed to do that for her, needed all these physical gestures to make up for what had happened to her. None of this was his fault, of course, but Wes was the type of man to take on that responsibility. She bet he made an amazing SEAL.

"What are their names?"

"Quicksand is the buckskin, Twilight Star the paint, and that gorgeous appaloosa is Saragon."

"Saragon?"

"Yeah, I think it sounds like a dragon, so fierce and loyal. He likes shiny things, too." He was looking at her in a way that made her stomach flip flop. "I always take Quicksand first. He can be feisty."

He clucked and approached the buckskin easily, clipping the halter lead on him. He took them into the barn one by one.

"Any other ways to get into the barn?"

"Yes, a back door through the tack room, but I usually keep that locked. I'll check it out. The loft, too. Then we'll get to the horses." The dog went to follow him, and she realized that if Triton was already this attached to him, Wes sure had some major alpha mojo going on.

"Stay, boy. Watch," he said and Triton settled down in front of the big open doorway. It'd be hard to sneak up on them with Triton on duty.

"I'll get the grain ready."

"All right, but don't hurt yourself. If it's too painful, wait for me."

She nodded, and he disappeared into the back. She grabbed the three feed buckets from the stalls and set them near the large container that held the grain. Her wound protested as she opened the bin top, and she stopped, holding her side momentarily, allowing the pain to subside.

Wes came down from the loft and saw her. "Kia," he said with censure. "Don't make me hogtie you, woman." Grabbing her shoulders, he steered her to a hay bale that was up against the fourth unused stall where she kept several bales so she wouldn't have to get it from the loft above. She stacked it weekly to save time.

"It might be interesting to see you try," she said, the words just coming out in a husky tone she hadn't known she'd possessed. God, the way he'd grabbed her collar yesterday and brought her up to his mouth...she had to breathe around the sudden arousal.

His whiskey eyes heated, and he gave her a don't-go-there look.

She gave him her first set of innocent eyes and then said "What?" very fast in a high-pitched voice. Yeah, he probably thought she was a freak, too. Maybe he wasn't into her piercings. Maybe they turned him off and he was just trying to let her down easy. But the way he'd kissed her, devoured her with that clever mouth of his couldn't really be denied.

She'd been there, and she'd felt him unraveling. Maybe losing control scared him the most. It scared most people, except for Kia. She realized that having control was an illusion. Accepting that might be the weirdest thing about her.

She leaned back against the wood, giving in to her need to rest some more. She couldn't pretend this hadn't happened early this morning, that her world hadn't been altered. That now she was entangled in the worst way and best way with Wes McGraw.

He prepared the feed buckets to her specifications, his movements natural, as if he hadn't been gone from ranching for ten years.

"What's this guy's story?" He rubbed Quicksand's muzzle, and he snuffled into Wes's hand.

"I got him at an auction. I don't know much about him except he's a handful and gets ridden the least because he's a headstrong jerk."

He chuckled. "You a pain in the butt, buddy?" Wes said as he set the bucket inside and Quicksand dipped his head in. "Most horses just need to do what they were born to do. Maybe he was a cow pony? Needs to ride the herd to feel like he's earning his keep."

"I don't have any cows. Just the Notorious C.A.T. and Triton." Wes chuckled. She had plenty of names for BFA. Oh, yeah, and she suspected she would find more. "And that dog wants to herd as well as being a great guard dog. Maybe he's just too much horse for me."

"Maybe. I was surprised to see that you had horses. You didn't ride in high school. Where did you learn?"

Oh, man, here they were getting into her terrible secret territory, and she wasn't ready to tell him anything about it, rock his world or his past. She wasn't sure how he would take it, but she was sure of one thing. It wouldn't be good or an "in stride" thing for him. Maybe then he'd lose some of that restraint that had him locked up. "I took lessons. I had a great teacher, but I was in love with horses long before I ever rode one." Keeping the particulars vague worked for her, but she felt guilty for not telling him the truth. "Mostly because of you."

"Oh, yeah?"

"Yeah. The way you talked about ranching stuff always involved Sunshine—Sunny."

"A cowboy and his horse have a strong bond." He rubbed Quicksand's forehead before moving on to the next stall. "Saragon, huh? It does sound very regal. You have fanciful notions, Kia, that is for sure." He hung the appaloosa's bucket, and he dug in.

She felt her cheeks heat. Was he making fun of her? "I live in my own little world."

He turned to look at her—maybe her defensive voice gave her away—and she bit her lip, squirming a little at his scrutiny. "Did you think I was funnin' you?"

He came over and crouched down. "You wouldn't be the first one to have something to say about my clothes, or my piercings, or my fanciful names." Damn, but he looked good in the morning with that dark stubble. Typical of men in Texas who worked the range, he didn't go anywhere without his hat. It was pulled low and set his thickly-lashed eyes in shadow, but she could see clearly that he was sincere. And she should try not to focus so much on his mouth, but the ruggedness the stubble gave to his face emphasized those full lips, the hat accentuating not only his sculpted mouth, but her weak spot—the dark hair that curled just behind Wes's ear.

"I was just making a comment is all."

Not that she would apologize for who she was. That

would be like admitting she might as well disappear. Normal was her goal. Just try to be normal. If only she knew how.

"Here's the thing, Kia. You're the most authentic person I've ever met. In a world of conformity, it's easy to act the same as anyone else. But people want real. We're starving for realness. So you name your horses anything you like."

"Even if I think lizard people run the government?"

He chuckled and rose, going to Twilight and hanging the bucket for him, his back to her. She held her side as she pushed herself up from the hay bale. Twilight was the most patient of the three of them. When Wes turned, he almost ran her over. An instant later, two strong hands palmed her waist and steadied her. He looked into her eyes. "I might have to agree with you there."

There was no need to say that putting his hands on her was not the way to steady her at the moment, but she was too busy trying to rally her thoughts away from imagining him manhandling her like this while they were both naked and tangled in tousled sheets.

Or up against the shower tiles. There it was, that hot memory between them. The unfulfilled, aching memory. His head dipped, and his mouth hovered close to hers without touching. It was excruciating as the silence stretched out and the awareness expanded until the intimacy was screaming for contact, begging for release.

He shuddered and stepped away. "I think some people in government are as cold-blooded as lizards."

The moment over, they left the barn. For the rest of the day, Wes drove her around to her errands, watching diligently for any kind of danger. This must have been what he was like on patrol, and it was daunting to think he could be so intense for so long, like maintaining that kind of focus wouldn't be exhausting. But Wes didn't seem to tire of his hypervigilance. They picked up his luggage from the rental, and she called Sally Jean to let her know to check him out, so his card wouldn't be charged. She was relieved that it went to her voice mail, not prepared for her twenty questions.

Back at home, she was starting to feel pretty tired and sore. So she popped some of those pain pills.

"Is there anything else you need me to do? Besides dinner in an hour? Tank should be here close to one."

Tank again. What kind of name was that for a man? How intimidating was it already? She was going to have two hypervigilant SEALs in her house. Two alpha males and she was already drowning in males at the moment with three horses, Triton, and Catzilla.

"Yes, I need you to wash my delicates and then I was planning on changing my polish today."

"It still hurts to bend over at the waist?"

"Yes, too much for me to reach my toes."

"I've got you covered. Where are the...delicates?"

"In a white mesh bag hanging on the doorknob in my bathroom. I usually wash them in the dual sinks. One for suds, the other for rinsing, then set them in there to dry."

She went up the stairs with Wes behind her and Triton trailing her. "You can rest while I do this. You look beat."

"I am a little tired," she admitted as BFA came charging down the stairs and out the cat door as if his tail was on fire. "That animal is crazy," she muttered. When she got to her room, she let out a stream of curses. Bending down with a grimace and a soft groan of pain, she picked up the ruined lace panties. "That damn Lucifurr." She had been too distracted to make sure all her stuff had been dumped in the hamper. "I'm trying not to feel hurt because it is obvious that BFA likes you, Wes. Genuinely likes you. But he's clawed up another one of my garments and still acts like I'm the opposite of catnip." She threw her hands in the air. "I'm catnot."

He rubbed her back. "No, you're not. Have you thought he might feel threatened by you?"

"How? All I've done is feed him and *enjoy* the little dead treats he leaves on my front porch. I've given him a home, the ungrateful monster."

Wes went into the bathroom, and Kia followed him. "You're an orphan. He's an orphan, and maybe he's latched on to Triton as his territory. Maybe he thinks you're going to take away his home base."

"I never thought of that." Triton made a soft sound in his throat as if in sympathy. She sat down on the vanity chair, and Triton settled down next to her. She looked down at the dog and sighed. "Am I bogarting you, Tri?"

"Why did you name him Triton?"

Her head came up, and Wes's reflection in the mirror under the bright lights of the bathroom took her breath away as usual. It was tough being in here with him when this room was the location of that heated memory that still hung between them.

"I also noticed that forty plays a prominent place in your life. The Back Forty, the number forty spelled out on top of your cabinets, and the heart on your backside with forty inside it."

Her mouth went a little dry. She couldn't expect a smart man like Wes not to make the connection. She shrugged in a nonchalant lift of her shoulders. "Forty is a mystical number, a master number, and you find it a lot everywhere."

Oh, ho, he was calling her out. She met his smart-ass eyes dead on. She gave him a smirk and started to tick things off her fingers. "The saying, "Life begins at forty," the expression "forty winks," the highest number counted in Sesame Street, many references in the Bible, like "forty days and forty nights," the standard number of hours in a work week, the number of weeks of a woman's pregnancy, the number of spaces on a *Monopoly* game board, the—"

"My jersey number in football."

Her eyes fluttered and went all innocent again. "Really? I don't remember. You didn't even let me get to the math stuff."

He dumped out the bag, and she lost him for a moment as he looked at her collection of lacy, racy unmentionables.

He took a deep breath as if he was trying to gain his voice again. After a few more moments, he said, "Yeah, it all adds up. The name "Triton" is also very closely related to the sea, our trident, and, therefore, symbolic of us." Triton raised his head at the sound of his name. Wes's voice had gotten tight, but his ability to focus on the conversation and deal with his obvious addiction to looking at her underclothes was admirable.

"And here I thought men had one track minds and couldn't multitask."

He met her eyes in the mirror. "I can multitask, darlin', better than you know." His voice went soft and deep. "I can also one-track mind it until the cows come home. Don't change the subject."

Oh, my. Was it getting hot in here? She gathered her hair and pinned it up on the top of her head, so many tendrils falling down, but she didn't care. She was feeling no pain now. The meds were damn good.

"The subject was *supposed* to be you handling my delicate washing because you were being a high-handed, pushy...*man*."

"That so? I stand corrected."

Damn, could his shoulders be any broader? That wide back tapering down to his slim waist. She already knew the ridges of his hard, six-pack abs and his flat belly were just a lift of his T-shirt away. His butt. Wow, tight and firm, filling out those Wranglers to full and distracting capacity. She'd seen him naked. He'd stripped right in front of her. The contours of his body were etched in her mind with laser beam strength. She'd never seen such a well-muscled, delineated torso in her life. And, the part of him that made him male—thick, engorged and jutting up against that flat stomach. His equipment was as large and beautifully proportioned as the man who owned it.

"We'll have to defer the "forty" discussion for some time later."

Oh, poo. He wasn't going to let it go. Well, she would work at tying him into knots so that he wouldn't be able to get back to his football jersey. Even though he was completely, one hundred percent accurate about her obsession with the number forty and her ill-advised and drunken-decision tat on her backside.

"Christ," he whispered when he'd filled both sinks and added the soap she used to keep her hand wash items clean. He fingered a studded, punk rock inspired camisole.

"I wear that spiked collar with that one." Her voice was low and seductive; the wordless promise in her eyes to him was that she would wear it for him. You couldn't talk about that kind of piece without getting a little turned on.

"How do I wash this?" he asked, his voice sounding strangled, meeting her heated eyes in the mirror. She could see her own arousal reflected back at her. She was sure Wes could, too.

"Immerse it and move it around with your fingers." She

rose and went to stand next to him. His hands were big and strong. She would have thought it would have been difficult for such a virile man to manage it. "Easy." She slipped her thumb between his closed fist, caressing his palm. "Don't grasp it."

She ducked under his arm and set her hands over the backs of his, her spine and butt curled against his chest and groin. The pain meds were mellowing her out, and her need to be close to Wes was just too overwhelming to feign.

"Gently, so you don't break off any of the studs."

He slowed his movement, and she closed her eyes, inhaled a deep breath and let it out real slow, trying her best to ignore the erotic thoughts drifting through her mind. Another long, slow breath as she relaxed and enjoyed touching him, those big, capable hands of his that had touched her so gently. How could she be surprised that he would have a problem washing her dainty articles?

"Okay, now just squeeze out the excess water." She ran her soapy, slick fingers over his knuckles and up his wrist. "Now set it in the rinse water." He followed her directions.

"What about these...bras?" His voice sounded winded.

"Bralettes."

"Huh?"

"They're bralettes, the flimsy cousin to bras. They have no support."

"Then why wear them? Isn't that the purpose... ah...of bras?"

She smiled at him in the mirror. His expression of confusion was so endearing. Poor, sweet, dumb men. "I'm sure you remember I'm not exactly hugely endowed in that respect, and to be perfectly honest about it, I hate underwires and thick bras. They always make me feel like I'm trying to enhance what I have, which I'm not. I like my breasts just the way they are."

"They're as beautiful as you are," he whispered. She rubbed at the underside of his wrists with her thumbs, enjoying the feel of him around her.

She so wanted to respect his no sex rule. She did, but it was clear that they both wanted to explore each other from head to toe. It was clear what Wes wanted. It was also clear from the stubborn cant to his chin that he was the most controlled man she'd ever met. Then, when she thought he would continue with the task, he closed his eyes and buried his face in her hair and breathed deep. "Jesus, Kia."

This was torturing him and her. She hated that she was making it more difficult for him. With a quick movement, she ducked back under his arm, and his eyes opened as she moved away. "I'm sorry, Wes. It's just so hard to keep my distance. But I promise I'll try harder."

He swore like...well...like a sailor.

"You probably don't even want to kiss me. It's probably the piercing. Not many guys like the lip ring. A turn—"

He pivoted abruptly as if he had finally gotten to the end of his rope. He curled his damp hand around the nape of her neck, the coolness of it barely soothing the heat he had already generated. His mouth came down on hers harder than he'd ever kissed her, like he was making a point. His fingers buried in her hair, he pressed her up against the vanity with his hard, undeniably aroused body. With a low growl encompassing both frustration and urgent need, he slanted his mouth across hers and sank his tongue deep, kissing her just as recklessly as he had the night before. His mouth promised sin and unrestrained, bodily pleasure, and she matched him stroke for stroke, chasing his tongue with her own, letting him know that she was with him all the way.

The feverish intensity between them was sizzling hot, the strength and immediacy of her arousal making her knees weak. She slid her arms around his waist and skimmed her hands down to cup his buttocks through soft, worn denim. The muscles tightened under her palms, and the long, hard length of him pushed insistently against the crux of her thighs. She felt the bite of his belt buckle against her hip, but she was too swamped with the desire and need coiling tighter within her to care about the minor discomfort.

His cell went off, the ringing as insistent as his mouth. He hesitated, then curled his tongue around the lip ring, then his lips sucked her right there as he drew away, her bottom lip still in his grip until he finally let go. The message was pretty clear that her piercings turned him on.

"Fuck." His breath was ragged. He set his forehead against hers, then pulled out the cell. "Damn, it's Tank. Probably checking in. Why don't you go lie down?" he said. "I'll finish up here."

She nodded. "All the lacy stuff gets set on the drying rack. The knit tops just need to be reshaped and dried flat, including the studded camisole."

"Okay." His eyes followed her as she exited the bathroom.

Feeling unsatisfied and grumpy, she left the room. Stretching out on her bed, she closed her eyes. All her stuff for the pedicure was on her nightstand. She woke several minutes later when she felt him removing the polish. Then he lifted her and set her on the vanity, gently placing her feet into a pan of warm water. When her nails were clean and buffed, he painted on the deep red color she'd chosen.

After that she went downstairs with him, and he made dinner. Once they'd finished eating, he built up the fire, and she fell asleep again until Triton startled her awake, alerting them someone was on the porch. Wes picked up his gun and went to the door, peering out onto the porch at the huge silhouette there.

He relaxed and then opened the door. "Fuck, this place is tucked out of the way," a deep voice said as he came into the foyer. Then Wes moved and, *holy hell*. Now she understood why his call name was Tank.

It was hard to miss that he was big. It was also hard to miss that his features were drop-dead gorgeous, but dangerous at the same time. There was no doubt in her mind that this man was a SEAL through and through, alpha to the core. The way he handled Triton was masterful, his confident energy telling her dog this was someone who was in charge.

With a face leaner and more angular than Wes's, he had a wide forehead, heavy, dark brows over thick-lashed, mesmerizing dark brown eyes with a bone-deep confidence radiating out of every pore. His black hair was shaved on the sides and long and wavy on top, almost punkish as if he knew what it was like to wear his hair in a mohawk and like it. His mustache was more pronounced, with a light beard coating a strong jaw as dark as his hair. He looked rough and ready, a carved slab of granite, even after twenty odd hours in the car.

He was tall, at least six four, his massive arms and shoulders bigger than Wes's, but his waist was tight and lean. The plain black T-shirt he wore was flat against his stomach, the sleeves straining at his bulging biceps. He had a tattoo on his upper arm that she couldn't quite make out.

"Petty Officer Thorn Hunt, this is Kia Silverbrook."

He stopped moving when he saw her sitting like a deer caught in the headlights of an incredibly beautiful Mack truck barreling toward her.

He stared at her as if he was absorbing her. Her attention cut to Wes, and even though it was clear he was trying to keep it under wraps, it was evident he didn't like the way Tank was looking at her.

"I pegged it, Cowboy." He grinned at Wes. "She's a freaking babe." He reached out his big hand, all but engulfing hers. "Kia, pleased to meet you. The cavalry is here, ma'am." There was something else about him; he was a gentle giant, his handshake brief and warm. She couldn't help but like him right away.

"You must be exhausted and hungry," she managed as Wes was now openly scowling. She thought it was cute and wonderful that he was acting so...proprietary. She wondered what kind of relationship these two men had.

"We ate an hour ago."

"We?"

"I have a Military Working Dog with me." He bent down and fondled Triton's head, his hand huge.

"Tank's our dog handler."

"I've heard of that. What's his name?"

"Echo. It's best that we introduce them outside and preferably by walking them in neutral territory before housing them in the same space. It'll allow them to bond as a pack before I introduce Echo to your home. He's well-behaved, but this is Triton's turf. I have a portable kennel for him as well."

They took care of the walk, both dogs a bit agitated at first, but she kept a firm hand on Triton, and Tank was amazing with the compact, beautiful Belgian Malinois. The brisk walk felt good, and back home, she entered first followed by Cowboy, then Triton. After that, Tank entered, then Echo. Both animals settled down near the fire. "I can show you to the guest room, then. You must be tired."

He looked back at Wes. "I ain't here for no damn garden party." The meaning was lost on her, but Wes, even with the scowl, looked amused.

"I'm sure that's some kind of SEAL speak." She rose and said, "The guest room is this way."

He followed her out of the room and past the stairs.

She opened the door, and he smiled. "Nice room, great view."

"Yeah. The bathroom is right through that door, linens are in the closet, towels, extra blankets, etcetera. Please make yourself at home and help yourself to the kitchen." Yeesh this guy was so big. He filled the doorway. She was starting to feel better after all.

"Thank you, ma'am."

"Thank you for coming here and helping me. It's much appreciated." They went back out to the living room. "All right. I'll go to bed. You guys look like you want to talk. Good night, Wes. Mr....ah...Hunt."

"Call me Tank."

She nodded. She looked at Wes one more time before she went up the stairs. She'd already showed him his guest room, sandwiched between her bedroom and home office on the upper level. It felt strange to have people in the house, men at that. Gorgeous men. Tank might be attractive, but her heart had belonged to Wes—Cowboy—for a long time. Their eyes met, and her body ached. She'd miss sleeping close to him tonight.

8

"Wow, damsel in distress, hometown, high school reunion, probably family drama. What's up with her? Who'd want to hurt her?"

Cowboy was still feeling the waves of tingles every-where, hot and alive with sensation from Kia's look as she climbed the stairs.

"Aren't you chipper for getting no rack time for almost a day?"

"Help me with this kennel," Tank said and blew out a breath. "I took a few twenty-minute power naps. Echo slept just fine. Fill me in."

Cowboy followed him out of the house, and they got the pieces out of the back of Tank's SUV. "I don't know who the guy was in the alley trying to knife her, but it didn't feel like a common mugging to me. The guy was trained."

Tank frowned, his eyes narrowing. Cowboy was sure he was as pissed as he was to know some elite warrior had been sent after a seemingly innocent, defenseless woman. "As in spec ops?" He unlaced his boots and toed them off.

"Yeah, he had that feel." They trundled the pieces into

the guest room and set it up. Tank dropped the black bag that held Echo's feed bowls, extra collars, grooming supplies and leads. He'd already set his dog food into the kitchen.

Tank whistled. "A freaking merc? Professional assassin? And her background? She owns a bar, right?" He unzipped the bag and pulled out a soft fuzzy blue blanket and spread it on the black bottom of the metal wire enclosure. "Echo," Tank called, and the dog immediately responded. Tank pulled out a small bone and said, "Kennel." The dog entered and Tank gave Echo the bone. He settled down while Tank latched the door.

They left the room. Triton was still by the fire and looked to be out for the night. "Not just that. She's a hacker, one who's not been so particular in her clients."

Tank settled into one of the leather chairs. "Wow, a bad girl damsel. My favorite kind."

Cowboy sat down on the cushy couch across from his team member. "We're here to protect her. That's all."

"Right. *I'm* here to protect her. I believe *you* have a different agenda."

He sighed. "Change of plans."

His brown eyes gleamed. "What? Now that she's in danger you don't want to nail her?"

Leaning back into the couch and hooking his ankle across his opposite knee, Cowboy crossed his arms over his chest. "I swear to God, Tank." His jaw was so clenched, his words came out as if under mountains of pressure, a tight growl. He'd known this was coming since he'd asked for Tank's help. He'd just meant to confide in Kid, but as was typical, his teammates were as nosy and opinionated as old biddies.

Tank listened with an indulgent smile, rolling his eyes.

"Fuck, you're uptight. We all know you have a thing for this looker, so cut the crap."

When he didn't answer, Tank leaned forward. The guy was intense even when he was sleeping.

"It's complicated."

Tank laughed. "It's body slots A into B. Everyone's happy. Providing you know which is A and which is B." He chuckled.

"Sex isn't A into B, you Neanderthal. She's not a hooker." Cowboy didn't bother to hide his irritation over Tank's nonchalance when it came to sex. He was an earthy guy, Cowboy got that, but geez. This was Kia. *His* Kia. He could tell himself this was about protecting her, but that didn't remotely explain why he couldn't stop thinking about her, touching her, kissing her, when he was the one to set the ground rules. He was chafing at the bit he set in his own mouth.

Tank's smile turned knowing and grew wider. "Sure it is. It's easy-peasy, man." He set his hand through his dark hair. "You want her. Guys know these things because we're guys and we have the same one-track minds, but you, my friend, keep everything under wraps and maybe you're more afraid of showing her who you are than what goes into slot A or B or C for that matter." After dropping that bomb on him without so much as a breath in direction change, Tank rose. "You know I am kind of hungry. What you got to eat?"

After going into the kitchen and showing Tank the fridge, Tank made a sandwich, bypassed the beer, and went for the hard lemonade. Tank wouldn't compromise his focus with alcohol, but the alcohol soft drink wouldn't even faze that huge metabolism. He sat down at the table to eat it. He might be a Neanderthal, but he was one with manners. He chewed, his features thoughtful. He smirked. "Nice shirt. Girl power. I like it."

Cowboy ignored him. That much was true, he was attracted to her. He did want to nail her if he was being crass, and Kia was definitely the opposite of him—bold, unconventional, outgoing and quirky. But something about the way she looked at him, and handled his attention, had definitely gotten to him in ways he didn't want to understand. But his body certainly had. Which was the last thing he was going to share with the caveman here. "It doesn't matter whether I'm attracted to her or not. What is important is that she's got more going on than meets the eye. She's in trouble, Tank. The kind that makes you dead."

His features leveled out, finally serious. "What's she into then? Did she tell you? Are you sure she's as innocent as she looks?" He was all business now, and Cowboy finally relaxed a little.

"Thank you." Cowboy shifted when a log dropped in the fire like the proverbial other shoe.

Tank grinned unrepentantly. "Oh, I'm far from being done needling you about this, but if you really think something is up here, I trust your judgment. I wouldn't have gotten LT to release Echo to me or driven fifteen hundred miles in twenty hours if I didn't. More importantly, Cowboy, I've got your six and hers, too. No one is going to harm her."

He nodded. "I hate that she's terrified, and she told me that she's also had a break-in. I don't think that was coincidental."

"That son of a bitch is going to die, I swear."

"Not if I get to him first."

Tank's jaw hardened. "I don't believe in coincidences."

"Me either. As to her innocence, she told me she's a Black Hat, but her clients are confidential."

"DoD?"

"Yeah, it's what I was thinking."

"Could be some homeless vet in need of some cash. We could be reading more into it than there is."

"Maybe."

"Any activity since the attack?"

"No, nothing."

"What's our plan then? Lay low?"

"I wish. We have this reunion, and she's part of it, so she's adamant about keeping her promises."

Tank polished off the sandwich. "What's the schedule?"

He rose and went to her notebook and brought it back. Tank looked it over. "Hmmm, the only problematic functions on here are the car wash and tailgate football game. Anyone can get into those. The other functions look like they're only for your former classmates."

"That's my thought, too."

"Can she forgo the car wash and tailgate?"

"I don't think she's going to agree with that." Cowboy got a thought. "Then let's use it to our advantage. We could flush the bastard out. He knows I'm here, but not you."

"Yeah, an ambush. I like being a sneaky bastard."

"Could give us some answers."

"Yeah, I hope you like the answers you get."

WHEN COWBOY CLIMBED THE STAIRS, he was beat. They decided that Tank would also go to bed. If anyone came around, the dogs would alert them to any danger. He looked at her door, then decided checking on her would allow him to sleep better. Slipping into her room, he moved soundlessly across the covered rugs on the hardwood. As soon as he got close to the bed, he could hear her thrashing.

He rushed the rest of the way. "Whoa, darlin'," he said gently as she came awake, made a soft sound, and wrapped her arms around his neck. He couldn't help noticing she was wearing the collar again. He wondered what significance it had to her. It was obvious it comforted her. But, for him, it turned him the fuck on.

"Wes." She clung to him, holding him so tight, he ached to soothe her, erase the memory of her attack, allay her fears.

"You're safe, sweet darlin'."

He held her in the dim room as her body got heavy. What Tank had said to him held truth...more than a bit of truth. He closed his eyes and breathed her in. Dammit, the Neanderthal was freaking right. He had the kind of focus that wouldn't budge no matter what he was doing, whether it was moving through jungle, going over a battle plan, or protecting one beautiful little freak.

So many years, he'd kept everything under wraps, learned to handle his emotions alone and in private. Ever since his dad had pulled that trigger, Cowboy had shut down. It was only becoming evident to him now how much he had cut himself off from life. Living alone, staying away from his family and keeping everything to himself.

What was he afraid of? He shifted, and she clutched at him, her head coming up. Their eyes met in the dim light, and Cowboy was done, at the end of his rope, his patience. He'd come here for a second chance, and he was putting up roadblocks to taking the risk. It was so much easier to shut down, stay neutral. But what he hadn't realized was that also numbed him.

Kia reached up and traced his face with her fingertips. "I

used to dream about you being in my bed. I never, ever in a million years thought I'd have you here."

Against his will and every ounce of his common sense, he looked down at her mouth.

And took a breath.

"Please kiss me," she said in her bold, off-kilter Kia way as if she'd never grown out of that small-child-demanding way, her voice kind of raw and throaty, as if they'd already been kissing the heck out of each other for the last couple of hours.

Without the dark smudges at her eyes, her face hadn't lost one ounce of its dramatic contrast, none of its beauty. Her lashes were half-mast over her stormy eyes, her lips a softer shade of pink. Her hair was wild, so Kia wild, as if she'd been heaved across pillows and dragged across mattresses, the way a guy might, if he was...crazy or lucky, or simply out of his ever-loving mind.

"Wes," she breathed his name, her hands going to the hem of his shirt and starting to draw it up.

He didn't stop her. He was too busy thinking, remembering, and wondering if she might be a practitioner of witchcraft, because he was not his normal, clear-thinking self. He felt a little bewitched, as if he were under some kind of spell.

He fought it a bit. "Condoms," he said.

"I don't have any, but I'm on the pill. It'll be okay."

She was pulling the rest of his T-shirt over his head. She was gone, over the edge, and the part of him that had resisted, let go.

She was sweet, hungry for him, needed him.

Needed him inside her.

Needed him to anchor her world.

Kia had barely changed from the girl he'd known. She

still smelled like her, looked like her, acted like her, and Christ, she still had the same mind-blowing effect on him.

But she wasn't the same and neither was he, and he'd been taught a hard lesson in the most brutal way. *Could people really be trusted?*

He cupped her cheek and smoothed his fingers over her skin.

Hell, would they even still be together if he'd taken that risk?

He knew better than to kiss her, but he did it anyway—just let go of every freaking thing he thought was stopping him, tilted that impish face up to his and brought his mouth down on hers.

Heat, as hot and stirring as all get out, washed through him. He groaned with the pleasure of it, gave himself over to it. Her skin was so soft, and he was breaking out in a sweat. He suddenly knew it didn't matter that she was his charge. This wouldn't compromise him one lick.

She wanted him, and deep, deep down inside in a dark place where he'd locked, bolted and chained the door and thrown away the key, he opened it up. At first it felt rusty, then it hurt, then it hurt so good, then it felt so damn good, so damn right.

He'd let his dad's suicide stunt him emotionally. That included everything from friendship, except where it came to Kid, to allowing himself to love.

One of her hands slid through his hair, across the nape of his neck and up toward the top of his skull, holding him for her kiss. His brain was fogging. Her mouth was so soft, so silky. He clasped her around the waist and settled her on his lap, a hand on the silken softness of her thighs. Her other hand was sliding beneath his waistband, heading south, driving him wild, and he knew she was going to take him in her hand, stroke him, get him even harder than he already was, and he was going to let it ride.

Let it fucking ride.

She called to him like a siren away from nights so dark he'd thought they'd never end, away from fear and pain that had dogged him whenever he wasn't vigilant. Away from grief so deep, he was terrified to let it surface.

He'd gone into the navy to escape, to lick his wounds, to prop up his sagging pride. They had made him into something because he worked hard, took it into both his hands like a lifeline. In turn, they had honed him and enhanced him for near indestructibility.

Yeah, she'd seen right through him.

He was transparent to her.

He slid his hand around the back of her neck, and she captured him with her smoky-eyed gaze. Yeah, she wanted this.

Combing his fingers up through her hair, he closed his fist around a handful of silken strands and brought them to his face, and he breathed her in, the rich combination of all she was: the girl of his forgotten dreams.

She intrigued him like no other, enchanted him, everything about her. If he couldn't open up to Kia, if he couldn't let go of his shame, he would die inside. He would shrivel up and expire without her. She was like air, water, light.

The navy had kept him on the move, and he had made no effort, none. He was on the hunt for America's enemies, but deep down inside him, always on the hunt for her, the rarest thing on earth, a woman who knew him and cared.

After his dad's betrayal, he lost track of who he'd been, but Kia hadn't. She knew him. His longing for her had a past, and his need to be with her had taken on a life of its own.

Lowering his mouth to hers again, he kissed her, gently sliding his tongue inside when she opened for him. A small groan escaped her, and he deepened the kiss, the way a man does when he's going all the way. And she knew it, her body softening against him in a thousand lush and lovely ways.

This was all he needed.

Her.

He'd needed to sink himself into the sweet mystery of a woman's sensuality—this woman's quirky, goth cowgirl with the backbone of steel.

She pulled off her T-shirt, exposing those pierced breasts, the bats glinting in the moonlight. Every part of him that was hard got harder—the curvy mounds of her breasts beckoning him.

Grabbing her hands, he pulled them behind her, then manacled her wrists in one hand. He kissed her neck above the collar, then grasped it in his teeth and pulled. She groaned. Very gently he pushed against her wrists, using the pressure to arch her back until her nipples were jutting out hard, delicious nubs encased in metal and driving him crazy. He closed his mouth over one, and she cried out softly.

"Wes," she whispered. "Pull on them. It feels so fucking good."

He groaned softly, tugging.

She moaned. "After I had them done," her voice was barely-there breathless, "the ride home was so crazy, the vibration of the car so erotic. Still in full adrenaline mode, I came so hard, I had to pull the car over."

"Fuck, Kia," he whispered. "Tell me what it feels like."

He rasped his tongue against the hard tip. "Wrap your tongue around me," she sobbed. "I'm coming. Oh, God...Wes."

He sucked, and her body bowed while she shuddered. He grabbed her breast a little roughly, tightening his grip so her nipple thrust out even more. Using his tongue again, she cried out, the ecstatic sound of her guttural moans driving him wild. Her hips thrust against him.

Cupping her face in his free hand, he pressed her back toward the headboard and kissed her like there was no tomorrow. She slipped into him like a drug as he opened his mouth wider, kissing her deeper, longer, exploring her. She sighed in his mouth.

The wind whistled outside. He remembered that wind like an old friend, the way it had blown across Sweetwater, rattling his bedroom window. The taste of her filled his senses, turning them on, heightening them even more than they had been. She moved with him, her body all curves and desire, the sheer eroticism of her running like high-powered, pure adrenaline from his heart to his groin.

The scent of her was so feminine, so profoundly rich. She was like a storm queen, all dark hair clouds and silver-eyed power, gathering to strike him and infuse him with her domination.

"Wes," she murmured, and for the first time in a long time he remembered he was Wes.

"Darlin', sweet, sweet darlin'," he whispered against her lips. *I'll protect you with my life.*

He was finally in the here and now, in the moment with her, not in the past, not worrying about the future, but here.

"I've never felt...this feels..." Her voice trailed off as she pressed out-of-control kisses to anyplace she could reach—the side of his face, along the length of his jaw, to his lips.

"Real," he murmured. So real.

He remembered lying in a ditch in the wilds of Afghanistan looking up at the stars thinking Kia was seeing the same brightly lit sky. She was like a star, sinking into his cells, filled with light and air, beyond the physical, the lushness of her body, beyond the compelling enticement of her kiss, freeing him from the bondage of his own wasteland, his own loneliness, of always and forever being alone.

"I missed you," she murmured. "Even if you weren't mine, I missed you."

She restlessly shifted her hips, and he cupped her bottom. "Let me go," she demanded, and he released her wrists for now. Her fingers went to the top button of his jeans.

"Wesley McGraw," she whispered. "*Cowboy*."

Yeah, that was him, the guy she was unraveling one button, one kiss, one seductive move at a time.

He reached down and yanked off her shorts, and her clever hands had unzipped and were shoving his jeans and boxer briefs over his hips. She pushed him over onto his back, and she rose, turning on the light. The glow from the lamp made him squint. She was looking down at him, her eyes not missing an inch of him.

"Oh," she said, staring down at him. "Oh, my."

It was surrender to the heat of the moment, the strung-out sweetness. It was hot and getting hotter with every soft kiss she pressed to his mouth, with every single sashay of her hand over his body, with every time he teased her with his fingers. She couldn't get enough of touching him, her hands going over his chest and shoulders, molding over his biceps, trailing down his back, kneading his buttocks.

Her gaze made him ache with wanting her, sent a surge of pleasure through him. In a move that galvanized him, had his hips thrusting up from the mattress, she licked him from the base of his erection all the way to his head, taking the tip of him into her mouth. His hoarse, gruff cry burst from him.

He wanted to be careful with her. He wanted to take things slow, to really savor the taste and feel of her —next time.

This time glided past "caution" the moment he slid his hand between her legs, into the soft, secret warmth of her, into intimacy. He reared up, using a martial move on her that swept her knees out from under her. A SEAL ninja move that was pure commando.

He was a big man, covering her, drawing her leg up against his hip, making room for his large self in the cradle of her hips, and he rocked against her.

"Ohhh," she breathed, moving with him, pressing herself against him. When he was only partway in, she caught her breath on a small gasp, and he took it into his mouth as he kissed her. Feeling how ready she was for him, he plunged into her and her hips met his with the same frenzy.

"So slick," he whispered, using his thumb on her core, and she arched up, taking more of him, the look of her so intensely erotic, an electrifying hard-on, turn-on. Pulsing with the sound of her pleasure, he sighed, and the deeper he went, the softer she groaned.

"*Wes...damn...oh, Cowboy.*" She spread her legs a little wider, taking him in, taking all of him, her hands on his biceps, her hips moving with him on every thrust.

"I cried for you," she whispered against his mouth, then dragged her tongue across his lower lip and bit, hard—and he didn't know what tore him up more, the love bite or her confession. Both went straight through him on a wave of desperate need to fuck her so sweetly, to dry her long-gone tears, and somehow to love her until she was his.

Kia. He'd known the first time he'd seen her, known there was something between them, some connection making her impossible to ignore. He'd seen her so many times, and every time she'd made an indelible impression on his heart.

Now they were here, wrapped around each other, drenched in desire and need. All he wanted to do was thrust into her harder and faster, more and more and more, to find his pleasure in her body, to let the sweet, slick heat of her consume him and take everything he had. The gasping sound of her moans and the way her hips convulsed signaled her climax.

One deep slide after another, he pumped into her, again and again, reaching and striving for the moment of inevitable release. When it came, it came on him slow and hard, pulsing through him and damn near driving him goddamn crazy.

He pushed deeper, burying himself to the hilt inside her, and she tightened around him. He groaned with the pleasure and pushed into her again, loving the feel of her around his dick. This was life. My God, he'd missed this like a complete idiot. Her breath was warm on his neck, coming in short gasps. Her breasts were pressed against his chest, the erotic feel of the metal sensually scraping his skin.

He could feel her heart racing, feel the heat of her satisfaction. Whatever else he was, he was safely, surely, wildly, intensely alive deep inside her.

She turned her head and opened her mouth on his shoulder, her teeth closing on him not so gently.

"That all you got, darlin'?" The toughness of men's skin could take a lot more damage than a sweet woman's. She tried again and it hurt so good.

He propped himself up on his elbows and looked down

into her flushed face and sated eyes, the storm banked for now, a soft gray. A sigh escaped her, and he tightened his hold on her. God, for so long he'd been dormant, not under-standing what he was missing, and maybe that's what held him back. Maybe if he knew this, it would change his world. Turn it upside down.

And it had. She had.

He'd been in limbo emotionally for so long. Taking this pushed him beyond the limits of eat, sleep, fight, repeat, made him understand why he'd kept such a tight grip on his emotions all these years. If he hadn't...he'd have to face what he hadn't faced ten years ago.

She felt like life to him.

He could protect her. He could protect her without fail, no matter what she'd done, no matter what or who came after her. He was the tower of strength against which all others were broken. Until his last breath, he would be her protector down to the marrow of his bones. Whatever she was tied up in, he was bound as well.

9

Kia opened her eyes to the sight of Wes...Cowboy gloriously sprawled belly down against her, the pillows and blankets awry in all his morning-after sexiness, his hair mussed and sinfully tousled on his forehead. He was always so impeccably groomed that seeing him like this touched her in ways that she hadn't thought possible, that she could feel any more tender towards this big, beautiful man. His face was softer in sleep the way it never was when he was awake. There was just too much intensity for that. He seemed vulnerable with his jaw relaxed, covered in that dark stubble that had teased her skin with a sensual burn.

She didn't want to move and disturb this moment, this benchmark moment when she'd opened her eyes and finally, oh-so-finally had this man in her bed, beside her like she had dreamed and fantasized for so long. But it was no longer a fantasy.

Last night...*my God*. It had never been like that before.

His breathing was deep and measured, no doubt from exhaustion after their night together. His beautiful body needed time to recover. She, too, had slept soundly, no more terrible nightmares, although she would welcome them if she ended up in his comforting arms. She sighed with the memory of how utterly insatiable he'd been last night before he finally let her drift off to sleep wrapped up in his arms.

Her stomach did a free-fall tumble that had nothing to do with being hungry for breakfast and everything to do with her intense attraction to Wes. The man was so wickedly gorgeous there ought to be a warrant out for his arrest right now because it had to be illegal. Even asleep, completely ruffled, he managed to exude an earthy, sexual magnetism, one she was finding dangerous on so many levels—physically, emotionally, and mentally. The fact that this man had the ability to affect her so completely for so long was a scary prospect she was still dealing with.

She sighed again, loving the heaviness of his arm curled around her waist, the way he'd tucked her tight against his body during the night. And she'd reveled in his closeness, his presence filling that vast loneliness that had been such a part of her life for so long. She'd allow herself the luxury, if only until his short vacation was over and he left Reddick for San Diego and his warrior life.

She didn't want the real world to intrude, but her stomach pinched and her heart lurched thinking about how much danger he must be in every day out there in such a violent world. Here in Reddick, not much had changed. The crime rate was low. People went about their lazy days, enjoying each other, the outdoors, entertainment, good times while Wes was putting on body armor, going out to keep the world safe while armed and dangerous.

He was definitely armed and dangerous when all his male attributes culminated into this sleeping hunk occupying more than half of her king-sized bed.

"If you stare at me any harder," he murmured in a rough, sexy voice, "I'm going to think you have a thing for me, darlin'."

He stirred and his gradual move from drowsing to full wakefulness was mesmerizing. His whiskey eyes looked like chunks of amber with the way the light caught them. One brow lifted lazily, as did one corner of his sensual mouth.

"Newsflash: I do have a thing for you."

He chuckled, a low, rumbling sound that vibrated through her chest. Then he rolled over to his back and stretched his long, lean body, and she took advantage of watching all those muscles ripple. His glossy hair was a tousled mess around his head. "That's puttin' some spurs into my giddy-up."

"Isn't this supposed to feel awkward?"

"Do you want it to be? I can be like: Well, thank you kindly, ma'am. Let me grab my boots and my spurs and git outta yer hair. Go ride the range and mend me some fences. I ain't used to a soft mattress and an even softer gal. I usually bed down with my horse, but you know somethin', he don't smell as good."

She giggled at his thick Texas accent. "That was a huge side of cowboy there."

"Hey! Get your lazy asses out of bed. Sun's been up for ten minutes. Rise and shine, marshmallows! PT time."

"Give me a break!" Kia yelled. "I'm not in the navy. I don't take orders from you."

"Doesn't matter! You get sucked in by association, woman. Now get out of bed and get going."

She rose up on her elbow and pushed back the sheet. Cowboy gave her a quizzical look. "Are you going to give in to his bullying tactics? He called us marshmallows."

"He's a huge, Tank-sized pain in my ass. It's always got to be his way or the highway."

She smiled softly, trailing her fingers over his skin, marveling at the satiny texture over such hardness. He watched her face, then his cleared.

"I can go on record here as saying that you might be buttoned up, have a will of steel and take forever to get a clue when a woman is trying to get you into bed, but you're no marshmallow." She bumped her index finger over the ridges of his abs, through the silky hair that disappeared under the sheet all the way down to his hip, then smoothed her palm back up along his ribcage, enjoying the feel of this hard, hard man. She hadn't missed the tent his erection made beneath the covers.

As he flexed his legs, the sheet dipped lower on his hips, and she already knew what kind of heat he was packing there. She'd thoroughly enjoyed his well-endowed ministrations more than once last night. The man didn't just walk tough. He carried a big, gorgeous stick and he knew how to use it.

Speaking of supports, she reached out brushing her fingers along the jut of that tantalizing silhouette. "What kind of tepee pole do you have going on here, Kemosabe?" His amber eyes got this melting, challenging glint in them. "I can only hazard a guess, mind you, but I'd say you have some morning wood there, or am I just turning you on?"

He gazed at her through lashes that had fallen half-mast. Hooking his finger underneath the leather of her collar, he brought her mouth down to his. "You keep that up and there's going to be some hard breathing, some groanin', and some sweatin', missy, but there won't be any runnin' involved."

"I think I'll take my chances."

He grinned.

"Hey! I've seen the schedule. Don't we have some decorating to do, dumplings?"

"Again, with the fat insults. Is he always like this? The designated nudge, something like a SEAL yenta?"

He laughed out loud. "Pretty much, but I don't think he's Jewish." His mirth was so sexy, that wide, beautiful smile, the way he drew up his knees a bit, scrunched up his handsome face and clutched his flat stomach was so endearing. "I'll start using that. Believe me. With a team of smart-asses, it'll stick, especially if I get Kid Chaos on my side."

She giggled. "Who's Kid Chaos? He sounds like he's fun. Why didn't you bring him instead?"

"Ashe Wilder, he's the point man on the team, sniper and my best friend. He's batshit crazy, but in a good way. He just got married, and I didn't want to ruin the honeymoon. Besides, him and Paige are sickening with the kissy face all the time. Yuck."

"Are you a PDA Scrooge or are you just jelly?" She kissed him all over his face.

"Yes, both, bah, humbug," he growled, nuzzling her neck.

"So, now you have to tell me about your team. All of them. I already know Tank." She rolled her eyes. "Who else?"

"Our lieutenant, or LT as we call him for short, is Ruckus —Bowie Cooper, best damn leader on the teams, smart as a whip and gets right in there on our missions."

"Call names, huh?"

"Yeah, it's easier."

"Who else?"

"Arlo Porter, Scarecrow, Southern badass and our comms guy, but he's no pushover. When the bullets start

flying, he's deadly. Orion Cross, Wicked, gourmet cook and
Olympic rower, amazing dart player and hardcore all the
time. Ocean Beckett, Blue, our corpsman, god-like healing
talent, quiet but deadly. Lastly, Jude Lock, Hollywood, best
trash talker on the team, pick-up-artist ladies' man, and top-
notch ass-kicker. He's our heavy weapons handler."

"Daylight's burning, cinnamon buns!"

Both of them sighed. "Okay, now I'm starting to get
hungry," she grumbled. "Don't you have a granola bar or
a gun?"

There was that laugh again. "I'm fresh out of granola
bars, and yeah, I've tried shooting him before. It only makes
him mad, and the gosh darn uptight navy...they frown on it.
Like, zero sense of humor."

She threw back her head and laughed, choking out,
"The stick-in-the-muds. They have no vision." He brushed
his mouth against her neck. Her mirth died and her breath
hitched. "Is there any way we can stall him, gag him, tie him
up?" she whispered. "I do have handcuffs, duct tape and
old socks."

He raised a brow, his eyes heating. "He isn't called Tank
for no reason. But, I think you'll fit right into the team." He
cleared his throat. "I've got an idea, but you need to give me
a minute after that bit of information," he rasped. He closed
his eyes gaining control of his voice. "Shut the hell up, Tank.
Give us thirty minutes, and that's a freaking order,
meatball!"

"That's not even a breakfast item, but hoo-yah, sir!"

She smiled at him. "It's so good to have a man in
charge," she cooed. He chuckled and rose and tumbled her
onto her back, and before her peal of laughter could
subside, he captured her mouth, kissing her hard
and deep.

"So what call name would I have since I'm an honorary SEAL? Please don't go with something obvious like Raven."

"Fits because of your hair, but no, it's much too common for you. It has to embody the person, the attitude, and fit with something that you're known for that makes it much more personal."

"Now I'm intrigued. Don't make me tickle it out of you."

"I'm *not* ticklish."

She reached for his ribs, and he jerked away from her with a burst of laughter.

"The big, bad SEAL is ticklish."

He grabbed her wrists. "I have an order for you, and if you comply completely, I'll tell you my suggestion."

Her eyes narrowed. "Blackmail, huh? Since I think I might like the order, yes, sir," she said, her voice breathless. "I'm at your command, Cowboy, sir."

"Spread your beautiful thighs," he growled in his best deep, drill sergeant voice.

"What is it, you terrible tease?"

He waited a beat, his eyes twinkling. She preferred this sweet, open man to the one who had arrived in Reddick just a few days ago. "Fishnet." She was in deep love stuff here. "Tactically speaking, there's no buttons, bows, snaps, zippers, buckles, hooks or fastenings. The enemy will be so mystified how you got into the getup, we'd get the drop on them. Not a shot fired."

She smacked him. "I like it, but I have to point out you left "darlin'" off your order."

"So, I did."

"Now you'll have to make it up to me." She thrust out her bottom lip, and he sucked it into his mouth.

"Hoo-yah...darlin'," he breathed against her mouth. "I'd better get to commencing, then."

A low moan broke from him as she gently grasped him, stroked him and guided him into her. He was so hard, being careful as he filled her, but she didn't want his restraint. She wanted him hard, deep, and out of control. She thrust up, taking all of him at the same time she bit his neck, trailing open-mouth kisses to the hollow of his throat, his skin salty and delicious. Her whole body collected and tightened as she arched her head back when he pumped deep, then withdrew and plunged even deeper.

"Yes," she whispered. "So good." She arched again, choking out his name. He shuddered, then clutched her against him, drove into her in rapid succession, finally sending her over the edge of a high, splintering cliff. He thrust into her once more, grinding against her, then stiffened, an agonized groan wrenched from him as he freefell with her.

THE MORNING WAS a flurry of running for an hour and working to keep up with two SEALs—*although, note to self. Running behind two fit men in skimpy shorts and no shirts with deliciously muscled backs, achingly broad shoulders, trim waists, and butts of steel wasn't such a hardship*—then a hot shower with Wes *Umm...cough...to conserve water.* After all that it was on to the time-consuming task of feeding canines, equines, and one cagey and ornery feline. The most intelligent of the bunch, *homo sapiens*, had to take the last breakfast call. It was a surprise they arrived at The Barn on time. Tank and Cowboy, carrying a box each, flanked her as she walked in. Several heads turned toward the door; the males in there looked intimidated and the women looked...interested. She couldn't blame either gender. These men were deadly, sex on a stick. Setting the boxes near the door, Wes was dressed in a black T-shirt with a red plaid shirt open for easy access to the gun he carried in a shoulder holster, the open neck showing his strong throat, worn jeans riding his lean hips, the black Stetson shading his eyes and blue-gray ostrich cowboy boots on his feet. Tank on the other hand looked like he just got off a motorcycle, with a stark white T-shirt with "Speed, let it make you breathless," across his broad chest beneath a leather vest that mimicked a military tactical vest, hiding his shoulder holster, paired with a pair of olive green racing pants, the ends tucked into panty-melting, black-buckled, shiny metal boots.

Evie came forward. "Hi, Kia," she said, and the spot between her shoulder blades tightened. It was that mean-girl look that Kia remembered from high school. She took a breath, reminding herself that she wasn't in high school anymore and she didn't have to put up with that crap. "We were so sorry to hear about your mishap. Are you feeling better?"

"Mishap?" Wes growled. "You mean when she was almost knifed in the alley?"

Evie gave him a tight smile. "Well, hello there to you, too, Wes." She turned to Tank, her eyes glowing. "And, who do we have here? I don't remember you from high school."

"Babe, if I was in your high school, you would remember me."

Kia smirked, and Wes snorted.

"I'm sure I would." Her voice softened.

"Thorn Hunt. Wes and I are buddies."

She gave him the once over, clear that she thought he was quite gorgeous, but Tank looked away as if bored.

Tank nudged her. "Tell me what you want done, girl."

"Start with stringing the white lights and globes." She

opened her notebook and popped out the page that had the diagram.

"We need the table decorations," Evie sniffed.

"The flowers I ordered should be here any minute. The other stuff is in the boxes by the door, including the table-cloths and napkins. Wes, could you get the props I brought out of your truck? The posters of where our classmates have travelled, travel destination map for people to pin, and large postcards are in the back already. That's where you'll find the lights and the etched earth lanterns to hang, Thorn."

"Roger that."

"I found these fabulous globe sky lanterns as well. We can light them and set them free over the lake after the dance." The flower delivery guy pulled up and unloaded the stuff. The food wasn't going to be there until closer to the mixer start time.

Cowboy and Tank went off to handle the stuff on her list. Evie sniffed and went with them. A woman approached her and said, "Kia. I would know you anywhere."

"Melody! It's so good to see you. I hardly recognize you."

She blushed and smiled broadly. "I lost a lot of weight."

"You look amazing."

"I won't bug you too much because we have a lot of work to do, but I just wanted to talk to you for just a minute."

"Sure."

"You were so kind to me in high school when everyone thought we were so weird."

Kia nodded, remembering Melody as such a sweet girl who had been so horribly teased for her weight. Kia was glad she could get those embarrassing pictures taken down from the web showing Melody stuffing her face with donuts. She had loved horses and including her backpack. Any time Kia could, she defended her.

"Part of the reason I came was because I wanted to show everyone how I've changed, and the other reason is because I wanted to thank you."

"Thank me? Why?"

"Do you remember that speech you gave in class about using your weird?"

"Vaguely."

"Well, it was hilarious and changed my life. When I got out of high school, I decided to start working with horses. I volunteered at a local stable and started watching what I ate. I wanted to ride so badly. It paid off, but while I was there, I learned I was a natural. It was almost like I read their minds. So after that, I opened my own small training business. It went well, then I started doing horse rescue. I developed an app, *EquineBuddy,* for people to adopt horses. It took off and it was all because of you. You inspired me to use my unique talents. My obsessive weirdness for horses now allows me to make a difference in their lives. I met my husband through the app when he adopted one of the horses. We have a daughter. I named her Kia."

"Wow." Kia impulsively hugged her, her eyes stinging. "That is so wonderful."

"I see that you haven't changed one bit. You're still so very cool. You were right. Being who you are rocks."

Kia blinked a couple of times, thinking that she had been so isolated in high school, but somehow, she'd influenced Melody. Overcome with negative emotions, she headed for the porch at the back of The Barn. She saw both men watching her, their vigilance part of their training, but Wes indicated to Tank that he had her. She stepped outside and gripped the rail, her chest full. All her life she'd thought that by being strange, thumbing her nose at normal, she could protect herself. That people couldn't hurt her. But the truth of the matter was everyone wanted to be accepted for who they were. Trust they were enough just being themselves, and deep down inside, she had believed she fell short.

She hadn't realized that Wes was right. She had done everything for this reunion to ingratiate herself to her former classmates, but what she had been doing was trying to shoehorn her way into a select group of people who never got her, probably never would. It was that lost, lonely orphan who wanted to be accepted for herself. She realized that she would have to find the courage to do that, to let go of that need.

Wes's hands clasped her shoulders. "Darlin'," he said softly, "what's wrong?"

She abruptly turned and buried her face against his neck. "I just discovered that I'm an idiot."

Her chest expanded at the soft caring in his tone. "What do you mean?"

"All this time, I thought if I could do this or do that, I would finally fit in with these people. Finally be accepted for who I was...just me. But I was wrong. It doesn't matter what they think. It only matters what I think. I thought maybe, somehow, I wasn't enough."

He leaned back, his brow furrowed. "That's a dang lie."

"I know," she said as tears slipped down her cheeks. He thumbed the moisture, his touch so gentle and soothing. All this time she believed this about herself. If she didn't embrace it, she would die inside, lose her essence.

This reunion had been a catalyst for her in many ways. It had brought Wes back home to Reddick, threw her into crisis about the secrets she harbored from him, promising not only relief, but resolution. She'd discovered that she didn't have to sacrifice so much for an empty promise.

But what lingered was that her life was in danger. From whom, she didn't know. Her stomach tightened as she pressed her face against him again. Was it a threat from her investigation of the gun that had allegedly ended Travis McGraw's life by his own hand? Or had there been a sinister plot to snatch Sweetwater's land to build a damn competitive golf course?

She saw Roger "Red" Sweeny, Jr., enter and everything in her stiffened. Wes felt it and turned around. His jaw hardened.

Red was the rich kid, the one who got whatever he wanted from his overindulgent daddy, Roger "Big Red" Sweeny, Sr. Big Red wanted Sweetwater land for its beauty and proximity to the water. He wanted to build an upscale country club, tournament golf course, and marina. He had been around the last six months of Travis's life, pressuring him. It wouldn't surprise Kia to find out if Big Red had sabotaged Travis's business. She believed Big Red had killed Travis and staged his suicide. It was a gut feeling.

Wes didn't kowtow to Red, and that started a rivalry between them that started in kindergarten. Red was always trying to best Wes and had never been able to pull it off, whether it was sports, women, or popularity.

What Wes didn't know was that Kia owned Sweetwater and had for years. After the ranch had gone up for sale, she'd bought it as a cash offer. She had no idea how Wes would react. Red's father had wanted the ranch and now his son wanted it still. He'd hired Kia to find out who owned it, but Kia had no intention of telling him any time soon it was her. This kept him in the dark.

She could lose him. That sent adrenaline straight into her system, triggering a fast heartbeat and an irrational fear.

Oh, God, she could lose him so many ways. She tightened her arms around him as Wes drew her deeper into his embrace and rested his cheek on the top of her head. "It's a good thing to know who you are," he said huskily. "Coming back here has been...enlightening." She wrapped her arms around his neck, not exactly sure how she was going to handle any of this.

AFTER THE TABLES were assembled and all the decorations were in place, Kia assembled, stacked luggage near the entrance as props to reinforce her theme. In a big trunk with travel stickers all over it were goody bags filled with a raffle ticket for a trip to Paris Kia donated to add to the fundraiser coffers for the band and football uniforms, luggage tags with their theme "Oh, The Places I've Been," a travel mug with the school mascot and name and date of the reunion, and an itinerary for the rest of the reunion.

"You did a great job, guys. Thanks," Kia said after they got back in Wes's truck. "I need to stop at the bar and see how things are going. I'd already planned to have Sally Jean cover for me for the weekend, but Friday can be really busy."

"Sure," Wes said.

"You are quite the little organizer," Tank said. "That must have been a lot of work for you. The people who were supposed to be on your committee are a bunch of slackers."

She smiled at Tank. "Thanks. It was a lot of work, but worth it. The tables look amazing."

Wes parked right outside at the curb. "I can spring for lunch," Kia said.

"The food is excellent here," Wes murmured.

Kia led the way inside, and Sally Jean was talking/flirting

with the liquor deliveryman. She couldn't help it. Sally Jean preferred bad boys, rebels, and guys who were out for a good time, and nothing more. She didn't do long-term commitments or emotional entanglements. As soon as she signed for the shipment, she turned toward them. "Kia!" She ran out from behind the bar and hugged her tight. "I was so worried about you. How are you doing?"

"Much better. We just came from The Barn."

"I'm sure it looks fantastic. I wish I had been in your high school class."

"We'll need menus—oh, and did you do the deposits?"

Sally Jean nodded and then walked across the floor to grab the menus. Kia hadn't missed the way she had raked her eyes over Tank. Kia glanced at him, and he was following the movement of her slim hips encased in tight denim.

Throughout lunch, they kept exchanging glances. Finally, Kia left her bodyguards at the table and walked over to the bar.

"Oh, my God. He is gorgeous. Who is he?"

"He's Wes's friend."

"A SEAL?"

"Yes. I just stopped to check in. Call me if you need anything."

"I've got you covered, but completely jealous of you getting to hang out with two hotties."

"I would rather not need bodyguards, Sally Jean."

"Right, of course."

Back in the truck, Wes's cell rang, and he answered it through his truck speakers. "Hello."

"Mr. McGraw, this is Sarah Ferguson from Jasper Realty. I'm having a difficult time discovering who owns Sweetwater Ranch. I've even visited with the foreman who told me it's a corporation, Summit Enterprises, but I can't get anyone to phone me back. Do you have any additional information?"

"No. I don't."

"All right. I'll keep trying. I'll be in touch. Bye."

He disconnected the call, frowning.

"That's strange," Tank said.

"Yeah, it is dang strange."

Wes glanced at her. "Kia, do you think you could work your magic and find out who owns Sweetwater?"

Her gut churned and she turned to him in horror. Oh, no. This had to be her worst nightmare—now Wes wanted her to investigate who owned Sweetwater! Oh, man, what a tangled web she'd woven. "Um...all right." How could she refuse him?

Into the silence that settled into the truck, Tank said, "You're buying a ranch?"

As Wes explained, Kia sat silently between the two of them, feeling trapped and sick to her stomach.

10

The mixer was in full swing, and everyone was talking about the table decorations, which he had to admit were pretty spectacular. Kia had assigned them the London table. There was a place card with *London* in script and miniatures of the London Bridge, Big Ben, a small red double-decker bus, and an at-attention, expressionless Queen's Guard with the iconic tall fur cap. There were lit votives and pretty flowers mixed in with the tiny models. He had to admire her imagination. She was currently handling a small crisis with the caterers, and it still cheesed him off at how she was treated, but with that bunch, it shouldn't have surprised him.

He had to admit, it was more than strange to be back here with the people he'd gone to high school with. Back then, he'd had the expectation that his life was laid out for him. There was no deviation, no other choice he wanted to make. It had all been about Sweetwater, ranching, following in his father's footsteps. It was all about being exactly like his father.

He swallowed hard and walked over to the flat world map where people had been using the small red pins to show where they had travelled. Ever since he'd come to his realization that he had been numbing himself all these years, the memories were even more painful, but it was like draining a wound that had been festering for so long—a life-saving, required process that he wasn't really done with. There was relief in recognizing that he'd shut down and he'd lived ten years of keeping his emotions in check.

Even in this room, he could feel her presence filling him up. He'd been right. Taking Kia had lifted the fog, and he felt even more keenly focused. In fact, he felt like he was... more. More lethal, more sexual, more masculine, more rooted. She laughed in that easygoing way of hers, and his gut tightened.

Now that he was analyzing his actions all those years ago, he had to look at the ones that involved Kia. His relationships had always been lackluster and based more on getting laid than on any emotion he'd ever felt for the women he'd dated. He remembered the exact moment when he thought that he had really fucked up. That he'd never taken the chance on her. *You knew she would do this to you. Tie you up in knots, make you feel lost and challenge you.*

After his father's death, after refusing to talk about it, refusing to go to the funeral, refusing to deal with the loss of the ranch, he'd gone back to school, but it was like he was living someone else's life. Gone was everything he had ever believed, the whole foundation of his life wiped away with one pull of the trigger. Halfway into the semester, Lisa Palladino, his current girlfriend had broken up with him, and he couldn't generate enough energy to care. She had told him that she loved him, but she couldn't be with a man who was emotionally unavailable. She had tried to help him, but he didn't want help. He hadn't even blinked twice when she left. He wouldn't open up, and he wouldn't make

her a priority in his life. It wasn't that he wouldn't, it was that
he couldn't or he would have lost it. But that wasn't what his
father had taught him to do. A man provided for his family,
stayed in control and dealt with his responsibilities.

But that meant nothing to him because all his father's
words that had once been so full and deep were nothing but
empty bits and pieces of a hollow alphabet.

He couldn't even remember feeling anything...anything
but shame, a sick, awful, debilitating feeling that sat on him
in waking moments and buried in dreams that woke him up
with such anguish, he could barely breathe. The only thing
that got him through each day was exercise, specifically lifting. Looking back, he realized it was the catalyst that had
released all his tension, lifting something heavy, holding it
and getting the relief of then setting it down. Someone had
told him swimming would help with flexibility and running
would keep him lean, so he'd started using the pool and it
was there where he found comfort and support. Another
world he could disappear into. It was the only place in his
life where he felt almost free. Conditioning his body kept
him away from alcohol and drugs. But he spent more time
away from his studies and his grades started to slip. The
school tried to help him, but he rejected counseling and
kept telling everyone he was fine. But everyone knew he
wasn't, best of all him. But denial was a potent thing.

He hadn't even begun to sort through his SEAL service.

When he'd come across the navy recruiter, he wasn't
sure why he'd stopped. He wasn't sure why what the man
said had sunk in. He'd taken one look at Wes and asked him
if he'd ever thought about becoming a SEAL. Wes had to be
completely honest and tell him, fuck no.

The man hadn't lost his stride at Wes's rough language.
In fact, his eyes had lit up. The more Wes listened to the

"opportunities" of being in the navy, the more he thought about escape, getting away and running his body hard so that he wouldn't have to use his mind.

He'd signed up on the spot. He sailed through the testing, especially the aptitude tests and the physical conditioning. Some of the testers had to look at their watches several times to make sure they weren't seeing things. Excelling at the time was something that was ingrained inside him, and he was sure that perceptive recruiter saw that in Wes from the moment he met him. He got his orders and packed up his shit, shipping it home. He dodged his mother and sister's calls. Kept only essentials and reported to Naval Station Great Lakes and boot camp. He pushed his limits every day and his drill instructors looked to him to set the pace, his teammates struggling to keep up with him. He needed the exhaustion that came with eating, sleeping and breathing his training. It kept him even too tired to dream.

Looking back, he realized that the navy had taught him much more about himself than he had ever known was possible. It broke him down into pieces then reassembled them. He found he enjoyed working with other men, pushing them, inspiring them, leading them.

They were easy, uncomplicated, and didn't require him to touch any of the emotions he'd started to bury. He couldn't help it as his training progressed and he and his training class started to bond. It's where he met Kid, this brash, out-there knucklehead who met him stride for stride, pushed him harder. Kid had the kind of controlled chaos that left Cowboy awed. He admired his thirst for experience and how he embraced it and, more importantly, how his skewed way of looking at things solved intricate puzzles. They went to BUD/S together at the top of their class. He couldn't be happier that the boy wonder had found his happily ever after.

She came up beside him. Was Kia his HEA? Who was he kidding? She was embedded, and he was struggling to deal with emotions that weren't only rusty, but felt awkward and unfamiliar until she touched him and, like the witch he'd named her, magically felt right.

She just felt so damn right.

But, even with his realization, Reddick wasn't his home and the memories were still painful, still shameful. His time was limited. And how could he even build a relationship when distance was such a huge obstacle?

He picked up a pin and stuck it in Kabul. That would have to be representative of his time in Afghanistan, although his travel hadn't involved vacation in any sense of the word. He'd travelled extensively on Uncle Sam's dime to places that weren't even named on the map, crisscrossed oceans and land masses, fought, bled, and took down enemies. His throat tightened. So much of him was tied up in patriotism, pride, respect, and dedication, he realized that the SEALs had saved him from becoming something less than he was capable of, that the spiral after his father's death would have brought him to ruin.

He had to also acknowledge that he might have lived up to his potential as a SEAL, but he was still not quite there in his personal life. Bits and pieces of his father's guidance over the years kept surfacing everywhere he looked. The memories stirred up even more shit, and he suspected they always would.

He'd only known her for less than a full week. How he had fallen so hard in such a short period of time wasn't lost on him. SEALs measured their lives in reflexes and action. Anything worth doing was worth doing to the fullest.

Connecting to Kia, frankly, didn't surprise him one iota. Kia required action.

She tapped his temple. "What's happening up there, handsome?"

"There are so many places that I've been, I don't think you have enough pins here. I'll keep them to one place to signify the countries I've been to."

"All of them, I assume."

"Nope. I've never been to Canada. Not much going on there that requires SEAL involvement."

She smiled and ran her hand down his arm. "Here's an idea. Why don't you just pin the places that have meaning to you or that you have always wanted to go, instead of the places where you've been deployed?"

Her touch, her voice grounded him. He found he was more willing to figure out shit, make decisions, take a risk with her than he had ever been open to in the past. He wasn't sure where this was all going to end, but he couldn't leave Kia vulnerable to an assassin. It was frustrating that they had no information to go on, no clues as to who this man was who wanted to kill her. But after several days of nothing, he certainly wasn't going to be lulled into a false sense of security. His vigilance had to remain high.

He started to do as she asked, and instead of feeling the tension from those conflicts like the Darién Gap and Philippines, he thought how he wanted to experience Paris with her, watch her enjoy the nuances of each new place he pinned. He stuck a pin into Toronto, and she laughed softly.

He specifically would love to go to Florence because he had always admired Michelangelo, Renaissance architecture, and Tuscan food. When he set a pin there, she picked up one and set hers right next to his.

He turned to her, about to suggest a nice walk along the

wraparound porch to look at the stars and maybe steal a few kisses, when he heard his father's name. Conversation surged, and he missed the rest of the sentence, but he stiffened. Kia looked at him.

Then he heard "Sweetwater," then "tragedy." He closed his eyes and all the terrible memories surged, leaving him completely breathless. How could they not think of him as his father's son...that coward's son?

He pivoted and sought out the person who was speaking and, unable to help himself, he strode over there. "Don't you have anything better to do than gossip about my family?" he asked low and menacing. "Isn't it old news by now?" The man backed up a step, a guy who had been so into the rodeo when he'd been in school and had done well on the circuit once he'd graduated.

"What? I wasn't talking about that." Where Wes had expected to see pity, there was only respect. "I was stoked that your dad has been nominated to the Texas Cowboy Hall of Fame. I so admired him and still do for his accomplishments on the pro circuit and then the success he made out of Sweetwater after he left to start a family. I'm sorry, Wes, if I offended you. He's finally getting recognition."

Cowboy was caught completely flat-footed.

"You didn't know?"

"I'm sorry," he said, backing up. Confused was an understatement. His knee-jerk reaction had been to assume they were saying something derogatory about his dad, and it was the exact opposite. For the first time since his dad's death, he wondered if people had ever called him a coward at all. Or had they had sympathy for his plight? Faced with losing everything he'd built, his failure had pushed him to a drastic end.

Through these people's eyes, he suddenly saw his dad,

alone, the ranch he had loved so much on the brink of bankruptcy. The legacy he had been charged with maintaining and preserving for future generations—and more specifically, *for his own son*—lost. Had he judged his dad too harshly? Had he put him on such a high pedestal, worshipped him, and when he'd fallen from grace, condemned him?

The shame he had experienced before had all been tied to his dad's action, but now, he was ashamed of himself, heartsick that he hadn't had the kind of compassion his father had always told him was more important than judgment. People made mistakes, and they were fallible and fragile.

Kia wrapped her arm around his waist, filling the silence with how thrilled she was to hear that news, her tone so genuine.

Then she steered him toward the door that led out to the porch. His tight lungs loosened as the cool air blew across his skin. "Are you all right?"

"No. I'm not."

"Oh, Wes. Talk to me."

"I was wrong. I was so, so wrong. I need to speak with my mom. Now." The pain mixed with anger, an emotion he hadn't felt until just right now.

"I'm ready to leave. I'm here for you."

"Are you okay?" Tank said from the doorway.

"No," Kia said. "We're going."

"Okay. Is there a threat to you?" he asked, immediately intent.

"No. Wes needs to speak with his mother."

They got into his truck, and he drove. The pressure was too strong. He murmured, "I judged him. Unfairly. All this time. I thought they were talking about him being a coward.

That by association that made me one, too. I was devastated, torn apart inside. I thought how could he leave me like this? This shameful way. It ruined me back then and all I could think about was myself. I didn't have any compassion for my dad, Kia. I didn't even attend his funeral. I cut my family and my ties to home, a home I lost when Sweetwater was sold. He was supposed to be stronger, fight. We were supposed to fight...together. But he took the easy way out."

He pulled up at his sister's two-story house and parked. He exited the truck, leaving Tank and Kia inside and went up to the porch, knocking on the door. When it opened, his sister stared out at him. It was clear she was still angry about him missing their breakfast, but in the depths of her eyes was also a sadness, one he was probably responsible for.

"Where's Mom?"

"I'm here," she said stepping into the hall. She was in her robe, and he realized she was angry and fed up with his behavior. She had a right to be because he'd never explained himself. Never asked any questions. "When were you going to tell me that Dad got nominated for the Texas Cowboy Hall of Fame?"

Her face went white, her mouth compressed into a hard line. He could feel the indignation in her. She had aged well. Her hair had turned a perfect silver, and the lines on her face did not detract from her stately good looks. Yeah, she had aged well, but she hadn't aged softly. "Outside, both of you." It was appropriate that his sister was involved in this discussion. He and his mother might need a buffer.

"If you had bothered to show up for breakfast I would have told you." She clutched the robe, and Erin stepped close to her and wrapped an arm around her. It was clear that they had been each other's support for years while he'd been acting like a complete asshole. "But I don't know why I even bothered. You abandoned this family a long time ago."

He sucked in a breath. "I had to," he said.

"You had to? You had to go in the navy without so much as a courtesy call to your mother? Then ditch our calls? You put yourself in danger every day. You never come home, and half the time I have no idea if you're even dead or alive." Her voice crumpled. "My only boy. Do you know what that does to a mother?"

"No. I don't. I just have to explain something to you."

"Explain to me?" she snapped. "I'm so disappointed in you, Wes. I expected better out of you. We needed you."

"Why did he do it? He promised me we were going to handle everything together. Why?"

Her face went white, and she clutched the robe tighter. "I don't know, Wes. He was such a strong and noble man. I was blindsided. I couldn't believe it. You are right, he was going to fight. He had plans, wonderful plans. I know he would have turned Sweetwater around. That ranch had been in our family for generations—there's a responsibility that goes along with that kind of heritage. Your father loved that place, but more importantly, he loved us. Even to this day, I can't believe he would have left us willingly."

Her words eased something that had been so tight and closed off for so long.

"You want to know why I went into the navy? Why I didn't say anything to you?"

"It doesn't matter. You've made it clear that you don't want to be part of this family anymore. I'm tired of trying, Wes. I'm tired of your refusal to talk about this." She turned toward the door, and something ripped open inside him.

His control broke against his mother's pain and disillusionment, against her disappointment and condemnation. "I didn't do it to hurt you. I did it so I could breathe! If I hadn't shut down, I was afraid I would have destroyed my own life with my disappointment at what I'd felt was Dad's betrayal of all he'd stood for, making me an accessory, just an extension of Dad's cowardice because I had tried to be like him in so many ways. How could I even trust my own instincts, deal with my own anguish, forgive Dad when I was so raw and disillusioned? The navy saved my life, Mom."

She stood there staring at him, her face pale. She started to tremble and the tears that had threatened slipped down her cheeks. "Then go back to the navy; go back to your family. You don't live here anymore."

His sister's gasp was loud in the night. "Mom, you don't mean that. You're just upset."

She didn't say anything else, just slipped past her daughter and opened the door, closing it softly behind her.

Erin turned to him. "She doesn't mean it, Wes."

She took a step toward him, but he raised his hand, then leaned heavily against the porch post. He'd needed to release that truth to his mom, but now he wasn't sure what he felt. Everything inside him was raw and chewed up. Ten years of bitterness couldn't be overcome in the span of a few minutes.

She didn't heed his attempt to hold her off. She threw herself at him and wrapped her arms around his neck. "We have missed you so much, and for the first time since you left, I finally feel we have you back."

Her face was wet, and he opened himself to his sister's vulnerability, validated her feelings. "I'm sorry I hurt either one of you."

"This has been a long time coming," she murmured. "Give her some time. You take some time. We have missed you so much."

"I've missed you, too. More than you know. I love you both," he whispered against her wet cheek. "I understand how she feels. I took what I needed, darlin'. I had to, or I don't think I would be standing here right now."

She nodded vigorously, then pulled away. "When you didn't show up, she was so upset. She wanted to tell you about Dad's nomination." She smoothed down the lapels of his shirt. "The mayor was here that day. She wanted to ask you to be part of a hero's parade to honor our town's warriors and to raise money for veterans." She wiped at her eyes. "Mom was embarrassed and angry."

"A hero's parade. I don't know...I don't serve this country for parades and accolades, Erin."

"I knew you'd say that." Her hand went to his shoulder, and her eyes widened. "She flicked the material away to reveal his shoulder holster. Her mouth dropped open, and she looked up at him with surprise on her face. "Why are you carrying a gun?"

He looked toward the truck and found Kia and Tank standing at the curb. "I'm protecting Kia. She was attacked outside The Back Forty. That's why I missed breakfast. I was at the ER with her and then took her home."

"Oh, geez, Wes. You can be such an idiot. Why didn't you just say so?" She wrapped her arms around him and kissed his cheek. "But, you're my brother, and I love you. Please don't leave without seeing us. Mom will come around. She might not admit it now. But she has missed you, too. So much. It's been so hard on her to lose everything."

The door opened, and Erin's rough-and-tumble husband leaned out. "Babe, you okay?"

"Yes, I'm fine, Brew."

He gave Cowboy an I'll-kick-your-ass-if-you-hurt-my-wife look. He vastly approved of his brother-in-law. "We're good, Brewer."

He nodded once. "I'll get the kids ready for bed, babe." His attention shifted to Cowboy. "Wes, man. Don't be a stranger. And fucking be careful out there."

"Brew," she hissed. "Language."

He winced. "Oh, sorry. It gets away from me sometimes." She gave him an indulgent look.

"You got it," Cowboy said as he closed the door, and his sister kissed his cheek again.

"This was good for us, Wes. It feels like progress. Promise me you'll come see us before you leave."

"I promise, darlin'."

She waved to Kia and Tank and then went back into the house.

Cowboy pushed off the post and went down the stairs. He shook his head at himself. A hero's parade. It was now very clear to him that no one in this town ever thought either he or his dad had been any kind of coward. In fact, their compassion humbled him. Yeah, his perception sucked.

Again, there was complete silence in the truck. Kia reached for his hand, threaded her fingers through it, and held on. The small show of comfort and support was so welcome. He realized, as soon as he saw them at the curb, they had heard everything that had been said. It was strange to have the most traumatic event in his life witnessed by one of his teammates and the woman he was just getting to know. But with his newfound discovery freeing himself from all the baggage tied to his hometown and his dad, he was just going to let it ride.

He had no idea what Tank was thinking. He only knew a little bit about the big dog handler. His home life had been chaotic, he had two brothers and he'd been raised by a single mom. When they got back to the house, Cowboy did a perimeter check while Tank sat with Kia in his truck.

As soon as they were inside, Kia went upstairs to change, and Tank let Echo out of his kennel and took both dogs for a walk. Alone, Cowboy sat in front of the fire and just stared into the flames.

His regret at hurting Erin and his mom was deep, scored him with how much he'd cut them out of his life and hurt them. But he was different now, enlightened. His misconceptions may have warped his insights, but how he'd felt had been real and genuine. They had been his feelings and he would own them.

Tank came back in and closed the door. The dogs settled down in front of the fire. Tank went into the kitchen and after a few minutes Cowboy smelled the aroma of coffee.

He rose from the sofa and sat down at the counter in the kitchen. Tank slid over a cup of that delicious mocha.

"Families have a way of fucking you up."

Cowboy looked up and nodded. "They do."

"I'm sorry about your dad, Wes."

"It was a long time ago."

He took a sip of his own cup. "Yeah, but it still matters." He lifted his fist and Cowboy bumped it. "I won't mention this to anyone," he said before he headed to the living room. "Does your gal pal get ESPN?"

When he went upstairs a couple of hours later, Kia was sitting on her bed and had just closed her laptop

"How do you want to handle the sleeping arrangements?"

"Yes," she said softly. "I want you to sleep with me."

He raised a brow. "You have no imagination, darlin'."

She smiled and opened her arms. "Oh, yeah, I do. Sleep is way overrated."

He stripped and slid in beside her warm, soft body, the scent of her a boon, and they made slow, sweet, hot love. Every move she made showing him how much she loved being here with him. It was a balm to his heart, his ragged emotions, to his very soul. Afterward, she snuggled down with him and wrapped her arms around him as they fit so tightly together.

"I went to the funeral. Do you want me to tell you about it?"

Warmth flooded him. He closed his eyes, blinking away the stinging. She had a way of turning him inside out. The tightness in his throat made his jaw ache. "Yes, please," he drawled as she started to tell him how beautiful it had been and that the church couldn't hold everyone who wanted to attend. She went into detail about the flowers, the coffin, the service, and the weather that day, leaving no detail out, even the information about a carved headstone he'd never seen.

The heavy, silky weight of her hair tangled around his fingers, the loose fall like satin. She took a soft, tremulous breath, and he smoothed one hand across her hips and up her back, molding her tightly against him. This story and the soothing sound of her voice was all he needed right now.

11

Kia jerked up in bed at the knock, her heart pounding. Wes was already reaching for his gun. "Kia? There's a guy down here with a load of hay. He needs for you to show him where to unload it." Tank's deep voice coming through the door made Cowboy relax.

"Okay," she called. "Tell him I'll be right down."

"Roger that."

She got out of bed and threw on some clothes, Wes following suit. Downstairs at the door, she smiled. "Hello, Mr. Holbrook."

"Sorry about bein' so early, Miz Silverbrook. But I've got a lot of deliveries today."

"It's totally fine." She signed his clipboard and pulled on her stable boots. "This way." Both her bodyguards followed her out onto the porch.

Mr. Holbrook was a hunched over little old man in his mid-sixties. When a shadow fell over him, he looked up and his brows rose. "Yer a big fella, aren't you?"

Kia laughed and swiped at his arm. "Stop that, Tank."

"Fits," Mr. Holbrook said, not looking at all worried.

He got into the rusty, faded blue truck stacked with bales and drove slowly behind Kia as she walked toward the barn.

"You can unload here," she indicated.

He backed in, and Tank and Wes got to work unloading. When that was done, she waved at Mr. Holbrook as he drove off.

"He's a few days late." She shaded her eyes and looked up. "We need to get these into the loft. Plenty to do today, including the reunion car wash at ten."

She ducked into the tack room to grab three sets of sturdy gloves and then showed them the pulley system and how they could stack the bales on the pallet and winch it up to unload it in the loft.

The morning heated, and the T-shirts came off, leaving nothing but big, wide chests and shoulders bare and glistening with sweat. Wes didn't have any tats, but Tank had XXVI inked across his right pectoral and several rose blossoms on his right biceps with *Jelsena* inked above the cluster. Kia wondered what it meant.

Tank stayed on the pallet loading the hay then working the winch to come to a stop right at the open loft door. His balance was impressive as he handled eighty-pound bales with ease. Every time Wes bent over and grabbed a bale of hay, Kia wasn't sure what she liked looking at more—that tight ass in those jeans or the ripple of his thick, supple muscles beneath his skin.

Of course, she was getting a double whammy of half-naked hot male bodies. Tank was breath-stealing, his chest flexing with muscle as he manhandled bale after bale to Wes.

Once that task was done, it was to the horses. But Tank stood at the door, his T-shirt back in place, his arms folded over his chest. "You can't really muck out stalls if you're not in the stall," she said.

Tank took a step forward and then stopped when Quicksand arched his neck toward him.

"He's just curious to meet you."

"Stop being a wuss," Wes said as he handed Tank a pitchfork.

"Wes," she said, smacking him as he went past. Grabbing a halter and slipping it over Twilight's muzzle, he then snapped on a lead rope, guiding him out of the barn toward the corral.

"That's not fair for him to needle you about being afraid of horses. He's lived with them for most of his life."

"I'm not scared."

Quicksand nickered at him, the sound loud in the confines of the barn. Tank jumped back, and she had to keep the laugh bubbling inside from emerging, but it was clear from his scowl he saw the twinkle in her eye.

"I'm from East LA, ma'am. I've never even seen a horse."

"No, but you handle a lethal K9 like a boss."

He shrugged. "That's different."

"Horses are just bigger with less pointy teeth. They really have no interest in hurting you."

He gave her a skeptical look telling her he wasn't convinced.

She approached him and took the pitch fork out of his hand and set it against the stall. Grabbing Quicksand's halter, she handed it to him. "Just use all that alpha energy," she said gently. "He'll respond. They're just like dogs. Be the boss, and they'll follow you."

"Hoo-yah," he said low under his breath. He reached out and Quicksand nudged his hand. "Wow, soft." He rubbed the big buck's nose then up his forehead. The gelding grunted and closed his eyes. A wide, beautiful grin spread across Tank's face. He slipped on the halter and closed the buckle. She handed him the lead line, and he snapped it into place.

"I'll tell you something about handling horses if you tell me what this means." She tapped his upper arm.

"It's my sister's name. She died in a car accident when I was young."

"Oh, I'm so sorry."

"It's all right. It was a long time ago."

"The roses?"

"She loved them. Said they stink good." He chuckled softly, but there were shadows in his eyes. "She was so cute."

She nodded. "I think I have the other one figured out."

"Oh, yeah? Give it a shot."

"XXVI is the Roman numeral for twenty-six and that's the atomic number for iron."

"Aren't you the brainiac? That's exactly right. What's the tip on horsemanship?"

"Always walk right at a horse's shoulder. That way he can see you and you have better control for both leading him and avoiding his hooves."

Tank was a fast learner, and he led him out.

"Wuss," Wes growled. But she saw the teasing light in his eyes.

"Screw you," Tank intoned, and Wes laughed.

After the stalls were cleaned and the horses brought back inside, Kia caught Wes leaning against the stall door, obviously taking a breather.

She kicked his cowboy boot and sassed, "Stop slacking, McGraw, and earn your keep."

He raised his gaze and gave her the once over, a look of

heat in his eyes. Then he gave her a lopsided grin, keeping his voice low. "I think I've earned my keep, darlin.'"

She shook her head. "There's no time for lollygagging or any trips south."

His grin deepened.

"I think I have a cattle prod around here somewhere."

Wes shook his head and chuckled. "You my trail boss now?"

"Sure, you want a job? It's got good fringe benefits."

He managed a drowsy half smile. "I think I'd be better off wrangling wild broncs."

"That would be a whole helluva lot easier," she agreed. She approached him. "I know where you're ticklish."

"Them's fightin' words, and I think you would benefit from a toss into the sawdust bin."

"No, not that. It gets in my hair and it's hard to get that stuff out."

He shook out his arms, fixing her with a predatory smirk. Whipping off his hat, he hooked it on the vacant bridle peg near Quicksand's stall.

"I could call in reinforcements. Tank?" She raised her voice and Tank walked inside and leaned against one of the stalls

Tank chuckled. "Sorry, lady, but we're part of the brotherhood and teammates. I'd say she needs a lesson for all that sass. What're you worried about? He's a pussycat."

She started to laugh and back away. "Yeah, a big, lethal, brawny lion." Wes rolled his shoulders, and if she wasn't worried about all that sawdust, she would admire every solid inch of him. "Cut it out, Wes. You'll spook the horses."

"I'm not going to spook the horses," he said coming after her. "But I am going to dump you in the sawdust bin, and I'm going to enjoy every moment."

"No, you aren't."

He grinned and started to circle her. "Yeah, I am."

God, how she hated those shavings getting on her clothes and in her hair. Good for horse bedding, bad for long, black hair.

He focused those intense eyes on her. "Time for a sass lesson."

She put up her hand, trying a new tact. "Come on, Wes," she pleaded laughingly. "Don't. I hate it."

Realizing that he was backing her into a corner, she changed her tactics again, darting for the open door. His grin broadened. She had no intentions of fighting fair, not against a heavily muscled SEAL with lightning quick reflexes.

"Come on, Cowboy, can't you subdue one feisty filly?"

He threw Tank a challenging look and then focused back on her.

He had expected her to go that way, but he didn't expect an offensive. She landed a solid tackle, dumping him in the mix of dirt and shavings on the barn floor. He managed to catch her leg, and he brought her down. She put up one hell of a fight, but in the end, he was able to get her into his arms.

She was laughing and out of breath, but she was still trying to break loose as he carted her down the corridor.

"Wes, damn it! Put me down." She tried to push away from his back, but she couldn't see a thing for all her hair. She tried to kick free, but he simply tightened his hold on her legs, giving her backside a smart smack.

"Please, Wes," she pleaded, her voice breaking from laughter and exertion. "Come on—"

"Well, well, well, isn't this quite the horseplay? I was

wondering if you could set down my hacker for hire so that I can consult with her?"

Kia ceased her struggles, and Wes turned, steadying her as she slid down his chest. Securing her against him with an arm around her waist, he faced Red Sweeny, his expression hardening.

Kia felt like everything was closing in on her. What had started as a way to stick it to the family who she suspected had murdered Wes's dad was getting quite complicated. She was sure she was close to a breakthrough once she tracked down the shady dealer she'd heard from on the dark web.

Big Red would go down, and his son's efforts to find out who owned Sweetwater would be moot.

Every muscle in Wes's body tensed, the bad blood between them something that was based on their volatile history. She squeezed his forearm and said, "Why don't you and Tank finish up? I'll be right outside the barn door so you can keep an eye on me."

He gave her a stiff nod.

She left the barn and Red said, "Getting cozy with the hero, huh? Dream come true for a freak like you."

"What do you want?"

His eyes narrowed, and his voice went low and menacing. "I want results. I've paid you good money to find out who owns Sweetwater. I'm getting tired of waiting. I thought you were some genius hacker, but I guess your reputation was sadly inflated."

"I am good," she hissed, "But there is a lot to wade through, so get a grip. I've only been at this for a few weeks, and I have other jobs, too." She poked him in the chest and said softly, just as threatening, "If you call me freak one more time, *Roger*, you can just go ahead and find yourself another genius."

He lifted his hands, his eyes flashing at his hated name, but was immediately conciliatory. "It's just a pet name, Kia." She didn't give him an inch and he sighed. "My dad is...not doing well. I'm on edge. I want him to know that I have Sweetwater before he dies. So, get it done or I'll find someone who can!"

He stalked off and got into his big boat of a car and drove off. She had no sympathy for either father or son. Red was a bully, following nicely in his father's big footsteps. Big Red thought he owned Reddick and ran roughshod over the town, getting what he wanted by any means possible. When Red's father died, she would pray that he went to hell where he belonged.

Wes stood at the entrance to the barn watching the Lincoln disappear down her driveway. Even from this distance, she could detect the animosity radiating off him. Closing the distance between them, she placed a hand on his chest, tilted her head and brushed her mouth against his in a slow, sweet caress. His lips were soft and warm.

After a moment, she pulled back. The kiss wasn't nearly enough to satisfy her desire for him, but it was enough to trigger a deep longing to keep this man with her forever. She slowly smoothed her hand down his chest, igniting a slow buzz of sexual tension, relishing the heat of his skin radiating through his cotton T-shirt and the way those thick muscles of his flexed beneath her fingertips.

Lifting her lashes, she met Wes's gaze and smiled up at him. "Hi," she said huskily.

"Hey, yourself," he murmured. "If you think that's going to keep you out of the sawdust bin, think again," he said in a low, seductive drawl.

"What exactly would?" she asked as an amused smile tipped up the corners of his mouth.

"It's open for negotiation."

"That sounds promising."

"We've got a full day. We better be going," Tank said.

She tore her eyes from Wes at Tank's words, the heat lingering, a smile from him that promised things to come. If Wes knew that Big Red had killed his dad, there would be nothing to stop him from venting his anger. It scared her to think what he was capable of doing. All the more reason to keep everything about this investigation and her involvement in Sweetwater a secret until she could come clean with him once the evidence was collected, the police involved, and Big Red charged.

The car wash went off without a hitch—well, except the water fight that she so innocently instigated by accident. But they made a tidy sum to add to the growing total for the band and football uniforms, so getting drenched had been totally worth it, not to mention people had a blast.

Tonight was the tailgate, and after a shower, she checked on all the details. Tank and Wes were busy talking about her safety during the event.

But she was beginning to think this was all just a matter of coincidences since she hadn't been attacked again. The break-in was most likely a vagrant and the attack in the alley was probably a desperate special ops guy in need of some quick cash.

There was no sinister plot. She couldn't deny that she had done some things in the gray area, and when she'd been a teenager, downright illegal, but she was a Black Hat now. The most recent job she'd taken had been for an official with the DoD for a test of the security for Naval Base Coronado in San Diego. She had been eager to discover any type of possible breach as she knew that Wes was stationed there, and keeping them all safe made her feel good. The night of the test, she'd shut down all security and had then received the second payment to her account. She could only guess it had been a success.

TANK CALLED Echo and Triton as he headed for the front door and some exercise for the dogs. Cowboy had started lunch.

This had been an eye-opener for him. Finding out about Cowboy's past had made him understand his teammate's need for control. It explained a lot of things about the big Texan. Not that they were touchy-feely—they were men after all—but it wasn't lost on Tank that Kia was good for him. She was a cute, attractive package and Cowboy had it bad for her. He didn't intend to get snagged by any woman. He was too selfish to ever settle down and give up his time toward a wife and family. He knew a lot of guys wanted that, but it wasn't for him. He really didn't have much of a role model to emulate. He was sitting on the porch steps, throwing the ball, when the door opened, and Kia came out. Sitting down next to him, she said, "I don't think I've mentioned my thanks for you taking your time to guard me. I just think it might have been nothing but a wild goose chase."

His brows rose. "Yeah? Cowboy seems pretty sure, and in my experience, he's rarely wrong." It was true. The man had a sixth sense about things and was a master tactician. It's why their LT relied so heavily on him.

"They're sure getting along well," Kia said as Echo and Triton chased after the ball Tank threw.

His face went pensive. "Echo doesn't normally get this much freedom and usually, when I'm with him, it's a combat situation. I'm not allowed to have him when we're not deployed."

"That must be difficult."

"It's tough after spending so much time with him."

"I think he means more to you than any dog you've handled."

"It's that obvious?"

She nodded.

"I was always able to move on from other dogs I've worked with, but ever since I got Echo, it's been different. I try to tell myself that I can't get attached, but how can you help it?"

She smiled and squeezed his forearm. "You can't. I'm attached to all my animals. They have a way of worming their way into your heart."

"Even BFA?"

"Well, the jury's still out on that one."

"You know, when he brings you those dead things, he's trying to get into your good graces."

"Oh, yeah? I thought he was just telling me to fuck off."

He chuckled. Cowboy was a lucky bastard to have found Kia. Hopefully he was smart enough to hold on to her. "I think interactions with cats are much different than with dogs. Cats think we're just a larger, clumsier version of themselves, and their behavior toward us shows it. Dogs know we're different, separate, but they overlook our flaws."

"BFA can't overlook my flaws? Is that it?"

"No, he just wants attention and is worried about his bond with Triton. He clearly loves the dog, and I think for him, Triton's his territory. Then you come in and start bonding with him, leaving BFA alone."

"Wes said something similar, but BFA is so nasty."

"He's just scared and in defense mode. He's probably

always had to take care of himself. He's incorporated Triton into his physical territory, and at first, you were a trespasser."

"I know something about being alone. What do you suggest?"

"Play with him. Start off with something that cats can't resist. He reached into his pocket, pulled out a small flashlight and handed it to her. "This is like catnip."

"Thanks, Tank," she said, and her smile was so warm. Yeah, Cowboy was a lucky bastard. "So, if nothing happens after the reunion is over, you should be able to go back home."

"If Cowboy thinks that's a good plan. Do you know anything about self-defense?"

"No. I asked Wes to show me how to throw a punch, but we've been busy."

"I'll show you, but I'll kennel Echo. He's trained to attack if I'm in danger."

She puffed up. "You think I'm dangerous?"

He laughed. But, yeah, this chick was dangerous, and he wasn't going down that road. She was Cowboy's girl. "Echo won't care. I'll be right back."

He called the dog and kenneled him before going back outside. "Okay, disclaimer, although knowing the fundamentals doesn't exactly make you Rambo, it should help in defending yourself. Just don't go out and pick a fight. Unless you're in prison, then deck the biggest person there. Or at a big girly sale and some Amazon has just grabbed the dress you want."

She laughed. "Okay, got it."

"I'm going to teach you the right way to make a fist, how to orient your wrist, what part of the person you should hit, and what you should do after the punch." Her attention was riveted on him. "You need a fist, but your thumb should always be on the outside. If not, you will break it. Most people think you should hit a person with the flat of your fingers, but that's a good way to hurt yourself. You want to aim to use your knuckles—and not the ring finger and pinky combination, but the index and middle together."

She made a fist, and he repositioned her thumb and touched the soft knuckles of her hand.

"Angle your wrist slightly down, but keep it aligned with your forearm. This is going to keep you from injury and allow you to make correct contact. Your shoulder will automatically rise and help you to block, too." He raised his hand palm out to her. "Hit me."

He was impressed with the way she picked up on it. "Good. Now, we're going to aim for one punch, but not to the face."

"No?"

"No. Knocking a guy out is usually a lucky punch. I would suggest a body shot or neck. Groin works as a great finishing move if you really want a head start. Also, if you want to distract and run, you can go for the nose. I do suggest that if you come up against a more experienced opponent, go for the neck, then follow through with a cross punch. It will disturb the attacker's breathing and give you time to bolt. That's your mission, and what you do after you punch. You run away."

She giggled. "Exactly." Then she got serious. "That's not what you do."

"No, but I'm spec ops, and the guys that are usually trying to kill me have automatic weapons and any close work is done with a knife. If I have no other option, then, yeah, it's a beatdown, no quarter, no mercy."

"You're fighting for your life. Makes sense."

"Okay, try to hit me to get a feel for it."

She got into the fighting stance and got ready. Tank focused on her. Then Cowboy yelled, "Tank, what the hell are you doing?"

That distracted him for just a split second and was enough for Kia to clip him on the chin, which rocked his head back and made him lose his balance. He stumbled.

"Oh, I'm so sorry," Kia said as he regained his balance and rubbed at his chin, glaring at Cowboy who was laughing loud and hard.

Cowboy came up to Kia and held up his fist, which she bumped. "Way to go, slugger." Kia thumbed her nose, then danced around like Rocky.

Tank could tell that Cowboy wasn't too keen on Tank getting near his girl. He grinned. Too bad. He liked Kia.

THEY ARRIVED at the tailgate early to make sure all the nifty dinner boxes for their reunion attendees would be available during halftime.

When dusk settled and the lights brightened the field, they all assembled at the designated spot to go to their reserved area up in the bleachers.

The game got underway and the teams came onto the field amongst a lot of cheering and fanfare. During halftime, everyone enjoyed their boxes and with the home team winning, were in great spirits, the conversation lively. Kia noticed that Tank was conversing with Sally Jean who had come out for the game. The way Wes had looked at him after he'd taught her how to throw a punch, it made her wonder if he was worried about the big man getting under her skin. She curled her arm through his. That would never happen. Tank was a nice guy, and although she could admire him as purely a gorgeous male specimen, she liked him like a brother. No tingles or heart palpitations there.

When the game wrapped up, Kia headed with them toward the exit, but then realized she'd left her sweater at her seat.

"Oh, my wrap," she said.

"I'll get it," Tank offered and took the steps two at a time to reach their bench. She waited with Wes in the middle of the small stadium.

Suddenly, a man attacked Wes, and when Tank went to come down to aid him, another man appeared and challenged him. Wes and his attacker were in a vicious fight, punching and wrestling. Tank was now facing off with the other guy. From behind her she heard footsteps. A man in a ski mask was running toward her.

She took off, and the only way to go was up. When she reached Tank's level, he called out, "Kia!"

He elbowed his attacker, and he went down. She pelted toward him as fast as she could go with Ski Mask right on her heels. Tank grabbed her up and without even missing a beat tossed her in an arc down the rows toward Wes. He pushed his attacker hard and caught her on the run against his chest. She scrambled for a handhold on his neck. Ski Mask ignored Tank and came after them, a knife glinting in his hand. The other man was already in pursuit of Wes.

"Tank," he yelled, and Tank started to come down the bleachers until he was about three up, and Wes's attacker was almost on them. She felt his muscles bunch, then with a powerful thrust, he propelled her up the three rows, the metal benches glinting in the moonlight, as she hung for a split second airborne, then landed right into Tank's arms. She hit with an *oomph* knocking the wind out of her.

What the hell was she? A football?

Tank rolled her up his body without breaking a sweat and draped her over his shoulder, facing Ski Mask. She couldn't see a thing as she gripped his belt and held on for dear life.

Suddenly, he whipped her around, and she was unceremoniously tossed back to Wes, who set her down right behind him.

Ski Mask knocked Tank over, and he tumbled down a few rows before righting himself, but he was too far away. Wes, dispatched his attacker, and it was only Ski Mask left.

He grabbed her hand and dragged her up and away from the prowling assassin until they were at the top.

Ski Mask's eyes glittered in the holes of the mask, but when he swiped at Wes with the knife, Wes grabbed his wrist and hurled him over his shoulder. Ski Mask sailed over her head and off the edge of the bleachers, his shout cut off abruptly only moments later.

Wes turned around and looked over, leaving nothing to chance. Tank was calling the police after dragging the two unconscious men together.

Wes pulled her hard against him. "Are you all right?"

"Other than feeling like a cross between a sack of potatoes and a football, yes."

He laughed softly, and she buried her face in his neck as sirens sounded in the distance.

Once the sheriff and several deputies arrived, Wes, Tank, and Kia had gone down to where the dead man lay. Wes bent down and removed the mask, and she got this sick sense of dread in the pit of her stomach.

"He's been in The Back Forty," she whispered, her skin crawling. "I've served him." But that wasn't the only place she recognized him. He'd looked familiar even then, but she couldn't place him. She realized if someone wanted her dead, whomever that someone was would send another killer. Her only hope was to figure out who was after her and end the threat once and for all, or she wouldn't be able to get back to her life.

Wes and Tank couldn't stay here indefinitely and guard her.

Once again, as reality intruded, she was on her own and in much more danger than she had anticipated. She'd have to get proactive.

12

"Are you sure you're up for this?" Cowboy asked for the umpteenth time. But he couldn't help himself. The thought of losing Kia...it was tying him up in knots about what to do at this point. His leave would eventually run out. With the death of the assassin, he hoped there would be answers. It had only been twenty-four hours since she'd recognized the guy, but she couldn't figure out where she'd met him other than serving him in The Back Forty. The sheriff had concluded the man's death didn't warrant any arrests as Tank and he were attempting to protect Kia. Luckily there had been witnesses who had been happy to corroborate that fact.

But Jerry did say he would be proactive in trying to identify the dead man. Maybe the two lackeys who had been part of the attack could shed some light. Where that investigation was at this point, Wes had no clue. His job would be to continue to protect Kia any way he could.

"Yes, now let me get ready for the dance. You look amazing, by the way, very handsome." She smoothed her hands down the lapels of his Western cut, dark brown suit. A bolo tie with an eagle cinched under the collar of his tan button down shirt. Her expression sobered. After having lived in a uniform for most of his working life, the suit felt a bit strange. The best thing that came about dressing up was the brand new dark brown felt Stetson on his head.

He stared into her eyes, and then she bit her lip. "I'm scared, Wes," she admitted after a moment. "This is feeling bigger and scarier by the minute. I'm not a conspiracy theorist, but this is making me think twice."

He hugged her, then closed his eyes, holding her hard against him. "I'm here, darlin'," he whispered. "I can handle anything that's thrown at you."

"Or throw me around, you beast," she said her voice breaking on an unsteady laugh.

"Yeah, that, too." He drew a deep, uneven breath, his voice raw with emotion. "I think you're amazing, lady."

Rising on tiptoe, she molded herself tightly against him as he shifted his hold, bringing her fully aligned with him from shoulder to thigh. He shifted his head, his mouth connecting to hers in a kiss that was much more about how they felt for each other than anything physical.

He held nothing back because he couldn't. He felt the way she reciprocated, the wonderful, hot, all-consuming fire that seemed to come from her very soul.

He let her go, and she disappeared into the bathroom.

He headed downstairs and found Tank sitting on the couch rubbing Echo's ears and head. The dog was half in his lap. He'd gone for more casual attire, black slacks, black T-shirt and a black leather jacket.

"She all right?" he asked. Ever since Wes had seen the way he touched Kia while teaching her to throw a punch, there had been this undercurrent of animosity between them.

"She's putting on a brave face."

Tank nodded. "That's Kia for you. She wouldn't shirk any of her responsibilities. Not for this reunion and not when it comes to whatever is going on with this assassin shit. I don't like it."

Tank wasn't his rival. He knew that. But the way he looked at Kia put Cowboy on edge. Cowboy was heading back to San Diego soon, and he wasn't sure what would happen between him and Kia. Tank's admiration of her only made him completely aware that other men would find her attractive. Without him in the picture, she would move on. He wasn't sure he could handle that, but the reality of him being a permanent fixture in Reddick was iffy at best. There were just too many memories here. Even though he was trying to mend fences with his mom, dealing with their baggage from the past, her resentment and feelings of being left out of his life still between them, he couldn't see himself here. Not in his mind. He'd moved on with the SEALs, and his loyalty was to them.

"I don't either, but until we get some answers, we're in the dark."

The SEALs were his future, and no matter how much he had clung to Sweetwater, he knew now he was going to re-enlist for another four years. He still wanted the ranch, still couldn't let go of his heritage and a large part of his past. The responsibility for it was ingrained in him, a part of his flesh and bones. Getting that ranch back in the family was still his goal.

With the realization that he had tied his personal honor to his dad's actions, he was beginning to understand with the hero's parade and his dad's nomination that honor was more personal than public, that what mattered was how he conducted himself, his accomplishments, not his dad's desperate, last-resort act.

"Not a place I like to be unless I have my combat knife, my weapon, and the rules we make for getting the job done."

Cowboy was all for that. "I hear you, pardner."

Tank's expression changed, went blank with admiration, and he straightened. Echo jumped down and Tank said, "Wow."

Cowboy turned around and Kia stood in the hall doorway leading to the stairs. Her glossy dark hair was piled on top of her head in a haphazard style with tiny silver butterflies perched and nestled into the mass. Her dress was sheer, sandy-colored tulle with strategically placed pansies and delicate fairies embroidered with pink, silver, gold and copper thread to give her a barely-there look. Matched flesh-toned fishnet stockings and beautifully delicate pink and silver butterfly sandals took his breath and wouldn't give it back. She blew him away, and all he could do was stare. She looked like she was fresh out of the Garden of Eden or some secret fairy hideaway. Wow, indeed.

Both of them were spellbound.

She blushed, and it made him want to just throw her over his shoulder like a caveman and drag her upstairs, keep her in her room forever until any threat against her had ended.

"You guys are great for my ego, and as much as I hate to stop this awed jaw-dropping party we have going here, Cinderella has to get to the ball."

He walked up to her and offered her his arm. Tank smirked at his gentlemanly conduct. But Cowboy didn't care. "You look amazing, darlin'." Her blush deepened.

There had never been anyone that affected him like Kia,

and that long-ago time back in high school he knew she would do something to him no woman could. What had he been afraid of back then? He wasn't sure, but this woman had gotten deeper than any woman had ever...or maybe... just maybe, she had always been there.

She took a steadying breath as he kissed her temple. "I'm so glad you're here," she said unevenly. "I don't know what I would have done if you hadn't come."

He smiled and together they headed for the truck.

When they arrived, The Barn was lit up at the edge of town like a bright sun. It sat perched just at the edge of a wide lake. Cowboy wheeled his truck into the empty parking lot near the front door.

Kia picked up her binder with all her information and her delicate handbag, the light breeze caught and ruffled the butterflies in her hair as if they were alive and flapping their wings. She looked so enchanting as she exited on his side, Tank slamming the door to the passenger side. His eyes moving as he scanned the perimeter, he opened one of the big double doors for her, and they entered the big area, a dance floor now taking up the space where the tables had been before. The tables were lined up on either side of the open area, a riser for the band against the back wall.

He kept an eye on her as she went about her organizing, especially after people started to arrive and the room filled up.

After staring at her for most of the night, Tank came up to him and nudged his shoulder. "Ask her to dance for Christ's sake, knucklehead," he growled. "I've got you both covered." When he didn't move, Tank rolled his eyes in disgust. "Okay, I'll ask her to dance."

"You do, and I'll break you in half," Cowboy said, smiling for effect.

"You can try, pardner," Tank drawled.

Cowboy walked over to Kia, who was talking to some of her former nerdy classmates. He touched her elbow as a slow dance started up. "Wanna dance, sugar?"

"I thought you'd never ask, and I would feel like this awkward wallflower all night."

He chuckled as she pinched his ribs. He glanced down at her. "You're no wallflower, and the reason no one else has asked you to dance is because I'm glaring at any man who even approaches you."

"I hadn't noticed any man but you," she murmured. "I never did."

He stared at her; then he looked away and swallowed hard, his grip gentle as he took her hand. His heart contracted. "I think we missed this dance ten years ago," he said.

"I think we missed a lot ten years ago." Regret was never stronger than now. With her tremulous smile, his second chance with Kia was turning out better than he could have imagined. But his first chance with her was a missed opportunity, and now he didn't know what was going to happen, how it could happen.

It was a romantic cluster fuck.

But one he couldn't seem to get enough of.

Insulated by the crowd, he drew her against him, the weight of his hand against her back pressing her deeper into his embrace. Her forehead nestled against his jaw, Kia cupped the back of his neck as he fought all the emotions rolling through him. It was on overload after being so rigid and controlled for such a long time.

Inhaling unevenly, Cowboy rested his head against hers, his arm tightening around her as they began moving to the music, drawn into the intimacy of their own private space.

The sensual, intimate tempo folded around them, the power and eloquence of the lyrics expressing the soul of their own private love song. And it was Cowboy's love song to her of how she gave him hope and consolation, how she gave him the strength to open up his heart.

Easing back into his embrace, she looked at him, her eyes shimmering with unshed tears, her gaze revealing everything she was feeling. "I'm so glad you came back for the reunion," she whispered, a deep, heartfelt joy making her voice tremble. Moving to the rhythm of the music, he stared down at her, unwavering, searching. Tightening his hold on her hand, he pressed her knuckles against his mouth, his throat tight with emotion. Drawing a deep breath, he pulled her closer, urging her head against his jaw. Then he tucked their joined hands against his chest, letting the melody and lyrics enclose them in their own private space.

The rest of the weekend passed in a blur and, as usual, the brunch went off without a hitch. Kia announced the winners of the Paris trip and the couple were overjoyed. He could only think how special she was to be so generous to people who had treated her like a pariah.

~

THE TWO DOGS wrestled with each other, knocking over a lamp until they were reprimanded. Then it was Wes and Tank. They argued about how to boil pasta, how to set the table, how much wood to put on the fire, but when they got to arguing about old naval battles and then about the difference between pirates and privateers, the final flicker of annoyance pumped through her.

In the morning, they had gone to the Sheriff's Office, but

the only thing he had to report was that the two lackeys who had been with the man now identified as Paul Lambert were nothing but local muscle, had no clue about why he wanted to kill Kia, and served up another dead end. He said he had found that NCIS was looking for any information regarding the assassin, and he would let them know any new information as soon as they had it. With sleight of hand, she snatched the phone off the desk and with an upset trip to the bathroom, she cloned the assassin's phone, then turned the ringer off.

Now if the person who had hired him called. Kia would be the one to answer the phone.

She had been doing some work, but ever since Jerry had mentioned NCIS and that they had information on Lambert, she couldn't stop herself from working on hacking into their database. The assassin's phone hadn't so much as beeped. What connection could she possibly have to a man who was wanted in conjunction to a murder of a suspect in custody? What was this about?

The Cat Who Must Not Be Named, yowled, growled and swiped at her ankle, then sat there staring at her with his golden, unblinking eyes. She tried harder to concentrate on what she was doing. This was her paying job. The job that supported this house, horses, and these freaking out of control animals. It helped with her expenses at the bar and made her a very comfortable living.

"Stop it, BFA." She nudged him away with her foot. But he was relentless, pawing at her again just as the two dogs started at it again and Cowboy insisted that privateers, buccaneers and pirates were all the same.

Something dinged in the email she kept for business purposes, and she felt a headache coming on. Her heart jumped into her throat when she saw it was a real estate broker inquiring about the ranch. She wanted to talk to the owner about a possible bid on the property. Her heart started pounding when she saw the client's name: Wes McGraw.

It was highly amusing to her to string Red Sweeny along because he was such a surly so and so and his father had staged Travis McGraw's suicide. But it was another to have Wes ask her to find out who owned Sweetwater when she was the owner! This wasn't at all funny, but it was ironic at the very least and horrible to be in this predicament in the extreme.

They had such a wonderful time this weekend, all except that guy trying to kill her and the bruised ribs to prove she wasn't as resilient as a football, nor as hardy as a bag of potatoes.

Wes's voice boomed across the room, and her stomach fell in on itself. It hit her that she had this thing with the ranch hanging over her head. The investigation into the gun she'd just gotten access to had just gotten started. Now she was going to break the law and hack into NCIS to find out how much crap she was really in—without looking, she'd have to say neck deep.

"Just because you have government sanctions to rob and pillage doesn't make you anything other than a pirate."

"But they weren't called that, and they served a specific purpose, a guerilla band that helped to control the seas. It was more patriotic." The two of them filled her house to bursting.

The information she held could really affect Wes, and she just didn't have anything to share with him right now. Not anything that was going to make a difference. She wanted to have it all worked out, then spring the information that she owned Sweetwater. Had since it had gone up on the auction block ten years ago. She'd amassed a fortune hacking with sneaky ways to make money that weren't legal. Back then, she felt justified in her teenaged rage at being who she was, how she couldn't, didn't fit in, was ridiculed for the way she dressed. It only made her more determined to be different. She didn't want to be like all the unorphaned teenagers. But that defiant attitude only masked her real desire. She did want to be like them, but she never could. Her parents were dead, and no one understood her. No one.

"Pirate is pirate," Cowboy said through gritted teeth. The debate raged on, and Kia felt the control on her life slipping backwards. The stuff from her past crowding her in on all sides. Back then she hadn't had anything to lose, but loss was something she remembered keenly. She glanced at Wes, and she took a painful breath. Hurting him in any way just wasn't an option, but how could she avoid that? She didn't see a way out of it.

Tank was in thoughtful mode, his brows furrowed. He was just as intelligent as Wes, just as intense, just as...alpha. There were definitely too many males here. She was outnumbered.

"How about the Barbary corsairs?"

That email looked like a doomsday message. She closed it without typing back an answer. She didn't have an answer. The ranch would never be for sale. Ever. It belonged to Wes, and it would go back into his family.

"Are you kidding me with this?" He sat straight in his seat and got in Tank's face. This argument didn't have a damn thing to do with pirates. It was buried aggression. Wes was reacting to the way Tank talked to her, looked at her, and generally interacted with her. He was jealous. It was clear to her. That revelation should have made her giddy, but it only made her stomach feel like lead. It meant that Wes was *involved* with her, falling in love with her, maybe?

"Just because they were French and drank their stinking tea with pinkies extended doesn't change a dang thing. Still freaking pirates."

That's when BFA bit her and she snapped, rising from the sofa, her fists clenched, shouting, "That's it! What a freaking zoo!"

At the tone of her voice, the dogs stopped in mid-wrestle, Catmageddon yowled, but it was from across the room. Cowboy and Tank straightened, looking at each other, then in her direction.

"Could the both of you come with me?" she said, a tight smile on her face, her tone deadly calm, crooking her index finger at them.

They rose, giving each other the kind of look that probably passed between them when they weren't quite sure if they were dealing with a suicide bomber or not. The message was clear. *Danger: Use extreme caution.* Crossing the room warily, they were primed for action.

She went to the front door and opened it. They came to stand in front of her, and she shoved them both out onto the porch, threw their boots out, grabbed both dogs by their collars and sent them out there, too." Catcujo was nowhere to be found. Smartest one of the bunch.

"Kia?"

"Go and argue outside. I don't want to hear it. I have work to do. Work that pays my bills! Whatever has your alpha shit all riled up, you can duke it out and SEAL it into submission. Use your words or your fists. Whatever works for you to get this aggression out." She groused under her breath and set her hands on her hips. "It's bad enough that I have this ornery *male* cat who hates me, three *male* horses, one of which fights me every step of the way, and two *male* alpha dogs to deal with, but now two alpha *males*...yeesh. Stay out!" The dogs, quite aware who was the alpha bitch, sat on the porch, subdued, watching her; the horses moved restlessly in the corral, nickering. "Don't try to butter me up!" she shouted. "That goes for you three, too! No horses in the house." Her voice got watery. "There's way too much testosterone in this here Gray Havens! I'm freaking *alphaed* out. So just deal with it."

In the ensuing silence, BFA padded up the stairs and dropped a dead mouse on the WELCOME mat.

Everyone looked down, dogs and humans, and uncharacteristically, he sat down, curled his tail around his hindquarters, picked up one delicate paw and started to wash his face. "Well, I've made my point and he's made his."

She slammed the door, grabbed her laptop, and went to her room. Throwing herself face down on the bed, she squeezed her eyes closed. Turning over, she kicked her legs and flailed with her arms and fists into the mattress. *Wes.* So *wonderful.* Why couldn't this just be easy? She'd had the best intentions, but now that so much time had passed, what would he think? How would he really react? All she knew was that she had no evidence to back up her claim, and if she told him about the ranch, the information about his dad would come out, and her suspicions and her silence all these years would definitely put him in a tailspin.

She wanted to come clean, but she just wasn't prepared for any of this. Dammit. She didn't have the social skills to deal with so many people, animals...the fact that she was hopelessly in love with Wes.

She sat bolt upright. *That's nothing new, Kia.*

But her inner voice mocked her. *Yes, it is. You didn't know him before which made what you felt for him infatuation and based on airy-fairy fantasy. But, now? Now you know him, a complicated, gorgeous, heroic, living, breathing man who has quite simply taken you by storm. Now you have a basis for how you really feel, have a strong foundation to build something wonderful with him. He's been in your bed, been deep inside you and is embedded in your heart. It could all come crashing down, and that is a scary thing for you to deal with.* Then it mocked her. *Orphan. You know what it's like to be utterly alone. You remember the pain of abandonment. Do you really want to go through that again?*

She dropped her head into her hands. That stinking voice was right.

After a moment she opened the laptop, and with her hands shaking, sick that she had to once again illegally obtain what she needed before she went insane, she worked at hacking into NCIS. They had some strong measures in place, but Kia was just that good. She'd hacked all the way into the President's email one time just to see if she could. She sang "Hail to the Chief" every day for a week after that. No one had a clue.

But she'd given that up. She had put illegal and dangerous stuff behind her. When she got into the database, she searched for Lambert, and that led her to Bryant Anderson. With a shock she recognized that name. He had been the man who had hired her for a specific job. He gut churned. When a file popped up on Anderson, she accessed it. The Special Agent's name was Paige Wilder.

In growing horror, she read every word, a litany bursting from her lips, her stricken eyes widening as each word burned into her brain and seared her heart. "Oh, God, oh God, oh, God..." over and over again. Then she sat back against the pillows. After a moment, she covered her mouth and ran for the bathroom and was sick. The cold seeped deep into her bones as she kneeled on the tiles. She burst into tears, frightened, remorseful sobs that echoed in the small room. Anderson had tricked her, completely pulled the wool over her eyes. He and his accomplices had gotten her to hack the security and then stolen weapons and warheads. She could barely breathe. Then, her face crumpled again and she sobbed softly. Two military policemen had been killed. Their blood was on her hands, too. She felt the enormous weight of their deaths pressing in on her, the betrayal by the people she'd worked for making it all that much worse.

She got up and rinsed out her mouth and brushed her teeth, tears of anger and betrayal now coursing down her cheeks.

The assassin's cell rang, and she rushed to her bed and picked it up. The number was blocked. She pressed the accept button.

"Is it done?"

Her heart slammed into her throat at the sound of the voice on the other end of the line—a voice she recognized, a voice she'd *trusted*.

Then like a lightning bolt out of the blue, Lambert's face slammed into her, and she remembered where she'd seen him as clear as day. It had been the day she'd gone to the DoD. She knew who was behind this. It would only be a matter of time before Special Agent Paige Wilder figured it out. This DoD bastard was going to pin everything on her, make her the fall guy. Without any evidence, she would be arrested and go to jail. What would Wes think of her, then?

"You son of a bitch!"

"Fuck. Kia! You're a dead woman walking." Then he disconnected the call. In shock she dropped onto the bed, a sick, horrible feeling churning inside her. She thought she was going to be sick again. She trembled all over, and then she got angry. Good and angry. They had tricked her into something so heinous and were willing to make her the fall guy. Bryant Anderson had died for his involvement. He'd been cleaning up loose ends and she was left dangling.

She went to her closet and packed a suitcase, setting it back inside and out of sight. Then she pushed her clothes aside and opened the small safe tucked away in the back and took out the documents she needed. She was done with being the hunted.

Her biggest regret was that she was going to have to leave Wes behind. She couldn't compromise him or Tank. Not active, dedicated Navy SEALs. Not Wes.

She was on her own.

Again.

⁓

"You think she locked us out?" Tank asked.

Cowboy just looked at him and he backed up a step. "Hey, this isn't my fault. You're the one who's on edge."

He turned and sat down on the top step. The two dogs were still a little traumatized after their beat down and went and laid at their feet. Cowboy knew how they felt. Something was up with Kia. He wasn't sure if it was the trauma, the stress, or something else she wasn't telling him.

And he was peeved at Tank. But it didn't have to do with thinking he was after Kia. He was tussling with his own emotions, and arguing with Tank helped him to combat some of the frustration.

"I would never step into your girl, man. I swear. I think she's great, but she's only got eyes for you."

"So if she didn't just have eyes for me, that would be a game changer?"

"No, that's not what I meant. She reminds me of my sister. You know I'd follow you into hell and that buddies don't poach other buddies' girls, but she's something special. I hope you see that."

"I'm not sure where the hell it can go," Cowboy growled. "Here I thought I would come home, try to get the ranch. I had this stupid notion that I would quit the SEALs, get out and ranch again."

"But?"

"I don't want to leave the navy. That ranch doesn't belong to me anymore. I lost it a long time ago."

"Kia and I overheard what you said to your mom. We didn't mean to, we were just concerned. You looked pretty spooked there."

"Yeah, that nomination...I thought no one would ever look at my dad again without thinking about him taking the easy way out. About him being a coward."

Tank looked off into the distance. "I've never had anything like that, mostly just crappy apartments and my dad bailed long before I became a man. So I'm not the one to give you great advice about the paternal stuff or lost birthrights. But I can say that you have to be honest with your family. True to form, you were brutally honest. But if you don't get that shit off your chest, it festers." He sat down, deeming it was safe. "Did you join to prove that you weren't, by association, a coward?"

"Maybe. All I know is I was working myself ragged, and it felt good. I let everything go except the exercise. People were worried. I could tell. I guess I needed a reason to work out to the extreme."

Tank chuckled. "That's basic, man. I guess you got what you bargained for."

"And then some, but I wouldn't trade it for anything."

"Not even her?"

That question hung in the air between them, and Cowboy came to the same blank dead end he'd been wrestling with for a while. "My gut ties up in knots, and the thinking just stops with her."

"Maybe you should talk to her. Maybe she feels the same way."

"She's grounded here. She has a business, a home, horses. What can I offer her? I'm gone all the time, the distance would be too much, and coming back here, even to visit my family, has been tough." He closed his eyes, fighting against what he had believed for so long, but he had to remember what he'd discovered. His personal honor wasn't tied to anyone but his own actions. The fact that he wrestled with it told him that even now, he wasn't fully convinced.

"It's really none of my business, but I think if she means more to you than just something casual, if that mushy feeling is strong—"

"Mushy feeling? Is that the official term?"

"It is for guys like me who don't like to talk about mushy feelings."

"It's strong."

"Then you've got to say something. After this is over are you just expecting to walk away from here and tell her, 'It's been fun, babe. Catch you when I'm in town.'"

"No. That doesn't fit, but telling her how I feel may not solve anything."

"Or it may solve everything."

"I'll think about it," he said.

13

After composing herself, she came out of the house. Tank and Wes were playing horseshoes, *with* her horseshoes. She shook her head when Cowboy got a ringer and did a little two-step.

"Is there anything you can't do?" Tank growled.

Then they saw her and both of them watched her warily. "I'm over my snit," she said. "Wes, can you ride with me? I need some fresh air."

"I'll hold down the fort," Tank said.

"Exactly." She walked up to them and said, "Wes is right." She patted Tank's massive chest. "They're all pirates."

He chuckled. "You would take his side."

"I'll take any side I can get," she said as she continued walking, throwing a sultry look over her shoulder. If she masked the turmoil inside her, maybe Wes wouldn't notice. Tank nudged, him and Wes shoved him lightly on the shoulder.

"You coming, Cowboy?"

He hurried after her. Once inside the barn, a fragrance of horses and dried hay rose up to meet her, and Kia squinted, waiting for her eyes to adjust to the dim interior. Her tack room was in the back, and with one quick glance at the large box stalls lining the structure, she stepped toward Saragon's enclosure. The loud whinny from the big buckskin when Cowboy materialized made her smile. "I think you've made a friend. I bet he behaves for you."

"I've been dying to ride him." He nuzzled Wes's shoulder. Quicksand had never been that affectionate with her. Looked like he'd formed a special bond with Wes. Then, who could blame him? Wes was a consummate horseman and confident working with them. That would transfer easily to Quicksand's high-strung disposition. Her throat got tight thinking about losing all this, losing her freedom, losing Wes. She turned away as her face contorted, and she had to work to keep from sobbing.

She opened Saragon's stall, and he immediately shifted against her as if he had sympathy for her sorrow. In the next stall over, Twilight Star nickered softly as if he, too, was picking up on her distress. "Sorry, Star baby. Not today." Regret welled that she wouldn't get a chance to ride him before she had to leave. She cross-tied Saragon and went to the tack room and grabbed his blanket, saddle and bridle. Wes was doing the same with Quicksand.

He looked over at her as she headed out of the room. "Had a mighty big meltdown there. Are you sure you're all right?"

She smiled, working to keep it natural. "I am still surrounded by alpha males and plenty of testosterone." He gave her a small half smile. "I'm fine, Wes. It's been an exhausting and scary week."

"You did a great job with the reunion. Everyone enjoyed it." He followed her back out into the barn.

"Even with the excitement?" She placed the blanket and

hauled the saddle onto his back. Wes made it look effortless. He did most things with very little struggle. Just the thought of doing this on her own was terrifying. She was a hacker for God's sake, and even though she knew how to throw a punch, she was far from a spec ops warrior. Something must have shown on her face.

He walked over to her. "Are you sure there's nothing else bothering you?" He reached over and handed her the bridle, and Saragon took the bit like a good dragon.

"Other than why this man is trying to kill me?" He wrapped his arm around her and drew her close. "No, nothing else." She had to keep everything to herself, which was pressure enough, but she was quite aware that Wes would try to help. Aiding and abetting a fugitive was a federal offense. She'd looked it up. He could be charged with the crime if he went with her to DC, and he would insist on it the moment she told him she knew who was behind this. She closed her eyes and breathed in his scent. God, she wanted him to go with her so much.

She couldn't risk it. She couldn't be responsible for him getting a dishonorable discharge or getting court-martialed. She swallowed hard against that sick feeling, blinking back the tears. She had blood on her hands. His honor wouldn't let him do anything else, and after struggling with it so hard during the ten years after his dad's death... No. That was enough. She'd take the decision out of his hands.

But she had enough time to spend one more afternoon and night with him. She couldn't risk much more. She'd already booked a flight out of Corpus Christi. Once she arrived in DC, she was going to be hiding and most likely on the run.

They led the horses out of the barn and mounted up. She wanted to be honest with him about something, and as they trotted off past the corral into the open country, she deliberately headed in the direction of Sweetwater.

The organization and execution of the reunion thankfully behind her, she actually could have gotten back to normal if it wasn't for this terrible situation hanging over her head. The end of the festivities also signaled Wes's departure. She knew he wasn't staying, and her attempt to get him to go may fall on deaf ears, but she was going to try.

She loved this part of the ranch—loved the vastness, the spectacular vistas, the untouched beauty of it. With the exception of fence lines, this area was just as it had been a hundred years before, and she was always overwhelmed by it.

There was a gap along the west fence at the top of the rise, and Kia stopped, shielding her eyes as she stared out at the view. It was breathtaking, this country. The mountains, the forested eastern slope, the spiny backs of the foothills, the distinctive green of the aspens. There was no place like it in the entire world. She wondered if Wes missed it. And there was a sense of unfettered freedom here. Shifting her gaze, she followed the majestic flight of a hawk as it hunted, the wind whipping loose hair across her face. It was as if all this space allowed her to take a full breath, to expand her lungs to their total capacity, to shed all her constraints —for now.

Wes had never talked about it, at least not to her, but she understood his commitment to the legacy of Sweetwater. She understood how deep his roots went. And she wondered if getting the ranch back would make him happy or if it would always be a reminder that his dad's blood had been spilled there.

Had she preserved his family heritage for nothing?

She looked over her shoulder. "You don't seem rusty to me."

"I guess it's like riding a bicycle. It comes back as soon as you get on."

"He's not giving you any sass?"

"No, he's being a fine gentleman," Wes said, patting his neck.

"Typical."

He chuckled.

"How about we give these ponies some exercise? I'll race you," she said.

Before giving him a chance to respond, she kicked Saragon and he jumped into a gallop.

"Hey!" Wes shouted, but when she looked behind the racing horse, he was gaining on her.

"Come on, my dragon," she whispered. "I know you can lead a horse to water, but you can't make him drink. Let's just get him there."

She saw the familiar outline of the ranch on the horizon, and she spurred Saragon a little faster. The appaloosa truly had the heart of a dragon, and he responded with more speed. They passed through a wide belt of trees, and Sweetwater's ranch buildings came into view. The arena was at the most eastward end of the complex, with a series of corrals between it and a huge red barn, and on a knoll to the west, the beautiful house. She'd just had it painted recently. As soon as she got to where she wanted to go, she slowed Saragon, and Wes pulled up Quicksand.

"You are very fast, lady."

Then he glanced to his right and his mouth tightened.

She stared at it. After ten years she knew every nook and cranny. She loved this place as much as he did.

"Kia..."

She dismounted and tied Saragon to a bush. "Have you even seen it since you got back?"

"No." His jaw hardened and flexed as he threw his leg over Quicksand in a fluid move to the ground. He tipped his hat a little lower. "I stopped on the way out of town when I was here for my cousin's wedding."

"Why do you want to buy it back?"

He turned to look at her, his expression closed.

"I just want a simple answer."

She could tell by the stubborn set to his jaw and the look in his eyes that simple couldn't ever apply to Sweetwater. With a sigh of resignation, she stuck her hands in her back pockets and looked away. He was about to brush by her when she laid her hand on his arm, and he jerked away, almost as though she'd scalded him.

It was an unexpected reaction and stung a bit.

For a long time, he simply looked at her, his eyes giving nothing away. But she sensed a deep discontentment about him, as if he were enduring some inner struggle. And she couldn't stand that. Reaching up, she touched his face, her voice breaking as she said, "Something is happening between us, and I'm getting in so far over my head, I don't know what to do. Without even trying, you overwhelmed me, and I can't even fight back."

He shut his eyes in a grimace as he pulled her hand away. "Kia," he whispered raggedly. "God, Kia...don't."

"Talk to me, Wes," she pleaded. "I'm not asking for much. I just want you to talk to me."

He opened his eyes, eyes that were dark and smoky, and as if drawn against his will, he cupped her face in his callused hands and softly stroked her cheeks with his thumbs. "I was born in that house. The boots of my grandfather, great-grandfather and the ones before him walked the land, tended the cattle, raised the horses and built a legacy. I was always proud to know that it would come to me, that I would get the opportunity to provide good stewardship of the land." He tipped his head forward, the shadow of the brim obscuring his eyes. "I lost sight of home, Kia, and it almost destroyed me. In the swamps, jungles, and deserts of this world, I was unhooked, unhinged, wandering with Uncle Sam's purpose, and home became the brotherhood where I belonged because we bled, sweated, and fought together. But I never forgot my roots." His hands dropped away from her, and to keep contact, she hooked her finger into one of his belt loops. "I fight for tangibles and people and for concepts that have words like patriotism, honor, justice. I fight for the American way as part of the force that keeps this country free. I thought I was ready to give that up. But I'm not. I'm not sure if getting Sweetwater back in my name is more about trying to overcome the betrayal of my dad or remembering that home has many meanings and that it can't be separated from the heart."

She reached out and ran her hand over the stubble on his jaw. She stepped closer and kissed him, lingered on his tantalizing mouth for just a few heartbeats.

"Wes, I know these ten years have been so difficult for you. But I need to tell you something that I left to omission. After graduation, I was attacked by several boys, and it would have been bad for me if it wasn't for a man who saved me from that fate with a shotgun and a disposition that brooked no argument."

Her heart was pounding, and she wanted to blurt everything out, but she couldn't—not just yet, not until it was resolved. She wouldn't give him false hope. She couldn't do that to him.

"He took me home, and he was kind to me, treated me

like a beloved daughter. He allowed me access to his horses and taught me how to ride, exposed me to his wonderful brand of humor and stories. I spent two wonderful years enjoying that man just because he was so genuine and warm." Her voice was thick, and she worked to keep the tears at bay. "That man was your father."

His eyes widened, then narrowed. "What? You had a relationship with my father?"

"Yes.

"When I was at school?"

"Yes."

"Where were you in the summer when I was home?"

"I stayed away."

"Why?"

"Because of Lisa Palladino."

"I see."

"You should. I've had a crush on you ever since I clapped eyes on you. I couldn't bear watching you and What's Her Name make out, be all close and lovey-dovey when I wanted that to be me."

"I felt the same," he said. "I was a fool."

"Then it's not just me, is it? It's happening to you, too." There was a flash of something in his eyes that resembled anguish, and it aroused such a fierce protectiveness in her she had to fight to keep her voice level.

"You are such a treasure, Kia."

"But—"

He pressed his thumb firmly against her mouth to silence her, gently rubbing over the lip ring. "We know this isn't an easy thing here."

For once she didn't argue. Not now, not while he was looking at her the way he was. She had a nearly uncontrollable urge to be with him here on this spot overlooking

Sweetwater while he was busy trying to put distance between them, him slipping and sliding away.

"No, it's not easy, but it's real, Wes. So very real."

"It is. The realest thing in my life, darlin'. I don't know how to get my head around it, you being here, me being gone so much, and the memories. I'm still working on all of that."

"I get that. I'm not asking you for anything, Wes. I just wanted you to know that it was something more with you. I need that." This would sustain her in what she had to do.

"It's more," he growled. "So much more I'm a pretzel."

"Aw, my poor beautiful Cowboy. Does it still hurt?"

"*You* make me hurt," he said huskily. He buried his fingers in her hair and pressed her up against his solid body. God, he was built like a slab of granite, and she loved it. That hard, undeniably aroused body.

With a low growl encompassing both frustration and urgent need, he slanted his mouth across hers and sank his tongue deep, kissing her just as recklessly as he had every time their mouths met. His mouth always delivered on that sin and pleasure he promised. She met him stroke for stroke, let him know that she was his.

The long, hard length of him fit hard in the crux of her thighs. He flexed his hips when she grabbed his shirt and pulled it out of his jeans. With one whip-like move, she split his shirt open, the snaps popping free in one big, clicking explosion.

"Let me kiss it and make it all better."

She leaned forward and captured one of his rigid nipples between her lips. She laved the erect nub with her tongue and grazed the tip with the edge of her teeth. A groan rumbled up from his chest as she navigated her way lower, spreading hot, moist kisses on his taut belly. She bit the edges of his abs and licked along each ridge while she undid his pants. Hooking her fingers in the waistband, she pulled both jeans and briefs off him.

He sucked in a breath when she came to his thick, straining erection, and even that part of him was as gorgeous and magnificent as he was.

She wrapped her fingers around his hard, velvet-textured length and felt him pulse in her tight grip. She took him into her mouth, his skin hot and salty against the stroke of her tongue. He shuddered and tangled his hands in her hair, and she sucked him, taking him in deep as she could. She pleasured him with her mouth, teased him with her tongue, and aroused him to a fever pitch of need that made his entire body shake with the restraint of trying to hold back.

"Oh, Christ," he breathed and frantically tried to tug her back up. "I'm going to come if you don't stop."

She wanted more of him than this, and with one more lick along his shaft, she kissed her way back up his body, working on the closure on her pants. He helped pull them down. She pressed him back until both of them were lying on the ground, her on top of him. "Save a horse," she whispered. "Fuck a Cowboy."

She straddled his hips with her knees and directed his erection upward. She was so ready for him. With deliberate slowness, she sank inch by inch on top of him, until he filled her completely and her sex stretched tight around him.

His nostrils flared, and stark desire heated his eyes. He clutched her waist and rocked her tighter against his straining body, setting a rhythm that would take him much too quick to climax.

"Buck, baby, buck me hard," he said, fiercely.

She was in control, and bucking him was exactly what she had on her mind.

"I'm going to buck you so good." His chest rose and fell heavily, his expression fierce and hungry as he sent his hands up her body and under her shirt, beneath her bra, and fondled her nipple rings, pulling and tugging.

"I'm begging you, Kia," he whispered raggedly, "take me, now. I don't care if this gets complicated. I don't care that you're scared. I want you."

"I am scared," she whispered. So scared of losing him.

"Take me." He pulled her against his body.

"Cowboy..." She was breathless—she could never catch it any time this man was close.

"Take me, darlin'," he demanded.

"Oh, God, Wes..." she murmured as he cupped the back of her neck and pulled her down to his face, her breasts against his chest, her heart beating as hard as his.

"Take me hard. Take me soft. Take me all the way."

More than eager to give him anything he desired, she wrapped her arms around his neck, locked their bodies so they were meshed from chest to thighs, and took him. Lowering her mouth to his, she pressed her lips against his velvet ones as her hips rolled and glided against him.

He gripped her hips, but he allowed her to set the pace, and she moved on him, shamelessly in love. She felt his thighs tense beneath hers, felt his stomach muscles ripple, and knew he was nearing the end.

Twining her fingers in his silky hair, she pulled his head back and dragged her damp, open mouth along his throat, then gently sank her teeth into the taut tendons where neck met shoulder and put her dark fairy mark on him.

He bucked upward one last time, hard and strong, and

his groan of surrender in her ear was the sexiest sound she'd ever heard.

The fiery sunset reflected their heated embrace, sending streaks of flame across the sky.

They clutched each other in the heather above Sweetwater and she was determined to be strong, tough, a SEAL at heart just as he'd named her. She might have to do this alone, but when she went into danger, into battle her way, she would have this man so deeply embedded in her heart, it would be like he was right beside her.

14

___

It was one of the hardest things Kia had ever had to do, to walk away without consulting with Wes, but to get him involved would compromise him and she couldn't... wouldn't do that. She smiled as he turned off the light and snuggled up to her, waiting until his breathing went even and he dropped into sleep. Once she was sure he was out for the night, she rose and very gently kissed his slack mouth. "I love you," she whispered brokenly.

She slipped from the bed, grabbed her packed bag and laptop. She deliberately picked up her phone and stuffed it in her purse.

Once downstairs, she rubbed Triton's soft velvet ears and kissed him on the head, then knelt down and hugged him tight to her, her tears soaking into his fur. BFA came and rubbed up against her, as if he finally realized that she wasn't the enemy. Tank had been spot on with his advice. Her heart heavy for betraying the men that she had come to care about—and with Wes, love with all her heart— she closed the front door quietly behind her. Once in the Jeep, her tears flowed heavily down her cheeks as she drove to the airport, her ticket booked under a different name. It had been so easy for her to manipulate digital data, including a fake ID. She'd constructed Raina Matthews on a whim when she'd been illegally hacking hardcore, worried that if she'd been caught, she'd have to run. Everything for that shadowy persona was still in place. The driver's license, the bank account, the credit cards. The house in the Bahamas.

She'd made up a whole story for Raina, how she was a ranch owner with a big family who loved her, including a mom and dad who were so proud of her. She had been so pathetic.

Her hands tightened on the wheel as she parked her car at the airport and with her bag, purse and laptop, started toward the terminal.

She squeezed her eyes closed, her insides still quivery, a huge load of anxiety trying to wash over her like a tidal wave. Doing her best to surf it, she was determined to neutralize this threat against her. Not only against her life, but she could lose everything if she didn't play this just right. When the officials arrived, and they would, she would be placed under arrest. She would go to jail for the part she played in the security breach.

She'd hacked NCIS, knew that Bryant Anderson, the man who had seemed so damned official at the time, had duped her into shutting down security at Coronado. Unwittingly, she had put Wes and his team in danger, was an accessory to the murder of two military policemen...with families. She had to stop momentarily just at the entrance to the airport and lean against the wall to absorb what her actions had done, feeling heartbroken and sick all over again. Even though she had thought she was sanctioned in doing the job Anderson had hired her to do, they had played her. Now the weapons they had stolen, including warheads were on the open market to be used against innocent people and military personnel around the globe. What had she done?

Would Wes ever look at her the same once he found out her involvement?

She called Sally Jean and her sleepy voice answered. "Hi, sorry to wake you. I know it's late, but could you take care of my horses and animals for a few days? I have to go out of town."

"Of course. You know I will. And the bar, too."

"You are the best friend I've ever had," Kia said, her voice catching. Then she gave her specific instructions.

Sally Jean's voice sounded more awake. "Are you all right? Where are you going?"

"To DC."

"DC? Why?"

"I can't explain, but thank you for always being there for me."

"Kia, wait!"

She disconnected the call, turned off her phone, removed the battery, and pocketed the SIM card. They could track her GPS and she was banking on that...later. She went to one of the stores in the airport and bought another phone. Then she caught her flight.

She was going to DC to make sure the man she suspected of being the mastermind of all this would not only get nabbed for his role in this fiasco, but also give NCIS any information he possessed to retrieve everything that had been stolen. If he got away, she was in danger of being hunted by his hired killer or helpless behind bars. Afterward, she would turn herself in and accept the consequences of her actions.

First, she had to get out from under the threat, then she

could deal with the rest of the fallout. But she wanted more. Much more. She wanted time with Wes to explain her actions. She desperately needed a chance with him to talk, to sort things out. She had no idea what he was thinking in the long-term, but with this mess hanging over her, she couldn't even begin to think of any future with him. Even if he wanted one with her. The investigation into his father's death, Big Red's involvement, the gun, and hacking the NCIS database were only a few loose ends that would have to be tied up. Without opening up to him, without taking the risk and telling him everything, she knew deep down inside her that before they could go forward, they had to go back. And that was the most frightening thing of all.

"I NEED to stop at the office on the way home to pick up my phone," Paige said, rubbing her husband's arm.

"Can't you just get it tomorrow? You'll be going in."

"It's been three days of wonderful white-water rafting, and I've been out of the loop. I don't like it."

"Roger that. We'll swing by, but you had a good time, right? Tell me you weren't worrying about work while we were having fun in and out of bed."

She kissed him on the cheek and then nuzzled his neck. "No, Ashe. When I'm with you, you're all consuming. I was focused on us the whole time. Mostly."

He laughed and shook his head. "It's why you're a good agent."

She grinned.

When she got home, she ran up, got it and then headed back to the car. It was close to being almost out of battery. She plugged it in, and as soon as she saw the email, she clicked the notification and read the message. It was from a Sheriff Jerry Jones in the Reddick, Texas Sheriff's Office.

Agent Wilder, I discovered that you are looking for any information on a suspect who matches the description of a man who attacked one of our citizens, Ms. Kia Silverbrook. She was accosted in the alley behind her bar on the eleventh of the month at approximately twelve forty-six am. The weapon he used was a military issue combat knife.

Subsequently, he then attacked her at the local high school football game. He was killed by one of our local boys. His picture is attached.

Why did her name seem familiar? Paige clicked on the attachment and pulled up the picture of Paul Lambert, aka Onekill, the man who had been identified by the signature assassin's bullet that had taken out Bryant Anderson. It was him.

A breakthrough in this case was what she needed. After the chilling information Ashe had given her at the beginning of the month regarding the warheads, she had renewed her investigation into the possible location of the weapons.

"But why did Lambert try to kill a hick bar owner?"

"What bar owner?" Ashe said as he peered over her shoulder.

"Kia Silverbrook."

"*Fuck*," Kid said.

Another email dinged, and Paige said, "Oh my, God."

"Who's it from?" Kid asked.

"Kia Silverbrook."

"What? What did she say?"

"That she's Quicksilver."

"*Fuck*," Kid said.

COWBOY WOKE UP AND IMMEDIATELY, before he even opened his eyes, knew something was wrong. A cold wash of dread snaked through him when he realized that Kia's side of the bed hadn't been slept in. Driven by a fearful kind of desperation, he yanked on his jeans, his heart pounding as he searched the room. Her laptop was gone.

He grabbed his cell and called her, but it went straight to voicemail...just like it would if she'd turned her phone off.

He rushed down the stairs, his heart pounding, frantically praying he'd find her in the kitchen making breakfast. She wasn't. But the full force of his escalating fear didn't hit until he opened the door and saw that her Jeep was gone. He leaned back against the wall and closed his eyes, so worried he couldn't move.

"What the fuck is wrong?" Tank growled, looking like a bear who had been roused from hibernation too soon with his dark beard and narrowed eyes.

"She's gone."

Immediate fear and concern rushed across his face. "What? She was taken under our noses! Fuck us."

"No, her car is gone."

"That doesn't mean anything. Someone could have taken her."

"No, there's no forced entry and if someone had come in this house, Triton would have torn him apart. Triton lay by the fire, his head on his paws as if the life had been sucked out of him. BFA was curled up against his side as if they were consoling each other.

"Where could she have gone?"

"I haven't got a damn clue, and I've got a feeling if she doesn't want to be found, we won't be able to track her down."

"What the hell? Why would she ditch us? She's in

danger. If anything happens to her, Cowboy, I won't be able to forgive myself."

"Nothing's going to happen to her," he said more to console himself than to allay Tank's fears.

"I'm going to check the barn." Tank went back to his room and let Echo out. Got dressed and came back. The animals followed him outside, and when they got to the barn and peered inside, it was clear that Kia was not there.

"Fuck! Fuck! This is a major cluster fuck! Where the fuck is she!"

Cowboy was just barely holding all his fucks in when Tank painted the air blue.

Cowboy grabbed his shoulders, the panic sliding inside him like crates on a tossing ship. "Get ahold of yourself. This isn't helping."

"How can you be so goddamned controlled all the fucking time? I'm sick of it. This is Kia! We've lost her, and she's out there on her own." Echo growled low in his throat, picking up on Tank's agitation. He turned to the dog and said, "Echo. Stand down." He licked his lips and stared at Cowboy. His loyalty was to Tank, and it was clear he felt that Cowboy was a threat. "Down," he said, giving Echo a hand signal, and he flattened out. "Don't you move from that spot." He turned back to Cowboy, fire in his eyes. "She's a fairy princess, not a damn ninja! I'm going crazy, and I'm not the one in love with her. Are you some kind of cold-hearted bastard?"

Cowboy hit him hard. One minute he had control of himself, and the next, Tank was flat on his back on the ground. With a roar, he sprang up and tackled Cowboy, getting a couple good ones in to his face and body. The man was a freaking Tank, that was for sure. But Cowboy never started anything he couldn't finish. He simply reacted and realized that if Tank didn't have such good control of Echo, he would be in trouble right now. The dog barked, but didn't attack him.

They were evenly matched, trained by the same instructor—combat and close hand-to-hand, kill-or-be-killed physical contest. The SEALs weren't called elite for nothing. Cowboy threw him off, and they wrestled for control as Cowboy worked to subdue him. Even in his anger Tank wasn't out to really damage Cowboy. The man could crush him if he wanted to.

"What the fucking hell is going on here!"

At the sound of their LT's voice, Tank and Cowboy broke apart, stumbling in their haste and shock.

"Attention!"

They both snapped into place, the movement so ingrained, muscle memory taking over. Blood from his cut lip slipped down his chin. Blood from a gash on Tank's forehead made a slow descent. Neither of them moved to wipe it away.

Behind their commanding officer, Kid Chaos and his wife, Special Agent Paige Wilder, stood. Kid's mouth was agape, and Paige reached over and pushed it closed with her finger. His other teammates milled around—Blue, Wicked, Hollywood, and Scarecrow. This was bad news, not just because of the fight between them that they all witnessed, but the fact that Paige and his whole damn team were here meant Kia was in really deep trouble. Cowboy's gut churned with an urgency that made his muscles twitch.

"There better be a damn good explanation for this behavior, gentlemen. And I use that term loosely."

"Permission to speak, sir."

"Granted," Ruckus ground out, his expression of disappointment shaming Cowboy.

"It was my fault," Tank said immediately. "I goaded him, sir. I take full responsibility."

Ruckus walked up to Tank and got right into his face. "I saw two men engaging in fisticuffs. *My* two men who are on *my* team! Supposed to work as a team! So, attempt to take the blame, denied."

He looked at Cowboy. "Nothing to say, Cowboy? You should know better than this."

He gritted his teeth. "Yes, sir. I have no excuse. I lost it. Kia is missing, and he called me a cold-hearted bastard. That's not true." He worked to keep his emotions contained.

Ruckus said to Tank, "You're dismissed and on KP duty. Whip us up some breakfast, pronto. We've been traveling. We're hungry and tired. I'll talk to you later."

"Yes, sir," Tank said.

"Dismissed."

"Blue!" LT called. "Patch him up."

Blue came over and gave Cowboy a sympathetic grimace. The worried look in his eyes made Cowboy's gut clench even more. He set down his kit and pulled out some alcohol swabs and dabbed at Cowboy's face. He pulled a bottle out of his backpack and handed it to Cowboy. "Rinse out your mouth and get some fluid into you," he said.

"Thanks, Blue," Cowboy said as the man rose.

"Go in the house and take care of that other knucklehead."

"Yes, sir." Blue started walking.

"The rest of you head in the house and get washed up. Shower and change if you want to. We'll be inside in a moment."

They all headed to the house. Kid hung back. Ruckus turned and fixed him with a glare.

"Maybe you can just give him a time out, LT."

Blue stopped in mid-stride, glancing at Kid with a resigned look on his face, his mouth twitching. There were chuckles from the porch.

"Kid, get your ass in the house before you're going to need Blue's tender medical attention."

More uncontained laughter. "Maybe a spanking is in order."

"Kid, I swear to God."

"But I'm worried he might like it."

Paige pulled on his arm, even as Ruckus's eyes glinted ever so slightly. Kid sure knew how to defuse a situation, and he would definitely go the extra mile for Cowboy. The look that passed between them said he was sorry he'd been out of the loop with his beautiful wife.

"But I still volunteer."

"Kid!"

"He's going," Paige said as she tugged him toward the house.

Cowboy was still at attention.

"At ease."

He relaxed. "I fucked up, LT. I'm sorry."

"What's been going on here? You dealing with shit about your past? And, this woman? Where does she fit in?"

"Yes, it's about my past, and Kia's part of it." He gave Ruckus a quick and brief rundown.

"I see." He leaned his shoulder against the barn. "We'll talk about Kia Silverbrook in the house with the team and Paige. She's up to her pretty neck in something dark and dangerous."

"That doesn't help."

"It's reality. We have to deal. Let's be honest. I couldn't get along without you, Cowboy. You help drive the missions, and you shoulder additional work or help others get their work accomplished. You work smarter, harder, and normally demonstrate a lot of discipline, motivate others, lead by example. You come up with solutions to problems and most of the time anticipate them before they happen. You're way too valuable for this incident to go any further. I'm slapping your wrist." He peered inside the barn. "Horses. Interesting." Then he looked at Cowboy, his face solemn. "I know why you are cool and calm in the field, and that's an asset. Tank can be a hothead and you rub him the wrong way sometimes, but he's a damn good SEAL."

"I agree."

"Use some restraint. He's a monster, and I can't believe you decked him."

At first Cowboy wasn't sure if LT was serious, but then his mouth curved up at the corners.

"That's going to get you some points with the guys. I don't think any of them would take him on...well...except Wicked. He's a deep-down, mean, lean, spooky machine." Ruckus said.

"Yeah, I wouldn't want to be on the other side of a weapon Wicked wielded, not even my fists."

"Kid's good crazy, that guy is bad crazy," Cowboy said.

"Kid's a pain in my ass. I don't mess with Wicked," Ruckus said.

"Yeah, but he's our pain in the ass. Wicked usually keeps his shit in the shadows."

"Too true." Ruckus looked around. "This is where you're from, huh?"

"Yeah."

"Beautiful country."

"It is."

"Come on. Let's go shower and eat. Then we'll get down to business."

Cowboy actually had to wait in line as both bathrooms were occupied. Tank was in the kitchen, Kia's Kitchen Witch apron tied around his waist, his hair damp. Echo was at his feet, and he gave Cowboy a wary look. He couldn't blame the dog. He was still a bit pissed at Tank.

He had to admit though, the bacon and eggs smelled great.

Kid and Paige came out of the bathroom to whistles and catcalls. She ignored them and Kid just grinned.

As soon as he saw Cowboy, he sauntered over. "Man, I can't believe you decked Tank." They fist bumped.

"I'm not exactly proud of it, but he had it coming."

"Yeah, he's such a grouch. But, he laughs at me...wait... shouldn't that be with...no he laughs at me."

"What's going on? What's up with Kia?"

"Can't really say, but it's not good, man. Paige would have my hide if I discuss it before the big pow wow."

"Damn Kia. If someone needs a spanking..."

"I still volunteer."

"Shut up. You haven't even met her."

"Maybe so, but she's a badass hacker. One of the best. Paige told me they had no idea how to track her down."

"Great. This is going to make it difficult to find her."

"Very. If she's off the grid...she's a ghost—a negative entity."

"She's an honorary SEAL," he muttered.

"I'd rather she was on our side."

"I'm not convinced she's not on our side." Did he think this because he was in love with her, or did he know in his gut that she couldn't be voluntarily involved in this type of scenario.

They consumed breakfast the only way eight full-grown, badass men can, Paige was smart enough and they were gentlemanly enough to let her serve first, then all bets were off. But Tank made plenty. They cleaned up and made sure Kia's kitchen was spotless before Ruckus gave Paige the floor.

"Kia Silverbrook was attacked several times here in town, and Cowboy and Tank took it on themselves to protect her. Cowboy killed the assassin who was after her. Because NCIS has been actively searching for him after Bryant Anderson's death at his hands, I got an email from the Reddick sheriff." She paced and said, "She contacted us early this morning and confessed that she was Quicksilver, and she was responsible for hacking into Naval Base Coronado."

Cowboy stood up so fast that his chair clanged to the floor. "What? That can't be true. Kia would never go along with stealing from a military facility. She's a Black Hat."

"That is confirmed by the DoD. She is a Black Hat, so why would she do something like this? We have no answers." She made direct eye contact with Cowboy. Even with her professional face on, he could see the sympathy there. "Because of that, we had no choice but to issue a warrant for her arrest as an accessory to theft from the U.S. Government and to the murder of two military police."

"No," he said softly. "There's got to be an explanation." His fist came down on the table, and his voice boomed through the room.

He wouldn't believe what he was hearing unless it came straight from Kia's mouth. He didn't for one minute think she was capable of such crimes. Anguish washed through him thinking about losing her. Her gentle soul would be crushed in prison. This couldn't be happening. There had to be a logical explanation.

"Cowboy," Ruckus said. "She's a fugitive."

"Yes, she is," Paige said. "A valuable one, so we want her alive. We're going to track her down. She could have valuable information on the possible whereabouts of the other five warheads that are missing and the weapons. As you all know, many lives are at stake and not just military, but civilians. We can't relent."

"When we find her, Paige is arresting her," Kid said with deep regret.

KIA STEPPED out of the hotel shower and grabbed a towel, drying herself off. She'd strategically set up all the players, and now it was just a matter of getting them all in the right location. She had already done the needed work to begin unraveling herself from this terrible mess.

For the millionth time, she thought about Wes and how he was handling all this. And she couldn't forget about Tank. He cared about her. She cared about both of them. But now she had to rely on herself first and foremost. Her unique ability, her thinking outside the box was going to get her out of this. And for the first time in her life, she was so glad she was a freak.

She hoped her animals were doing all right, wondering if Catmanian Devil was behaving himself. She actually missed her daily dead animal.

She got dressed and went shopping and bought herself a cheap laptop and the devices she needed to pull this off. If she hit her mark, she'd be off the hook.

When she got back to the hotel, she donned her disguise, then checked herself in the mirror. Her own foster mother wouldn't recognize her.

She'd already cancelled her target's usual cleaning

woman, and after monitoring the house, she discovered what time she came and the code she used. Taking a breath, she drove across the street and as nonchalantly as she could, pulled up in a white sedan with the required logo on the side. She went up to the house and punched in the code.

Her DoD contact liked security monitoring, and she was so glad he did. She went about her business of cleaning the house like she was the actual cleaning woman. But when she found a blind spot, she pulled out her laptop and got to work. She'd need to install what she had brought with her in her "cleaning supplies." As soon as she had the security system on a loop, she got to the real reason why she was there.

WES GOT up from one of the couches and stepped over numerous bodies to get to the bathroom. Days had passed, worry eating him as Kia's house was filled to the brim with big, burly men. Cowboy had given up his bed to the two lovebirds. Kid had tried to console him, but the urgency he felt from the moment he opened his eyes had no outlet. He had no freaking idea where she was.

After taking care of his bladder, he went into the kitchen and started coffee. BFA came padding in, and he wasn't happy, protesting and carrying on. "You miss her. Admit it, you fuzzball."

He wound around Cowboy's legs as if to say that he needed some tuna treats to console him. The big softie that he was, he gave them to him.

None of the animals were happy. Triton was hardly interested in eating, the horses were off their feed, and BFA was...well, just as ornery as ever. The guys loved him, and he protested, but that was his way. He'd taken his harassment to a new height, literally. He'd climb up something and then ambush one of them when they were walking by. Hollywood was spooked, always looking around for him, and called him Big Fucking Asshole. Kid called him BFAN (the N stood for ninja). Hollywood wasn't exactly a cat guy, but he was the one that BFA hung out with the most, as kitties tended to go to the one person in the room who wasn't too fond of them. He accepted them all. Maybe that Catastrophe was nothing but a hard to get little bastard.

He realized he was now making up silly names for BFA just like Kia had. Fuck, he missed her, was so worried about her he'd barely slept. He pressed the heels of his hands against the counter. Then he looked out the kitchen window and noticed a car parked near the barn.

The house was waking up and there were several of the team getting ready for a PT run.

He left the house, and like the curious, nosy bastards they were, most of them followed him, including Ruckus.

They came around the opening to the barn.

"Sally Jean?" he asked.

She whirled and dropped the bucket of feed, then stepped back and said, "Whoa, all the rodeos came to town."

"What are you doing here?"

She went from one face to the next, as if she wasn't sure where to look. "Kia asked me to take care of the horses. She told me specifically she would need me today and what time to get here."

"You talked to her?"

"Sure. I always take care of her animals when she's busy, and I run the bar for her, too."

He came up to her and grabbed her shoulders. "Do you know where she is?"

"Wow, dude, back off. You're one intense rodeo."

"I'm sorry. Just tell me where she went."

"To DC. She didn't tell you?" She looked around and said. "I'm going to kill her for not telling me to look my best."

"I think you look great," Hollywood said, and she looked at him and smiled.

Scarecrow called from the house, "Her cell phone just came online."

15

The lot of them, except Tank who had stayed because of Echo and to watch over Kia's house and animals, landed in DC six hours later. The GPS pointed them to a boutique hotel just on the fringe of downtown and back against a suburban neighborhood of upscale townhomes. Paige went up to the manager and flashed her badge.

"How can I help you?"

"We're looking for this woman. Is she staying here?"

"Yes."

"We'll need access to her room."

"Yes, ma'am. Let me get my manager."

Once the manager came out from the back, she explained the situation to him. He took them up to the room and then used his key card to unlock it. They burst inside, but even though all Kia's belongings were there, she wasn't.

Her phone sat on the nightstand.

Cowboy spied her laptop, and he walked over to the desk. The lid was up and there was a folded piece of paper sitting on the keyboard. It read: *Turn me on.*

"Dammit, I hate hackers," Paige muttered under her breath. "Wait," she called out. "Don't touch that. It could be wired."

"Kia wouldn't hurt...she wouldn't hurt me. She wants us here for a reason. She orchestrated it. Let's see what she's got in store for us."

He pushed the "on" button and the screen came to life. It was the foyer of an upscale house, the security camera pointed at the front door.

There was a noise, then the door opened and a man walked in. The screen split, and it now showed the living room. Kia was standing there just inside the wide doorframe.

He noticed she was encased in black fishnet. Cowboy smiled, remembering the name he'd playfully given her.

"Harold Jackson."

The man turned abruptly. He frowned, his face angry. "How did you get in here?"

Kia shrugged. "I'm not really here to discuss my excellent breaking and entering skills, and don't bother to check the silver. It's all there. With what you pay me, I can afford my own."

"You were stupid to come here, Kia. My guy might have missed you in your Podunk town, but the next one won't. I've gone international."

"Your guy. Right. The killer you sent after me. I thought I recognized him."

"He was an idiot. Who do you think you're dealing with here?"

"A backstabbing, treasonous snake. I thought working for the DoD was legit."

"It was. But, we needed you for the Coronado job. We

knew you wouldn't agree to it unless you thought it was on the up and up."

"You're damn right. You know I trusted you. You sent Bryant Anderson with his phony credentials, and I fell for it."

"Anderson...what a fuck-up. He hired the wrong pilot. If he hadn't gotten himself shot, we would have pulled it off. The only piece was the hacking, and we knew you wouldn't do it if you knew, reformed as you are."

Shots sounded, and Kia gasped as Harold's back hit the wall, his face showing his shock as blood blossomed on his chest and he sank down into a sitting position, his eyes open, his face blank.

"He was right. You are a fool dead woman walking." A man materialized out of the shadows, big and menacing. His accent was thick...definitely Slavic. Before Cowboy could blink, he fired at her point blank, four times in the chest.

"Kia!" His anguished shout reverberated in the room.

"Oops," she said as her beautiful face popped up on his screen. Forgot to turn on my screen," she whispered. His heart was pounding, and the fear and adrenaline was subsiding, making him tremble. "I didn't expect that to happen, but did you get what Harold said before he was brutally murdered?"

"We got every word," Cowboy said.

"Thank God. Look, this was supposed to be completely bloodshed free. A little candid camera, a little prodding, and he would spill his guts. Not literally, of course, but Ivan the Terrible showed up. And, FYI, he's still here."

"Kia. Where are you?"

"Oh, I'm in the pantry off the kitchen. That wasn't me in the living room. It was a hologram. Pretty good, huh? I hacked into his security feed and then projected to the laptop."

She was such a genius. A cute, sweet genius. "No, darlin'." He would laugh if this wasn't so dire. "Not where are you physically. The address!"

"Oh, right." She smacked herself in the head. "I'm across the street." She rattled off the address. "Hey guys." She waved, and all he wanted was her in his arms safe and sound. "Wow, that's a lot of people to track down little ole me."

"I think we better get over there before he discovers you're a hologram."

"I think he already has. He's looking for me. Hurry." Then she called out. "Oh, you need the code to the door." She rattled that off, too.

They got plenty of looks when they came pelting out of the elevator en masse and crossed the street at a run. The eight of them spread out. Cowboy, Ruckus, Kid, and Paige went for the front door and the rest of them covered the back.

Paige typed in the code and the door released. She nodded to Ruckus, Kid, and Cowboy.

As soon as she'd gotten the address, Paige had called an ambulance. The siren sounded in the distance.

They went in one at a time, guns gripped, fingers along the trigger guard. Like a well-oiled machine, they moved through the house. Wicked and Scarecrow headed up the stairs, and Cowboy slid around through the living room, heading toward the kitchen. Suddenly the guy popped up and open fire. They all dove for cover.

When he lifted his head to peer over the sofa, he saw a door slide open a sliver. Kia. *Don't.* But the door opened, and she moved very slowly, grabbing a frying pan off the stove. With two hands, she swung with all her might. There was a metallic conk, and then she looked over at him.

"Too bad Tank couldn't see me in action," she said proudly. "It wasn't a one-two punch, but cleaning a murderer's clock with a frying pan sure is effective."

"Yeah," Scarecrow drawled. "We should all start carrying frying pans."

She gave him a triumphant look while one of them flex cuffed the man she'd knocked out. She held up the pan as the guys laughed, then started to introduce themselves. Finally, Cowboy walked up to her, dragged her against him and kissed her in front of them all.

"I thought you were going to throttle me."

"I think a spanking is in order later."

The guys all made catcalls.

"Kinda half a garden party and half a goat fuck, but purely entertaining," Wicked said.

Finally, Paige walked up, and Kia's face fell. "I guess you're here to arrest me." She held out her hands.

"There's still an open warrant. We'll sort this out," she said as she pulled Kia's arms behind her back. Cowboy was worried on how this would all get worked out, but he trusted Paige. Kia would get a fair shake.

At the Navy Yard where NCIS was headquartered, it had been hours and hours since they brought her in. They were all waiting in the conference room when the door finally opened, and Kia walked in. The guys cheered, fist bumping her as she passed through them. Cowboy glared at them until they filed out.

"Hey," she said, looking disheveled, tired, and relieved.

"What's going on?"

"Are you mad at me?"

"You scared the bejesus out of me, so I'm a mite peeved."

"Ooh, on a SEAL, a mite could be deadly."

"Don't you dare make light of this." His was throat suddenly tight as he spoke, his voice husky. "I was going out of my mind."

Her eyes widened with that startled doe look of hers, then she released a breath, regret in her eyes. "Okay, I'm sorry. But I wasn't going to compromise you, not even to save my own skin." Her chin lifted in defiance.

God, when she did that, he wanted to absorb her into his body, a peculiar soft feeling filling up his chest. "What do you mean?"

She looked down, her lashes thick and dark, covering her expressive eyes. She toyed with the top snap of his shirt. "As soon as I realized that I was an accessory, that made me a criminal. I knew if you heard my side of the story, you would insist on being there for me." She looked up at him, and with her heart in her eyes, she whispered huskily, "I couldn't put your life in that kind of tailspin."

"My life is already in a tailspin, and we both know why." She blushed, and that was all he could take. He hauled her against him and covered her lips. Working his mouth slowly against hers, he shifted, and she clutched his shirt in both fists. "We both know I can handle the danger."

She pulled and pushed at the material, shaking him a little. "I know you can handle the danger, but your honor is so deeply ingrained. It would have caused you pain. Deep pain. You could have lost everything."

She had been trying to protect him, and what little anger was left over at what he perceived as her inability to trust him dissipated. "You're completely right. But if I had lost you, I would have lost everything."

This time she dragged him into the kiss. "You're so irresistible," she murmured as she softly brushed her mouth against his, the warmth and moistness of the kiss making his pulse erratic. She licked his bottom lip slowly—very slowly. Opening his mouth against hers, Cowboy dropped his head just enough to deepen the kiss, resolutely keeping his hands loosely around her waist.

He broke the kiss before it got even more heated, pressing his forehead against hers. "So, are you a free woman, then? Can we go?"

She nodded, still gripping his shirt. "They vacated the warrant after seeing the footage. They aren't charging me, even though ignorance was involved here. I was deemed as faithfully fulfilling my job duties under a conspiracy. I don't know if they made it up. Oh, and they offered me a job."

His head came up, his heart pounding. Did this mean she would even think about leaving Reddick? "What?"

"Strangest job interview ever. They said I was the best hacker they had ever seen and what I did with Harold 'May He Burn in Hell' Jackson was ingenious. Paige also confessed that if I hadn't wanted to be found, she doubts they could have found me. There was no trace to follow me back and discover who I was. They want me to become an agent and chase down criminals...um...through the computer."

He was so proud of her. "You're kidding me?"

"I turned them down, but agreed to hack for them for a fee."

Had he been a bit disappointed that she hadn't taken a job that would bring her to San Diego.

"I like freelancing, and it pays so much better. Okay," she rolled her eyes, "I'm a teensy bit a material girl, but I like my beautiful things and my horses." She moved closer to him. "Then I can do what I want with my free time."

He rubbed his mouth against her temple. "Is that right? What exactly do you want to do with your free time?"

She gave a shaky laugh and slid her hands into the back pockets of his jeans. "Well, there's this SEAL I kinda have my eye on."

He mimicked her hold, then leaned back and grinned at her. "You mean a rodeo as Sally Jean would say?"

She watched him, giving him a slightly scandalized look. "Yeah, so gorgeous...I think his name is...Hollywood? Or is that Wicked?"

His grin faded, and he brought his head up, his tone all business. "What?"

Kia gave a little shrug. "Might be Scarecrow. Isn't he the one with that dreamy Southern accent?" she responded dryly.

"It's overrated."

A wry smile lifted the corner of her mouth. "Or Golden Buzzcut...Blue is it...he can play doctor with me."

Cowboy pinched her bottom and grinned. "Like hell he will. I've got something for you."

She gave him a slow, lazy smile. "I think I've seen that. What else do you got?"

He threw his head back and laughed. "You like it." He leaned down and gave her a quick, hard kiss. "I'm afraid that's all I got, darlin'."

"Are you sure?" She ran her palm over his biceps. "How about you show me what this can do?"

He grinned, getting a charge out of how she'd caught him unawares again. "What? Flex?"

"Yeah, or I could go ask Hollywood to—" She let go of him and turned toward the door.

He reached out lightning quick and jerked her back against him. "I don't think so. I've got you covered." He tightened his arm and she sighed softly, molding her hand around the thickened swell. "I have another hard bulge you can check out. It might be familiar, but you know I always give you a bucking good time."

She looked around as if people were listening in, whispering, "I still have the hotel room."

"Do you now?" he whispered back.

"Yes. How about we go there and see what comes up between us? I'm pretty interested in this flexing."

"What else?"

"That thing you do when you're coming, that guttural noise. I'm pretty much addicted to that." She nuzzled his neck. "I believe you also mentioned something about a spanking." She bit him. "In case you didn't notice, I'm wearing my lucky collar, the one with the spikes."

"Christ," he whispered. "You're killing me."

"Yeah, that's the plan." Her sassy, too confident tone amused him.

LATER ON, they all went to dinner in the hotel. She got to know his teammates a little better. "So, what I want to know," Kia said, "is what is this garden party you guys keep mentioning?"

Cowboy looked over at Kid and chuckled. Kid shook his head. "You tell it," Cowboy said.

"All right." He leaned back and smirked. Several of the guys laughed or had big smiles on their faces. "So, we were training with some British commandos and man we were tired. We were going to this terrorist training op out in the

British countryside. Cowboy gets the intel about where we're supposed assault—a staged terrorist cell."

Hollywood chuckled. "Yeah, remember we were pretty tired, wasted from pub partying with those crazy bastards the night before."

Kid laughed. "Yeah, that was wild." He slapped Cowboy on the back. "Cowboy gets the address and we go there. When we get out of the truck, we're looking around, and I'm thinking this is quite an upscale place for a terrorist cell. I was expecting some farmhouse. Anyway, we surround the place, and I keep hearing orchestra music, thinking we picked up some kind of radio station."

The guys started to laugh. "LT gives us the go ahead, and we go in guns bristling—only to find all these women sitting at tables decked out with the works—candles, finger sandwiches, champagne, and little cakes. We all stand there dumbfounded. LT growls, 'What was that address again, Cowboy?' Cowboy says, 'I might have gotten something wrong there.' Finally, this elderly lady stands up and walks over to Cowboy because he was the closest. She says, in this proper British accent, 'Young man, I believe you and your commando friends don't have an invitation and are a wee bit confused. This is a garden party, not a war.' Cowboy apologizes profusely with 'dang it' and 'ma'ams' in that Texas twang which charmed the pants off most of the women there, including this amazing old girl. We all start smiling after Cowboy gives her this knee-melting grin. Then she pushes the muzzle of his semi-automatic down. We really wanted this woman on our team." The guys were really cracking up now. "Then she says, 'But in this case, I think we can make a few exceptions for brave, albeit unruly Americans. How do you take your tea, gents?'"

Everyone burst out laughing at the table. "Anyway, we

ended up sitting down and having tea and cake. I leaned over and said, 'This is a damn sight better than fighting a terrorist cell.'" Kid looked over at him. "Tell her what you said."

"I said, 'In the future, we'll go in blasting, unless it's a garden party.'"

IF IT HADN'T BEEN for Sally Jean's distraction ever since everyone left for DC, Tank would have run the hills with the coyotes, howling at the moon. First off, he hated being left out of any takedown, and even more importantly, he was attached to Kia. Like a brother and sister. She reminded him so much of the sister he'd lost so young. He closed his eyes; the rage at his father for his hand in her death had never subsided. He grew up as a primal, basic beast, running the streets of the hood. Taking what he could when he could get it and hating every minute of his life. But the primal basics had kept him alive. He survived survival.

"Thanks for the lessons," he said.

"It's nothing to be ashamed of, being scared of a horse, especially if you've never seen one."

He nodded. She stepped closer to him. The fire had been built up and they had eaten a great meal. "Look, I really want to fuck you. You interested in that? I bet you have a huge cock. I mean, look at you." She grabbed the waistband of his black motorcycle pants, but before she could run her hand over him, he grabbed her wrist.

"I'd say you're one hell of a straight shooter." He instantly recognized that look in a woman's eyes, and often it was in his direction. He wasn't a slab of meat; he was a man, and his appetites went to being as earthy as he looked. If he wasn't in the SEALs, he'd be pierced in other places, but his dick was somewhere that was private and didn't show.

"You have a girlfriend, you say the word, but I've learned in life that if you don't go for what you want, you don't get it."

"That's a true statement." He thought immediately of Becca, but they had a mutual agreement that what they had was casual. No exclusivity meant he could take Sally Jean up on her offer. He dragged her against him until her curvy, round hips were all up in his grill. "I have no attachments, but my dick is pierced. Some don't like that. If you don't, it's cool."

She breathed softly and looked down the length of his body. "Oh, man. Adds to the fantasy."

"How do you like to be fucked?"

Her quick breathing made those soft, full breasts jiggle. "Every which way but loose, rodeo."

He let her go. She pulled the T-shirt from his pants, and he bent slightly so she could get it off him. "God, the size of you makes me crazy." Moving closer to him, she slid her hand around to the nape of his neck and brought his mouth down to hers. She was a full-out, devouring kisser, her mouth soft.

As her mouth continued to arouse him, she pawed his chest, molding his muscles, skimming his ripped abs until she reached the button of his pants.

He caught her wrists to stop her, and a sound of protest rumbled from her throat. He lifted his head and gave her a slow, sinful smile. "Give me a sec, sweetie. I've got a loaded weapon on me, and we wouldn't want it to accidently discharge, now would we?" he teased.

She made a soft sound and gave him a moment to remove the holster and the gun he kept concealed in the waistband of his pants, which he placed safely on the coffee table.

Before she could go back to his pants, he grabbed her by the back of the neck, twining his fingers gently in her hair. Pulling it back, he raked her throat with his teeth. "Take your clothes off and make it slow. Then, I want to watch you get off."

She complied and he pushed her back and onto the couch, tightening his hand in her hair just enough for a bad girl to like it. "If you make it good for me, I'll fuck you with my mouth."

She released a hard breath, and she did make it good, then he lost his restraint and spread her out on the table and took her from behind hard, fast, and deep.

Sally Jean didn't stay, and he was okay with that. She was only into the physical aspect of being with a man. Whatever was up with her was none of his business and something he didn't want to know. He suspected she didn't have sex with a man twice.

When he went to bed, glad for the reprieve on worrying about Kia, his mind drifted to her and her relationship with Cowboy. Boy, those two were meant for each other if he'd ever been the judge of that, and he wasn't some yenta matchmaker Cowboy had, with a smirk, named him. But when he watched them, something hollow filled his gut. It had only begun lately after Ruckus found Dana and Kid had married his feisty Paige. It was a strange restlessness. He couldn't figure out what was picking at him, except that he had this itch that wouldn't go away no matter how many women he slept with. His gut tightened with a feeling that made him want to bust something. He clenched his jaw and rose stark naked. He stood at the window, moonlight limning his body in light and shadow and looked out at the wide-open spaces.

With a sharp, "Fuck," under his breath, he reached for a pair of shorts, let Echo out of his kennel, and padded to the front door. There he donned his sneakers and went out into the night. He didn't howl at the moon, but he came damn near close.

"KIA!" Tank's shout was full of joy as he came barreling out of the house when Wes and she pulled up. The rest of his team—what a delicious band of brothers—had all flown back to San Diego. She absolutely relished the dinner they'd had together; she really bonded with Paige, which was weird. But she couldn't fault the woman for doing her job. They were all so very unique. Kid was so out there, such a hoot, Blue quiet and contemplative, but oh, boy did he know a lot about everything. Hollywood was a terrible, irresistible, drop-dead gorgeous flirt. Scarecrow was wry and intense. She couldn't quite read Wicked; he was guarded as if he wore armor all the time, and she had to wonder if he'd been fostered as a child. Ruckus was quite intriguing, and she suspected his fiancée, Dana, had to be one hell of a woman. He was complex, commanded by just sitting there, one of the most intense men she'd ever met. She suspected he would tire her out. She absolutely adored Kid, and his story about the "Garden Party Job" had been hilarious.

She returned Tank's hard hug.

"You about gave me a heart attack."

She poked him in that wide, hard chest of his. "You're much too fit for a heart attack. But thanks for caring."

He cleared his throat and gave Wes a sidelong glance. "Sally Jean taught me how to ride."

"Oh, yeah? A horse?"

Wes laughed, and Tank smirked.

"Yes, ma'am, a horse."

Kia's brows rose. She knew all about Sally Jean and rodeos. "What else did she teach you?"

His jaw flexed and he looked away. "Plenty. She's a powerhouse."

That hussy, but Kia couldn't really blame her. Tank might be contrary and liked things his way, but he was a very nice man...at least to her. She suspected she was an exception.

"You coming?" Wes called.

"In a minute. I want to say hi to my guys. I understand they've been a bit off their feed."

She headed toward the barn. As Tank and Wes disappeared into the house, Kia turned toward the sound of a car. It was that damned Lincoln.

She went over to Red as he rolled down his window. "Where the hell have you been? I've been calling you."

"I've been busy."

"You're always busy. Have you made any progress?"

She had finally had enough of this charade. Something in her snapped. "Yes, I have made progress," she ground out, and it was all about her being strong enough to tell this huge jerk off. "I own Sweetwater. I bought it out from under your father ten years ago. You will never bulldoze over history or Wes's legacy ever, not as long as I live."

"You fucking bitch. You played me." He went to get out of the car and she slammed the door back.

"You deserved it." She bent down, channeling Wes's

tough look. "Don't come back here. This matter is closed and over with." Until she brought his father up on charges.

His face mottled with rage, he hissed, "This isn't over you fucking *freak*!"

She watched him drive away with deep satisfaction.

Later, after she'd visited the horses, she unpacked. She looked over at Wes who was quiet. "I could use a nice, hot shower. Care to join me?"

This had all started the night he'd been so tender and kind to her when she'd been traumatized in that alley. Now the mark Lambert had put on her was barely visible.

The shower spray was so pleasant as it massaged her tired body. She was so relieved to have all that "dead woman walking" threat against her life behind her. But she was far from off the hook.

She should tell Wes, but she hesitated again because of the missing evidence. An irrational fear climbed up her chest. "Kia?" Wes said, tipping up her chin. "I think we need to talk about me leaving."

Her stomach dropped, and she buried her face in his slick skin. "I don't want you to go."

"I know. But I have to mend some fences with my mom and visit with them before I head back. My time here is almost up. Have you had a chance to find out who owns Sweetwater?"

This was her chance to tell him everything. But she couldn't get the words past her thick throat.

"I'm still investigating."

"I can stay one more night." He rubbed her back. "Do you want...something more out of this?"

She raised her head and cupped his face. "Yes, I do."

He closed his eyes and pressed his cheek to the top of

her head. "So do I, but we both know that the distance is going to be an issue."

"We can figure it out. Can't we?"

"I don't know, Kia. I'm gone so much, and I feel disjointed right now. Reconnecting to my roots has been a rollercoaster ride."

"I understand. We'll take some time to think about it. Okay?"

He nodded and pulled her close, but now the water didn't help at all.

16

In the morning, she got up with a heavy heart. Both Wes and Tank were leaving today. She went downstairs and saw that Tank was already up, and through the open door she saw his duffel was on the porch. When she padded out to the warm wood, he was setting the last piece of Echo's kennel in the back of the SUV.

"Hey, you're not leaving without breakfast, are you?"

"No, just getting everything in the truck. Where's Cowboy?"

"He's still asleep."

"Lazy bastard."

She laughed. He followed her back into the house, and they got to making breakfast together.

He nudged her with his hip. "What's wrong?"

She gave him a startled look. "He's leaving today," was all she could manage.

He frowned. "Did you talk to him about...you know...you guys?"

"You're not a very good girlfriend," she said, nudging him back.

He scowled. "I can eat ice cream like a boss, but no chick movies or fashion advice."

She laughed softly. "I'm going to miss you and your grouchy disposition."

He brightened. "I'm going to miss you, too," he growled, hugging her one-armed around the neck.

"Something smells good," Wes said entering the kitchen a few minutes later.

"Yeah, no thanks to you, slacker."

He just gave Tank the middle finger.

After breakfast was done and they helped her clean up, Tank said, "Take care of yourself, Kia. I'm sorry for the circumstances that brought me here, but glad I had a chance to meet you."

She hugged him hard, and for a moment, his arms were out at his side, then he wrapped them around her. She pressed a small cooler in his hands. "I made you a few things to eat and there's some water in there. Some treats for Echo, too." Her throat felt tight. She knelt down and hugged Echo, and he licked her face. "Triton's going to miss his buddy."

"Yeah."

"The Catinator is going to miss him, too." He yowled from the back of the couch.

"Goodbye, fur ball," Tank said as he passed, but the cat just continued to lick his paws.

"He's broken up about it, I see." He shook Wes's hand. "I'll see you back in San Diego."

"Thanks for coming, Tank. I appreciate your help in protecting Kia."

He nodded, then he and Echo were gone. She already felt his absence. Wes had already brought down his duffel, and when he saw her face, he immediately took her into his arms.

"We'll figure it out, darlin', I promise. A few days with my family before they totally disown me, then we'll talk. Okay?"

She raised her face, unable to hold back the tears.

"Aw, damn, don't cry. You're tearing me up."

She wiped at her face and kissed him, wondering if he would come back. Hoping that he would. She needed to get this whole Sweetwater thing resolved and come clean with Wes about the ranch. Tell him about her investigation and let him know that she'd found the right gun dealer after hacking into the ATF's gun control database. She'd talked to him by phone in DC. He said that he remembered the guy he sold it to, a big, burly redheaded fella with a ten-gallon hat named Roger James, Sr. Big Red. He said he would tell the sheriff all about it.

Ten minutes after Wes left, there was a knock at the door, and she ran to it thinking it might be Wes coming back. When she opened the door, Red stood there. "What do you want?"

"I just want to talk to you." It was the eerily calm yet calculated look in his eyes that sparked a sense of unease deep inside. "Can't you spare a minute?"

She folded her arms across her chest. "After the name calling yesterday? No, I don't think so. Leave."

Triton rose at the sound of her voice, his eyes watching Red's every move.

Without warning, he grabbed her by the hair and dragged her onto the porch at the same time he slammed the front door. The dog lunged forward, but it was too late, he was trapped on the other side. She could hear the way he scrabbled against the barrier, his barking and growling frantically loud.

"What do you think you're doing? Let me go!" she shouted, her heart's frantic beating a hard pounding in her chest.

His eyes were mean and predatory. "I'm sick of waiting for what should have been mine. You're going to give me what I want."

Oh, God. She couldn't believe this was happening after all that she'd been through. His hold on her hair was punishing, and he dragged her across the yard toward the barn. As he walked, he shouted, "I've waited patiently for you to find the owner. For months, I dealt with your stalling tactics. For weeks, I've had to endure frustration after frustration." His voice rose with anger. "I'm done waiting." He'd caught her so completely off guard that she didn't even have shoes on. The stones from the yard cut her feet.

Once inside the dim barn, she fought him, but he backhanded her across the face. She fell against Quicksand's stall. The horses screamed, spooked by the thud, sensing her fear and the violence in the air.

He walked over and grabbed her around the neck and squeezed. Her oxygen was effectively cut off, and there was a frenzied light in his eyes. "I'll kill you right here, right now if you fight me again. The property be damned." He shook her hard, and she clawed at his fingers. "Do you understand me?"

She couldn't speak, but she managed to nod her head. He released her, and she doubled over, choking and dragging in lungfuls of air.

He grabbed her by the arm this time and headed for the loft.

He pulled her up the stairs, and when he reached the

top, he shoved her so hard she fell, sprawled out on the hard, wooden floor. She lay stunned for a minute, her hands stinging, her shoulder aching where she had hit, her upper arm throbbing from his fierce hold on her. He went to the loft door and opened it wide.

Then he came back to her and pulled out a sheath of papers. "This is a contract for fair market value. You're going to sign it."

She looked up at him as if he'd lost his mind, and maybe he had. "I already know what your father did to Wes's father. He's not going to be able to enjoy that property. I have corroboration that he bought that gun right before Travis was killed. Let me go now, and I won't press charges."

He threw back his head and laughed, the sound not full of mirth at all but something much scarier. "You are such a stupid bitch. My father didn't have the guts to get Travis out of the way." His eyes shone too bright, his smile pure evil.

She closed her eyes. She had been so totally wrong. It hadn't been Big Red who had murdered Travis. It had been his son, a son who needed to prove his own mettle to his father. Red had killed Travis McGraw.

"Yeah, you're getting it."

"How could you? You're a monster."

"You haven't seen anything yet, freak." He grabbed her by the hair and dragged her to the open door. He pushed her toward the edge of the loft and she screamed. The horses kicked and banged in the stalls below her, and her head spun as the ground looked so far away.

He jerked her back. "Sign the papers, Kia, now."

She closed her eyes. She simply didn't have a choice. "All right! I'll sign them."

He dragged her back to where the contract was and threw her down on the floor again. She heard a deep yowl and looked up. BFA was in the rafters, his eyes reflecting for a moment.

She signed them and then threw them back at him. "Now get off my property."

He inspected them. Then folded them and tucked them in his inside jacket pocket.

"Not just yet."

She tried to run when she realized that Red had no intention of letting her live. She tried to reach the baling hook that was stuck in one of the bales, but he grabbed her hair again and dragged her up. She kicked and screamed, but it did no good. He was too strong.

Her heart broke because she wasn't going to get to come clean with Wes. She was never going to have a chance to tell him, explain. She sobbed softly. He would come back here and find her broken, dead body on the ground. She couldn't bear the thought of him finding her like he'd found his dad.

Red dragged her to the opening, laughing. "It's not the fall," he said, his mouth close to her ear, his hot breath on her skin. "It's the landing that's rough."

COWBOY DROVE AWAY from Kia's feeling like he couldn't breathe. Who was he kidding? He didn't have to think about this. He wanted her. He had no idea how it was going to work, but he wasn't going to leave her with tears in her eyes and uncertainty. He did a U-turn after checking to make sure no cars were coming and headed back to her place. As he drove in, he saw the white Lincoln. *Red*. What the hell was he doing here?

As soon as he got out of his truck, he heard Triton's frantic bark, and he started toward the house, but then there was a bloodcurdling scream, and he froze in mid-stride, breaking into a run. The barn. Kia!

He went back to the truck and unlatched his case, grabbing the gun and the clip. He jammed it into the magazine on the run, racking the slide as he got to the open barn door. The loft. He rushed down the aisle. The horses were going crazy in their stalls.

He pelted up the stairs, and to his horror, Red had Kia by the hair and was shoving her toward the open loft door.

"Wes beat me at everything." His mouth twisted with rancor. "He's such a fucking hero. Wait until he comes back here and finds out what I've done to you."

Just as Cowboy lined up the sights with Red's torso, but before he pulled the trigger, a cream and brown, angry, spitting BFA dropped down out of the loft like a pouncing tiger, claws extended. He landed right on top of Red's head and dug in, swiping at his face, his back claws digging into his neck.

The man howled in pain and spun, trying to dislodge the cat who raked his face again and bit down hard on his cheek, yowling and hissing. As soon as he dislodged the attack cat, Kia balled up her fist and hit him right in the kisser. He clutched his nose as blood gushed, and he backed up and hit the barn wall, his face a mass of welts, deep bites and scratches.

He turned to look at Cowboy, who didn't move a muscle, the cold message in his eyes that all Red had to do was give him a reason. With defeat filling his eyes, he slid down the wall to the floor, a defeated, broken man.

She ran to him and threw her arms around him. "Grab my phone, darlin', and call the sheriff." He didn't take his eyes off Red.

Kia did as he asked, and when she was done giving him the details, Red used his suit jacket to press against his nose.

Sirens sounded in the distance and Cowboy narrowed his eyes. "You ever touch her again, and there won't be a hole big enough for you to hide in."

They heard cars sliding to a halt outside and the sound of running feet. Jerry came up and said, "Boy, you got yourself plenty of trouble here."

Cowboy looked over at Kia and said softly, "Don't I know it."

As Red passed, he pulled a sheaf of papers out of his pocket and threw them at Cowboy. "Did she dupe you, too, asshole? She's owned Sweetwater this whole time."

The sheriff and his deputy hauled Red down the stairs. But Cowboy was frozen in place. He turned to her, her dark hair a wild tumble around her shoulders, bruises coloring her cheeks, on her neck, her upper arm, a stricken look on her face. As if it was happening all over again, he remembered coming into the house. It was eerily quiet. He'd called out for his dad and laughed softly, thinking he'd fallen asleep in the study again. He'd gone inside and said chidingly, "Are you snoozing?" His words had cut off, his mouth going dry when he saw the bullet hole in his temple, the congealed blood and his dad's open and staring eyes. It was overwhelming, the feeling of betrayal that had washed over him, and he felt it again as he looked at her, trying to get his mind around the fact that she...*she* owned Sweetwater and hadn't said a word all this time.

Pressing her hands nervously together, Kia swallowed hard and met his gaze. "Wes, I can explain."

He didn't give her a chance to speak. His voice was quiet, controlled, and laced with anger. "I can't believe you would do that and not tell me."

"Wes, please."

She reached for him, but he jerked away. "There's nothing to explain. You had so many opportunities to tell me this information. You deceived me even after I asked you to find out who owned Sweetwater. You lied to my face."

"I can explain."

He turned away and started out of the loft, and she went after him. She caught him at the opening to the barn. "I wanted to tell you, but I didn't know how."

"It's a simple conversation, Kia," he snapped roughly. "I thought we had trust."

HER MIND REFUSED TO FUNCTION, and she stared up at him, groping for something to say that would cut through his fury. But nothing came, no answer, no explanations—nothing but a sickening fear. Driven by desperation, she made another attempt to reason with him, her midriff churning with a mix of guilt, alarm, and helplessness. She reached toward him, pleading with him. "Wes, please. You've got it all wrong, believe me."

He jerked away, his eyes blazing as he shot her a look of contempt before turning away. "You're the one who is keeping secrets, and you ask me to believe you? That's a hell of a joke!" Wes dropped the papers, and the wind swirled around them and carried them across the yard, like her dreams, blowing away. He walked purposefully to his truck and got inside. As he slammed the door, their eyes met through the windshield, then he backed the truck up and peeled out of her driveway.

She limped across the yard, a sick feeling washing

through her. She opened the door and calmed an agitated Triton. Walking to the couch, she sank down on it and drew up her knees and pressed her forehead against them. God, what had she done? What kind of damage had she caused? She had only wanted to protect him, but she had hurt him instead. Worse than that, she had resurrected the shame, the pain, the trauma that had been riding him hard for ten years.

A hollow, sinking feeling settled in her abdomen. Anything she tried to do now would only make matters worse. She turned and went up to the room they'd shared. Heartsick and overwhelmed by guilt, so alone in the bed where he'd made such passionate love to her, she finally let the tears come—tears that welled up from the bleak emptiness inside her.

That night as she lay in bed, she thought about Wes, and she so wanted to talk to him, but what could she say? There was so much that she'd held back, and she thought long and hard about why. She had said it was because she wanted the evidence she needed to convict Big Red, but that wasn't the real truth. She was afraid, and it was a dark and buried fear that she only realized now.

She'd hurt him in the worst possible way. By the sin of omission, she'd betrayed him. But what was most unforgivable of all was that she'd done it because she was scared. She knew that now. She'd been afraid of him abandoning her like so many people had in her life.

Even computers had homes: the desktop; websites had home pages, and Microsoft Word's first tab after File was Home. But this wasn't about her logical mind. This was about the heart she had never given to anyone because it had been flawed. She'd loved him from afar, and now she loved him for real. Her hands fisted as if she was trying to hold on to him, but she knew from her past that was impossible, especially when people always let her down.

She'd bought Sweetwater to preserve it, that was true. She'd wanted to save the ranch that Travis had died fighting for, but the real reason, the real truth, was that it was Wes's home. She couldn't bear the thought that he would lose it.

She knew now what home meant, and it didn't have to do with brick and mortar or wood and beams or marble and glass. It didn't have to do with a lost ranch or someone's hometown.

Home wasn't really a place...it was a feeling.

It was love.

17

Tank drove straight home, dropped Echo back at the kennel, and then he slept for ten solid hours, went for a run and showered. After his vigorous bout of sex with Sally Jean, he couldn't stop thinking about riding his bike. Just as he was heading toward the garage, his cell phone rang, and he answered, "Jordan, man I just got back in town."

"Perfect. Do you think you could come by and meet the Doc today, like now?"

"Sure, I was just going for a ride on my bike so that's perfect timing. What's the address?"

He drove straight there and parked the bike in the parking lot, then spied a coffee shop across the street. Man, he could go for some iced coffee. He'd missed that in Reddick. He dashed across the busy street and went inside, stood in line, and ordered.

As he left, he held the door for a beautiful woman and turned to watch her walk away, her smile for him flirtatious. When he turned back around, he ran right into something soft. The collision caused the top of his cup to pop off, followed by the distinct sound of his cold drink splattering just outside the entrance.

When he focused, he saw that he had spilled his whole iced coffee down the front of her.

There was a gasp and face contortions and a murmur, "Cold. Very cold."

"Oh, my God," he said, "I'm so sorry. I didn't see you."

She had her head down, her voice annoyed and beautiful, like liquid gold, the kind that could do car commercials and voice sexy anime characters. "That's because you were ogling some sexy woman's ass. You should watch where you're going, Casanova." She said "Casanova" like she knew what it was like to be with a guy who had a wandering eye and had kicked the bum to the curb.

She looked up then, and his breath caught in his throat at her eyes. This woman had the voice and eyes market cornered. They were a striking green with streaks of brown, almond-shaped and thickly lashed. Her long dark hair was pulled into a severe, tight ponytail, and she wore no makeup, not a stitch of it, not even lip gloss.

She had a light scattering of freckles across her cheeks and nose. Their implied innocence was so at odds with her knowing eyes and sultry voice. But then, she was a study in contradictions when it came to his reaction to her.

They were standing close to one another. He felt himself lean closer, breathing in her scent. Something that he'd never done in his life. She was dressed like an accountant, non-descript blouse a tan color, tight brown pants and a pair of serviceable shoes. This close he noticed how smooth and soft-looking her skin was. Then there were those freckles. They were cute, and she wasn't the cute type. She was no-nonsense and wore her confidence as easily as she did those chunky shoes.

She was so not his type. Not even close to the fluff that was Becca or the curvy Sally Jean. She wasn't really beautiful, but there was something exotic and unique about her that made men look. But part of that, he suspected, was the way she carried herself. She was tall, a touch over five foot nine, with small breasts and a long, slender body—and legs that went on forever and ever.

She pulled the soggy blouse away from her skin with a sucking sound, and his breath caught for a second time. Unfuckingbelievable.

Lace bra.

He couldn't help staring. She was wearing a lace bra beneath her wet shirt. The delicate lace outlined against the tan silk was unmistakable.

Lace.

So feminine compared to her Plain Jane look.

"Ugh, just great. Thanks, you big lug." She pivoted on her practical heel and started away.

Wow, he was transfixed by the way she moved, with the long-legged stride of a runway model, yet the grace and power of an athlete. He couldn't take his eyes off her.

A hand came down on his arm, and the woman who he'd held the door for and had caused the collision slipped her card into the pocket of his charcoal gray motorcycle pants.

But as soon as she moved away, he searched the street for the green-eyed woman, but she was gone.

He was irritated, and suddenly that itch started up again. Restlessly, he went back inside and got another coffee, this time careful when he left. He crossed the street and walked up to the Old Town Pet Clinic. Opening the door, he saw Jordan handing off a puppy to a blonde woman with a smile.

Jordan turned and saw him. "Hey, come on back. The Doc is in the bathroom. Be right out."

They waited, shooting the breeze about getting together for hoops when the door opened.

"I swear, men are so pathetic. This huge Neanderthal doused me with his iced coffee. If he could keep it in his pants, I wouldn't have to go through the morning wearing a soggy blouse and looking like I was in a wet T-shirt contest." She was dabbing at the mess he'd made of her shirt with a paper towel. "*And*, I had to miss my morning dose of caffeine. This is silk, too. It's probably ru—"

She looked up and froze. He couldn't get enough of looking at that face. But he never dated her type. Ever. The marrying kind, the girlfriend kind, the fall-in-love-and-lose-your-shit kind. No one would control him. Besides, she seemed tight-assed, straight-laced, as if she had a white picket fence up her ass.

"Dr. Alyssa St. James, meet my brother, Petty Officer and Navy SEAL dog handler, Thorn Hunt."

Shifting his iced coffee, he offered her his hand. "Uh, that would be Neanderthal to you. But my friends call me Big Lug, and all the women I seduce...they call me Casanova, but usually in a less deep and more breathy voice."

Her eyes narrowed, then that mouth curved up. Oh, look out, major babe earthquake. "Okay, so your brother has a sense of humor," she said with a laugh and a devastating smile as the world shifted under his feet.

He. Was. Not. Going. There.

WES COULDN'T FACE his family and realized that he wasn't

going to be able to function well in Reddick. He just hit the highway and started back home to San Diego. He apologized profusely to his sister, unsettled with leaving things the way they were with his mother, but after learning what Kia had done, he was heartsick.

All this time. *Ten years.* She'd owned Sweetwater, and from what he could tell from afar, she had done a bang-up job with it. His hands gripped the wheel as he drove. My God, she had preserved it, expanded on it. She had kept his legacy alive. Why wouldn't she tell him about that?

All the junk that he thought he'd worked through came rushing back. He was more mentally tough than this, he told himself. But when he tried to sift through it all, what stood out was Kia. She was the first person he thought of when he woke up and the last when he fell asleep.

For the next few days, he reverted back to his college days, running himself ragged. He didn't want to think, so he lifted, ran, swam. When he wasn't doing those things, he would stand in his crappy apartment in anguish, his past overwhelming him, the memories of her breaking him down.

When Tank showed up on his doorstep and took one look at him, he swore. "What happened?"

Wes told him, and Tank said, "I can't believe you left without hearing her out. That's low, Cowboy. She doesn't deserve that."

"How do you know?"

"Because she left to go to DC on her own so she could spare us the decision to throw our careers away and help her. She single-handedly saved her own ass in an ingenious way. She's a babe, funny, quirky, and works hard. Look what she did for that reunion. It was a success because of her. But you go ahead and act like a fool. If you can't see that, then you don't deserve her."

Days later, Tank's words tying him up in knots, he was ready to climb the walls. He headed out to the gym, and when he got home and picked up his mail, there was a large manila envelope that had an attorney's office return address. When he saw the Corpus Christi location, his gut clenched. He went inside, sat down on the bed, and tore it open. Feeling as if he'd just taken a blow to the midsection, Cowboy bolted to his feet. Warmth flooded him—gratitude and a sense of closure. It was the deed transfer of Sweetwater to him and a check for the proceeds of the ranch over the ten-year period she'd owned it for just shy of a million dollars. He sat back down on the bed, dragging his hand down his unshaven face, his throat cramped up, his eyes smarting. Unable to see, he gouged at his eyes, guilt slicing through him. He deserved this. God, but he deserved this. He'd been such a bastard to her.

A white envelope dropped out of the paperwork. His name written in a flowing script was the only thing on the envelope.

He broke the seal and read it twice. When he got to the part about his dad, everything went dead still—the sounds, his hands, his heart—and it felt as if every drop of blood had drained from his head. He slipped to his knees, and a soft sob escaped his lips. Tears dropped onto the page. He hadn't taken his own life. Losing his shit for several minutes, Cowboy felt as if a heavy weight lifted from him. She laid everything out for him, her reasons for her actions, the original reason and the real reason she hadn't told him. Red Sweeny had shattered everything he'd valued, and Kia, his beautiful Kia had preserved it all. He was infused with so much admiration for her, for her integrity, for her steadfast belief, for her determination. She had saved everything, and he'd never even known it. His second chance with her was in tatters because of his actions. But now it felt like she was everything.

Everyfuckingthing.

Feeling like a thrice-cursed bastard, he rose. His cell phone rang, and he pulled it out of his back pocket. The display showed Erin was calling.

When he answered, no one said anything, then he could hear crying, sniffling. "Erin?" But he already knew what must be wrong.

"Wes, you need to come home. Can you?"

"Yes. I know about Dad. I just found out." His voice broke, and for a few minutes neither of them could speak.

"It's like a nightmare. All this time and we believed he did this to himself. It changed me, changed you, just about killed Mom. How could he do such a thing?" She sniffled. "We just had a visit from Uncle Jerry. He said that Red Sweeny was arrested for Dad's death. He murdered Dad, then staged the suicide. Kia Silverbrook has been investigating his death all this time. She was finally able to find the evidence. He's also being charged with assault and battery for his attack on her. Mom is inconsolable. I need you here."

Shock rendered him speechless. His dad had been murdered. Everything he'd thought, believed for ten years had been a lie. Kia had suspected, and she'd followed through. "I'm on my way." Cowboy inhaled unevenly, his voice thick.

After he ended the call, a debilitating weakness rushed through him. He braced his elbows on his thighs and hunched over, pressing the heels of his hands against his eyes. He had to go home.

It was after two in the morning when he got off the plane

in Corpus Christi. The first seat he'd been able to get was on the red-eye. Erin met him, took one look at him, and wrapped her arms around him. They reached the house by two-thirty. His niece and nephew were with Brew's parents. They had been alarmed and upset by their grandmother's grief.

He went up to her room as soon as he walked through the door. She was sitting in a chair by the window, and she turned dull, grief-stricken eyes toward the door. There was a small spark when she saw him. "Wes," she sobbed as she rose, and he engulfed her in his arms.

"I'm here, Mom. I've got you. We'll get through this. I promise."

She buried her face in his shoulder and nodded as she clutched him to her, sobbing.

He helped her downstairs, broke the news about the ranch, and Kia's part in it. How she had preserved their birthright by her own toil. "It's ours again, lock, stock and barrel," he said. He showed them the check, and there was a stunned silence in the room, then his mom and sister burst into tears. As his brother-in-law consoled Erin, he held his mom tight.

After that, he got her to lie down and held her hand until she fell asleep. He let her talk about his dad openly now without the anger that always made him shut down.

He'd done his dad a terrible disservice, but he wasn't going to beat himself up over it. He hadn't known, and his reaction had been his reaction, but it was no longer valid. How he felt was, but not that anymore. He asked for his mom's forgiveness, silently prayed for his dad's, and he let go of the past, let it flow out of him like poison. Kia had healed him. He was no longer that coward's son...he never had been, and he shed the weight of that.

"That girl is a treasure," his mom whispered. "A gem."

"She is."

"Invite her over for supper, Wes. We all want to thank her."

"I will, Mom. Tomorrow when I see her."

After leaving her room, he went downstairs. Erin pushed him down in a chair and set a plate in his hands.

"After the word spread, we had more food than we know what to do with. So please eat." She studied him. "You okay?"

His throat feeling tight and raw, Cowboy answered, his voice gruff. "Yeah, I'm okay."

Erin stared at him for a moment longer, then said, "You're in love with her, aren't you?"

Without looking at his sister, he nodded. "Yeah, if I haven't blown it."

He was so numb with exhaustion that he couldn't regiment his mind, and bits and pieces of thoughts kept surfacing, like flotsam churned up by the tide. He had been so wrong. And so damned blind. What Tank had said had been true; he should have heard her out instead of letting the old baggage influence him.

If he was lucky—damned lucky—maybe she wouldn't turn and walk away.

The next morning when he woke up, he showered and changed. As soon as businesses opened, he went in and had a conversation with Uncle Jerry. He was just as heartbroken as they were, just as praiseful of Kia. After that, he went over to the bank and deposited the money into an account. It was just about the time she fed the horses when he turned onto her drive and passed under The Gray Havens sign. A moving truck passed him on the road.

She was moving? He felt a little panicky that he could

have missed her. It was a good thing he got here when he did.

He saw a horse trailer and her car filled with boxes. Quicksand let out what he could only describe as a loud, joyous whinny. "In a minute boy," he murmured as he went up on the porch. He knocked, but no one answered.

He couldn't have missed her because her Jeep was still here, and all three horses were in the corral, so she couldn't be out riding.

He heard barking and the tinkle of laughter around back. He hurried around the house, then came to a full stop.

She was watering the plants, and BFA, the cat that had saved her life, was batting at the flowers and lapping at the water as it came out of the can. Kia was throwing a ball for Triton and laughing deeply at the antics of the cat. Then before his unbelieving eyes, she picked him up and held him aloft, and she kissed him on his head. He nuzzled against her chin, then wiggled to get down. There was only so much he could take, Cowboy suspected.

Jesus. She was beautiful.

She turned her head and the laughter faded from her face. There were mottled bruises on both cheeks with a shiner of a black eye. The marks on her slender throat and arm were still there, and if he could go back in time, he would have taken that damn shot and put that miserable monster down.

She stood on the top stair of the arch filled with blooming honeysuckle, framed in pink and red blossoms.

"So this is where you have your secret fairy garden?" He stopped at the bottom of the stairs.

"I'm going to miss it." She took a step down.

"You're moving?"

"Yeah, three horses, one dog, and one ornery cat." BFA

yowled. "Okay, a reformed ornery cat." He yowled again. "All right, I did get carried away—semi-reformed."

Cowboy chuckled, his heart turning over. He wanted the whole lot of them.

"What is happening to Gray Havens?" He hated to think that someone else would live here.

"I sold it to Melody, the horse trainer from the reunion. She needed to expand, and her husband and daughter will love it here. I'm going to be one of the principle patrons of The Gray Havens Horse Rescue."

"That's perfect." He loved the idea that someone who had benefited from Kia's influence would own this place.

"What about The Back Forty?"

"I've made Sally Jean my manager. I can come back here when needed to make sure everything is running smoothly. We already have everything worked out."

"So, that only leaves you and your menagerie. Where exactly are you going with three horses, one dog, and one semi-reformed ornery cat?" He took a step up, his heart in his throat.

"San Diego," she said, taking another step down.

"You were in the city?" He moved up one more step.

"Only briefly to buy this beautiful place just outside of the city, near the ocean. It has this beautiful red barn and a quaint, gorgeous, remodeled farmhouse."

"You didn't come to see me. I deserved that."

"I wanted to see you, but..." She bit her lip.

"I read your letter, and I can only say, I'm so damn sorry for reacting instead of realizing that you would never do anything to deliberately hurt me. I understand you wanted to wait for the evidence, understand why you tried to protect me from the truth before you had a chance to figure every-thing out. Can you...forgive me, Kia?"

"Oh, God, Wes. I love you so much I can't breathe."

He rushed up the rest of the steps to her. All he could do was look at her. She was so beautiful. She'd knocked him senseless the first time he'd seen her, and he'd never really recovered—the wild color of her hair, the delicate arch of her brows, the shape of her face, the clear, sun-shot gray of her eyes. Her mouth. God, what she'd done to him with her mouth.

"I...I hoped..." she started, her voice trailing off breathlessly. Her cheeks were flushed. "You have perfect timing."

"I wanted to thank you for what you did for my family." His voice broke, and she wrapped her arms around him and he reveled in the comfort her touch brought him. "Can you forgive me?"

Her face went many shades of soft and tender. "Yes, I can. I did it for you, Wes. I couldn't bear for you to lose something so important to you. I'm so sorry about your dad. He was more a father to me in the two years I knew him than all my foster fathers put together. I'll never forget him."

Then it occurred to him. "You nominated him, didn't you?"

She nodded and buried her face against his throat. "Yes, every year. He showed me all his buckles. I was so proud. I loved him, you know."

"And you had to go through all the grief alone. Aw, Kia, darlin', I love you."

Her head came up so fast, she clipped him on the chin. He laughed softly, feeling so free. "Ow. What did you just say?"

He cupped her face in his hands. "I love you, Kia Silverbrook." Then there was nothing else to say, not right now when all he wanted, all he needed was to touch her, to slide his tongue in her mouth and taste her, to fill himself up with her.

Their lips met, hers parted, and a hundred emotions flooded through him. He'd expected pleasure, electrifying pleasure—but he also got relief, bone deep. This was home, being with Kia, their bodies touching. She came up on tiptoe, her mouth on his, her arms going around his neck, and he slid his hand down her back.

Then farther.

He tried not to devour her, but she was already there, and he was drowning in the love he felt—on the edge of desperation pulling him under, the heat of her skin, in the all-consuming soft wetness of her mouth.

This was going to be more than he could ever imagine as the future with her stretched out. She was fierce and independent, and she would handle him and his deployments in stride. He was so in love with her. How had he ever thought he could live without this?

It looked like he was damned lucky. There was nowhere to take her now that her house had been packed up. But he was sure if there was a bed in there, he wouldn't have made it anyway. Not when she was soft and wet, and his pants were half off. Not when her hand was between his legs and he could hardly breathe for what she was doing to him.

"Kia," he whispered, rocking against her. Then he lifted her in his arms and pressed her back against the arch. "Wrap your legs around me."

She did, helping him out, helping herself, and then he was pushing up inside her—and everything slowed down, way down.

It was so incredible, the sensations so intensely sweet, the rush of emotion overwhelming.

This woman had shown him so much in the ten years

that he'd been gone. She had preserved his family's legacy, searched for his dad's killer, believed in his dad; her determination was off the charts. She was a storm and she'd taken him by storm—took him deep.

He swore softly. She felt so amazingly good. He nuzzled her neck, thrusting into her, and felt himself die a little from the pleasure—and the pain of letting her down. He would make sure he never did that again.

With his arms supporting her, he had one hand wrapped around a fistful of vines, holding them against the arch, and the other threaded through her hair, flowers crushed in his fingers. The whole thing was amazing, the heat, the smell, the softness. Kia, taking him again and again. The powerful need for her slaked each time he slid into her, even as the thirst deepened. It would be a lifetime of thirst.

All she had to do was exist to make him crazy.

But she did more, sealing her mouth over his and sucking on his tongue and just flat-out filling his whole body with the sensation of love, the feeling of home from the top of his head on down. Everything. Consuming him. It was all sex and love and heat and Kia.

He moved one arm down to her butt, holding her tighter, lifting her, pushing deeper—and then he came, that first rush of the sweet power of release, and he was helpless against it. He didn't have the strength. He didn't have the will. Later would be soon enough to have control.

Oh, God. It was soul-wrenching, a melting orgasm that started at the back of his skull and the base of his groin and just flowed out of him, taking him deep inside himself, deep inside her. It was a timeless sensation, and it lasted forever, and all the while she kissed him, holding him, her mouth so hot and sweet.

"Kia..." he groaned, pushing himself deeper, his body shuddering. He'd needed her for so long—he'd been a fool to wait so long. The past was over, and there was only the future to plan, the present to live.

The wait was over, and she was his. Now and forever.

EPILOGUE

Two weeks later, Kia was settled in that nice little house with her zoo menagerie. Wes had just vacated his apartment and moved in with her. They had stayed in Reddick while Kia got acquainted with Wes's family, and she couldn't have had the best and worst times if she'd tried. Big Red had passed on after a massive heart attack, and most town folks speculated it was from the whole terrible fallout of Travis's murder and his son's arrest. The news about Red hanging himself in his cell just hours after he was told was the kind of irony that wasn't lost on any of them. It was the last part of Wes's past to be resolved.

All her life she'd wanted to experience that sense of home. Now she had it, and she'd been right—it was love.

She wasn't sure she'd worked through all her abandonment issues, because when Wes's deployment inched closer, she had a lot of anxiety, but that could be because he was going into danger. Being in love with a SEAL came with knowing your man was in danger when he was out in the field, but Kia also knew the passion and dedication that Wes gave to his brothers in arms. He couldn't live any other way, and she wanted him to be happy and fulfilled. She would be there when he came home.

His family moved back into their Sweetwater home, and Wes agreed with Kia to keep their excellent foreman to run the property. Wes and Kia would visit when they could, and he would take over ranching once he retired from the SEALs.

They were getting ready for LT's wedding, and as the best man, Wes would be wearing his full-dress uniform and Kia couldn't wait to see him in it.

They headed to the venue, Coronado Landing Park with a spectacular view of the San Diego skyline. The day was beautiful, but Kia was beginning to understand that it was idyllic weather here. It was very different from Texas, but she was enjoying her adventure. Triton and BFA were settling in nicely, and since BFA had saved her life, she was overindulgent with his tuna snacks. Quicksand had quickly become attached to Wes, who rode him with ease where Kia had to fight him every step of the way. He took him to a cattle ranch once a week when he was home and let him haze cattle. It also made Wes happy. Kia was content in switching off on Twilight Star and Saragon, riding Quicksand when Wes would be gone.

A tent had been set up for the wedding party to change in, one for the guys and one for the women. She waited patiently by the opening for him to come out. She wasn't disappointed.

"Wow," she breathed. He looked amazing. From his cover, a navy word to describe any uniform hat, to his shoulder boards, to the tips of his very shiny shoes, he wore the dress blues well, his broad shoulders filling out the jacket nicely, his ribbons impressive. He would be standing up with Lieutenant Bowie Cooper.

As the guests assembled, filling in the padded chairs, Kia took her seat on the groom's side up close to the front. After the procession, Dana and Ruckus stood on the gazebo decorated with bright, colorful flowers and exchanged their vows in front of family and friends. All these people were now her family, and here in the SEAL community, the girlfriends and the wives made her feel so welcome. She finally felt like she belonged.

Their expressions were full of the kind of love and adoration a person couldn't help but envy, and as Wes looked over at her, she was caught up in the ceremony and the genuine emotion between the couple.

Dana's boss, Sara Campbell, stood up with her along with two of her friends from college with Kid Chaos and Blue, whose eyes really stood out against his blue uniform, acting as ushers.

Then the minister was delivering the last line, telling Ruckus he could kiss his new wife. Cowboy moved into line with the rest of his team where they presented their swords. Each two men they came to dropped their swords barring the way until Ruckus kissed Dana, with the same action until they reached Cowboy. As they were stopped by him, he said, "You can't pass until you kiss." Ruckus gave her a quick one and Cowboy said, "Plant one on her."

And he did, bent her over his arm and gave her a deep kiss. Cowboy let her pass, but as soon as she walked past, he dropped his sword and swatted her on the butt with the flat of his sword. "Welcome to the navy, Dana."

She laughed and jumped forward.

After the reception where there was much dancing, drinking, kissing, and cake, Kia went home with her SEAL. Tucked against him, she ran her hands over his heavy muscles. "Keep that up and you're going to start something, darlin'."

"Maybe I want to start something."

"Is that so?" He turned toward her and brushed the back of his hands against the fading bruises on her cheekbones.

She ran her hand down his chest to his hip and cupped his super fine ass. "Geez, Wes, your butt is like granite." He followed the same path.

"I like yours better, especially the tat on your taillights."

She giggled. "Yeah, I was such a fool for you in high school."

He dragged her hips against his. "We are certainly older and wiser," he whispered against her mouth. Then he kissed her, and that was the end of the conversation except the purely physical one they fully embraced.

Afterward, Wes said, "Kia, one promise."

"What?"

"No more illegal hacking."

"Okay, I think I can handle that."

He grabbed her chin and she sighed.

"I'm going to miss you when you're gone, Wes."

"But you can handle it."

"Yes, there's no other man for me, not in this lifetime."

"That's a good thing, 'cause I'd have to kill him."

She said, "Maybe we can run a yellow traffic light every once in a while? You know, live on the wild side just a bit."

He chuckled. "Maybe we could." She snuggled down with him and drifted off.

SHORTLY AFTER THAT, Cowboy saw less of her as the SEALs began training. Word came down they were joining a NATO

joint task force to take down the Kirikhan Rebels and apprehend Boris and Natasha Golovkin. Retrieving the warheads
was the secondary task.

Three teams of eight were being mobilized: Team One
was going to take point and go in to try to get to the
Golovkins and capture them. Dragon's Team—a badass
sniper who had filled in for Kid Chaos on an op into North
Korea when Kid had been in Bolivia—was secondary with
Ruckus's team acting as back up. They all trained together,
and Cowboy could see that Ryuu "Dragon" Shannon was
well-respected amongst his teammates. No surprise there.
They often worked with other members of Team Seven, and
there were some tough guys working with Dragon. A set of
triplets—Errol "Pitbull" Ballentine, Flynn "Pirate" Ballentine, and Robin "Hood" Ballentine, their corpsman—then a
smart aleck former Royal Marine and elite member of the
Special Boat Service, the British equivalent of the SEALs,
Oliver "Artful Dodger" Graham. Their leader, a gearhead
that Tank got along with very well as they talked a lot about
muscle cars and motorcycles, was aptly named Ford "Fast
Lane" Nixon. Then there was Milo "Professor" Prescott, a
Rhodes Scholar with an encyclopedic knowledge and
photographic memory, and lastly, Justin "Speed" Myerson, a
quiet guy who did his job well, but kept to himself mostly.

HE CAME home tense and Kia picked up on it and insisted
that they go riding. That always relaxed him. She was right.

"You doing all right?" she asked.

"Yeah, just a lot on my mind. I wanted to ask you. What
happened to Sunshine—Sunny?"

Her face went a little sad. "He was despondent after you

didn't return. I took him home with me and he lived a happy life until he passed about five years ago. He was a sweet guy and after I got Twilight Star, they bonded. He perked up quite a bit after that and had a serene life."

Cowboy nodded. One more thing he could add to his growing list of why he loved this woman. His heart tightened a bit at the fond memory of that excellent horse but knowing that he was happy and well-cared for tempered his ache some.

As they clopped along, she said, "I know you can't talk about it, but know that whatever it is that you're going to be doing, remember that I love you, support you, and want you back."

He reached out and clasped her hand. "That means everything, darlin'."

He sat in the quiet of the meadow in the peaceful afternoon and said, "This...this is what I'm fighting for. I'll keep you safe, Kia. Every illegal, gorgeous, sassy inch of you," he whispered. "The last breath I breathe will be for you."

She tightened her hold on him. "Every single American should be thankful for that. I love you, Wes."

"I love you, too, darlin'."

He pulled her out of the saddle and she went with a squeak. Settling her solidly against him, he bent down and took her mouth. "This isn't going to be a garden party," she murmured.

He threw his head back and laughed. "It's going to be one hell of a blast party."

And, in the end, the score was: Stupid Girl Crush—ha! A measly four; Kia—infinity. She rather liked being a starry-eyed fool for Wes. "Hoo-yah, rodeo, hoo-yah."

Thank you for reading *Cowboy*!

Reviews are appreciated!

Book 4 in the SEAL Team Alpha series, *Tank*, is next. A mission gone wrong, a missing team member, and heart-breaking changes knock Thorn "Tank" Hunt off his game. He'll need the help of a caring, dedicated woman, someone like veterinarian Dr. Alyssa St. James. But she's the kind of woman who would demand picket fences, cause fraternization issues, was bossy, and drove him crazy. For a hell raiser like Tank, it might just all be too much out of his comfort zone.

GLOSSARY

- BUD/S - Basic Underwater Demolitions/SEAL training
- Comm - The equipment that SEALs use to communicate with each other in the field.
- CO - Commanding Officer
- DoD - Department of Defense
- DZ - Drop zone, the targeted area for parachutists.
- HALO - High altitude, low opening jump from an aircraft.
- HVT - High value target
- IED - Improvised Incendiary Device
- Klicks - Shortened word for kilometers.
- LRRP - Long-range reconnaissance patrol.
- LT - Nickname for lieutenant.
- LZ - Landing Zone where aircraft can land.
- Merc - Mercenary - guns for hire.
- MWD - Military Working Dog
- MRE - Meals, Ready-to-Eat, portable in pouches

and packed with calories, these packaged meals are used in the field.

- NATO - North Atlantic Treaty Organization
- NCIS - Naval Criminal Investigative Service
- NWU - Navy Working Uniform
- RIB - Rigid Inflatable Boat
- RPG - Rocket Propelled Grenade
- R&R - Rest and Relaxation
- Tango -Hostile combatants.
- SERE -Stands for survival, evasion, resistance, escape. The principles of avoiding the enemy in the field.
- Six - Military speak for watching a man's back.

ABOUT THE AUTHOR

Zoe Dawson lives in North Carolina, one of the friendliest states in the US. She discovered romance in her teens and has been spinning stories in her head ever since. Her heroes are sexy males with a disregard for danger and whether reluctant, gung-ho, or caught up in the action, show their hearts of gold.

Her imagination runs wild with romances from sensual to scorching including romantic comedy, new adult, romantic suspense, small town, and urban fantasy. Look below to explore the many avenues to her writing. She believes it's all about the happily ever afters and always will.

Sign up so that you don't miss any new releases from Zoe: Newsletter.

You can find out more about Zoe here:
www.zoedawson.com
zoe@zoedawson.com

OTHER TITLES BY ZOE DAWSON

Romantic Comedy

Going to the Dogs series

Leashed #1, Groomed #2

Hounded #3, Collared #4

Piggy Bank Blues #5, Holding Still #6

Louder Than Words #7 What Matters Most #8

Going to the Dogs Wedding Novellas

Fetched #1, Tangled #2

Handled #3, Captured #4

Novellas (the complete series)

Romantic Suspense

SEAL Team Alpha

Ruckus #1, Kid Chaos #2

Cowboy #3, Tank #4

New Adult

Hope Parish Novels

A Perfect Mess #1, A Perfect Mistake #2

A Perfect Dilemma #3, Resisting Samantha #4

Handling Skylar #5, Sheltering Lawson #6

Hope Parish Novellas

Finally Again #1, Beauty Shot #2

Mark Me #3, Novellas 1-3 (the complete series)

A Perfect Wedding #4, A Perfect Holiday #5

A Perfect Question #6, Novellas 4-6 (the complete series)

Maverick Allstars series

Ramping Up #1

Small Town Romance

Laurel Falls series

Leaving Yesterday #1

Urban Fantasy

The Starbuck Chronicles

AfterLife #1

Erotica

Forbidden Plays series

Playing Rough #1, Hard Pass #2, Illegal Motions #3

Made in the USA
Monee, IL
16 July 2023